REVEAL ME

BECKETT BROTHERS BOOK 4

L A GALLAGHER

For the readers who prefer their fairytales dirty and their princes dark instead of charming.

Chapter One

SEAN

I prefer to assert my power in an impeccably tailored suit with one commanding word than in leather, brandishing a whip—although, over the years, I have been known to do both.

I shrug off my suit jacket, remove my platinum cufflinks, and roll up the sleeves of my crisp ebony shirt. My current submissive, Samantha, kneels silently beside me, her porcelain skin a stark contrast against the black velvet cushion she's balanced on. She's naked, wet, and willing—exactly the way I commanded, but her eyes keep straying to mine—a privilege which I didn't permit.

'Eyes down,' I growl.

'Yes, sir.' Her head dips obediently, and I know she's waiting for me to tell her she's a good girl, but tonight, I can't.

There's a hint of something in her eyes that's making me uneasy. It might be time to rotate before she forms an attachment. God forbid she gets the notion that this thing between us is anything more than an arrangement.

I glance around Reveal, the bespoke BDSM club I created with pride. Twelve meticulously designed erotic chambers branch from this central lounge, each a unique expression of dominance and submission. Tonight, we'll be using the Discipline Suite. I had one hell of a day in the office, and I need an outlet. Samantha is only too willing to oblige. Being a Monday, the club isn't open to its one hundred and fifty members. We have the entire place to ourselves, bar the skeletal staff who've signed so many non-disclosure agreements, they may never open their mouths to anyone about anything again.

'Rise.' I beckon her up with a single index finger. Naturally, she obeys. Thankfully, her gaze remains fixed on my feet.

My eyes roam over her body. She's naked, save for the black bespoke leather collar I gifted her at the start of our agreement, and a black lace crotchless thong. Inch after inch of smooth skin gleams beneath the low lighting, ripe for taking—and tonight I'm going to shackle her to the Saint Andrew's cross and take it.

If my brothers had even an inclination of my preferences, they'd choke on their whiskeys. Well, my older brothers James, Caelon, and Killian might. My youngest brother, Rian —he'd probably come in his pants at the mere mention of a place like this.

'Follow me.' My shoes make a soft thwacking sound as I march across the marble. I don't need to look around to see that Samantha is hot on my heels. Even if she weren't so keen, the sound of her ragged breathing echoes off the black lacquered walls.

I step inside the Discipline Suite, eyeing the opulence with approval. When I initially dreamed up the idea of a BDSM club, I was adamant it wouldn't be another dingy, dark hole. Oh, it's dark, but its decadence is undeniable. The equipment is the most expensive and exclusive money can buy. Which is why the annual membership fee is a million euros.

Samantha hovers behind me, awaiting instruction. 'The cross.' I nod towards the centre of the room. The custom-designed Saint Andrew's cross dominates the space like a religious monument. Its polished ebony frame rises seven and a half feet high, arms stretching five feet wide. Chrome D-rings await their purpose at precise intervals along the frame: wrists, biceps, thighs, ankles, gleaming like surgical instruments under the lighting.

Samantha strides towards it. I watch as her ass sways seductively. I hope I'm wrong and she's not catching feelings, because I like our arrangement, but it will never be more than that. I'm incapable of more. She reaches the cross, turns slowly, lifting her wrists ready to be bound, a small smile playing at the corner of her lips. She loves being restrained and fucked. The rougher the better.

I'm at her side in seconds. She spreads herself wide and leans back against the cross. 'Not that way.' I make a swivelling motion with my fingers. I can't chance her staring at me with those doe eyes again.

She turns her back, spreads her legs, then lifts her arms. I fasten her into position using thick leather cuffs. Taking a step back, I survey her spread eagle on the cross. A ripple of satisfaction washes over me.

I need control like a fire needs oxygen. But being the fourth youngest brother born into Dublin's wealthiest family, my life was planned out for me from the day I was born. Which school I'd attend, which sports I'd play, which college I'd go to, what I'd major in. Manners and social etiquette were pressed upon me from the second I could speak. I'm privileged, ridiculously so, but also unfulfilled—unless I'm here.

My family would be horrified if they had any idea I'd

carved out my own lucrative business away from the Beckett enterprise, but the real wealth this provides me with is satisfaction, and the freedom to act out my darkest fantasies without the risk of being revealed.

Samantha whimpers and wriggles on the cross in front of me.

'Patience,' I warn her.

'Yes, sir.'

My eyes roam from her blonde hair, securely fastened with a hair tie, over her taut back, the smooth curve of her ass cheeks separated with that tiny sliver of lace, then finally to her spread thighs. I step closer, contemplating what to do with her.

I unbutton my suit trousers but I don't undress. I rarely do. I reach for Samantha's hips, gripping them firmly. She moans, tilts her chin up and angles her head round until her eyes lock with mine.

Oh fuck—she has goddamn fucking hearts in her eyes.

I glide my hands up over her body to cradle her head and reposition it so she's not resting on my body, but it's too late.

The damage is done.

I can't do it.

I don't do intimacy.

Not since *her*.

It's official—I need a new sub.

Samantha grinds her ass back against me. I should slap it for ruining our arrangement, instead, I simply unshackle her. Her cheeks are flushed, but the brightness in her blue eyes fades as they meet mine.

'Sir?' Her tone assures me she's aware she fucked up. Assures me she's aware she's been pushing for something she had no right to push for—more.

'I'll walk you to the Sanctuary Suite.'

There's a bathroom off of every chamber, but the Sanctuary Suite is a dedicated room where doms can provide aftercare for their subs. There's mood lighting, rainfall showers, an expansive lavender scented hot tub large enough to comfortably accommodate an orgy—which happens on occasion. As a rule, I never go into the Sanctuary Suite with a sub. Again, it's too intimate. But I always walk Samantha there and ensure one of the staff takes care of her.

'Is this it? Are we over?' She glances at me in her peripheral vision as she stretches the stiffness from her wrists and her legs. I press a hand to the small of her back and guide her out of the room.

'It's for the best.' Securing a new sub is hard work, not because they're hard to come by, no——they're usually clawing over each other at the chance to be mine. What's hard is finding a good one. One I can communicate with using a single look. One who innately understands my limits as well as her own.

Samantha's doe eyes and increasing neediness were too much of a test on mine.

'Can I ask why?' Her throat bobs, and she blinks hard.

Fuck. Don't cry. Don't cry. Don't cry. Crying women stir things deep in my sternum. She's the one who moved the goalposts.

'You know why,' I say softly, tucking a stray strand of hair behind her ear.

'I thought we were good together,' her voice wobbles.

'That's the problem.' We reach the Sanctuary Suite door. Two exceptionally talented masseuses are preparing a bed for Samantha inside, as instructed.

Understanding flashes across her face as she reaches for the collar around her neck and unclips it slowly. The ultimate acceptance it's over. She places it in my hands and swivels on her heel.

I breathe a sigh of relief as I go in search of Larissa

Laurent, the club's operations manager. Samantha might need another reminder about her non-disclosure agreement, and I need to arrange interviews for a new sub—immediately. I stalk through the dark marble corridor towards the offices at the back of the club. Larissa's is directly opposite mine. I step inside to find her tucked behind her tinted glass-topped desk, with her long, toned legs crossed beneath it. She looks up as I enter.

'Monday night fun, huh?' She squints at me through thick rimmed Marc Jacob glasses the same shade of crimson as her sharply bobbed hair.

I close the heavy wooden door behind me and dump the collar in the trash can. 'Samantha has to go. She's started looking at me with fucking hearts in her eyes, and it's freaking me the fuck out.' I drop into the huge leather chair in the corner of the room and rest my head back against the wall.

Larissa's low laughter pierces the air.

'What's so funny?' I rub my temple. A headache's threatening. I need two paracetamol and a double whiskey. Not necessarily in that order.

'You sound surprised, Sean.' Larissa reaches into her top drawer and pulls out a bottle of Beckett's Gold, my family's famous whiskey. Maybe there is a God after all. She pours two generous measures into two chunky glass tumblers then crosses the room to hand one to me. Her emerald eyes bore into mine. 'You're a Beckett. Even if you hadn't been blessed with big brown eyes, dimples, and a giant dick, your name is enough alone. Add in the fact your brothers are dropping from the singles market like flies, it's no wonder you're now considered Ireland's most eligible bachelor.'

Larissa has seen my dick many times. One of my favourite pastimes is fucking my subs in the main lounge where the voyeurs can watch. Not that it does much for Larissa, she prefers pussy.

'And that's how I want to stay—bachelor.' I accept the glass and drink deeply, revelling in the burn as the liquid hits the back of my throat.

'Why? Wouldn't you like to meet someone special?' Larissa backs across the room and perches on her desk.

'And give up this life?' I gesture towards the main lounge. 'You've got to be joking.'

'What makes you think you can't have both?' She cocks her head and eyes me thoughtfully over her glass.

'Experience.' Girlfriends are only interested in tying me down—figuratively, not literally, unfortunately. The woman who taught me about this life, Hannah Golden, also taught me not to mistake what occurs between a dom and a sub for love. It was a quick lesson—one I learnt the hard way, Back then, it was me who was stupid enough to sport hearts in my eyes. She broke me. Which is why I swore never again. 'I need you to set up interviews for a new sub, the quicker the better.'

Larissa is the only person I trust to do this. She's discreet, professional, and a perfectionist, a bit like myself. 'You know...' her eyes flash with mischief. 'It's been ages since we hosted a theme night. Maybe we could make your interviews into a show?'

I take another sip of my drink, and the tension slowly begins to seep from my shoulders. The members love a theme night. It practically guarantees a full house. We host a weekly masquerade night. Hell, some members prefer the anonymity of dressing up every night. We've held auction nights in the past, which proved hugely successful, but this? This has the potential to be massive.

'What are you thinking?' I rub my thumb over my lower lip, trying to work out the logistics. The prospect of lining up potential subs and taking my pick makes my dick hard just thinking about it. But the reality is, we'd need to grant the potential new subs access to the club, which risks exposure. Unless we offer them all one year's free membership and bind them all with NDAs.

'We could move the throne to the main stage where the members can watch from the observation areas. I'm thinking maybe three potential subs. We can get the members to vote on how they like to see the newbies demonstrate their devotion to their potential new dom.' Devilment dances in her pupils.

It does sound like fun.

'The members will go crazy for it,' she crosses one long leg over the other.

'We don't need to appease them,' I remind her. Their membership here is a privilege that they have to reapply for annually. 'How fast can we make it happen?'

'For anyone else, it could be weeks. For the country's most eligible billionaire—Friday.'

I roll my eyes at the bullshit tabloid description. 'Have Dominic host it. The man is a natural born entertainer.' He's also my best friend, fellow dom, and one of the most feared men in Dublin.

'He's a natural born psycho,' Larissa smirks.

She's not wrong. He controls the country's underworld, which is why he was the best person to organise security for this place. Naturally, I couldn't use my brother Killian's guys. Dominic's men are on another level. They don't ask questions, and they don't leave loose ends.

'This is either going to be the best idea we've had, or the worst. Either way, it'll be seriously entertaining.'

Chapter Two

LAYLA

You know how in Disney movies, princesses always end up with their happy ever afters, a cute sidekick best friend who's a snowman, a cute little cup called Chip, or a fat faced fish called Flounder? Well, the reality is far from that picture-perfect fairy tale. I may be Princess Layla of the House of Sinclair, the third daughter of the King of England, but right now, the only princess I can relate to is Rapunzel.

I glance around the draughty suite at Ardmore Castle, my mother's ancestral home, half an hour outside of Dublin. There are no singing mice to help me get dressed. Kat, my long-suffering lady-in-waiting—and the only true friend I have on this earth—doesn't even pretend I can choose what to wear. She's laid out yet another stiff conservative dress for me. It's not her fault. She's following orders, while I'm rebelling against them.

I haven't seen any spontaneous dance numbers in the village square where everyone somehow knows the choreography. But then again, I'm not allowed to leave the castle grounds, let alone venture into the village, so maybe they are hopping around to a merry little Irish jig. Who knows?

Everything about this "holiday" retreat is punishment disguised as privilege. The ancient exposed grey brick walls might look aesthetically pleasing, but no matter how many logs the staff put on the open fire, it's always freezing. There are twenty people on the premises at any given time, yet I'm constantly lonely.

Dead ancestors stare down at me from their oil portraits in every room, a full gallery of disapproving relatives whose idea of being rebellious probably amounted to two sherries before bed. Great-Aunt Prudence looks particularly miffed this evening, as if she can actually see me reaching for my riding jacket instead of the formal, floral attire Kat left out.

My darling parents have arranged another perfectly suitable bore to test my resolve tonight—Lord Finegan Montgomery. Apparently, they didn't get the message when I publicly shunned the last man they forced on me. I tried explaining that the glass of Bollinger I poured over Lord Harrington's head was an accident, but they didn't buy it. Perhaps they would have if they'd heard what he said first: "When we're married, you'll learn that a woman's proper place is in the nursery."

Then again, perhaps not. Knowing the Queen, she might even agree with that statement. Though I don't recall her spending much time in the nursery when I was a child.

Lord Harrington is a pompous twat.

A presumptuous, pompous twat at that.

But after what the tabloids called 'The Royal Splash— Princess Pours Her Heart Out', my parents banished me to the Irish countryside immediately after Christmas. They didn't even permit me to stay for New Year. Instead, I got sent to the arse end of nowhere to 'reflect on my actions and consider my options.'

Ha! Like I have any!

In their eyes, my duty is to marry well—someone with a

title to secure alliances between other influential families, and breed impeccably groomed, perfectly mannered royal robots —oops, I meant children. Lord Finegan Montgomery has a sufficient title and wealth, but all I remember from our last brief but painful meeting two years ago is that he spends most of his time discussing agricultural pursuits and tending to his mother's garden.

Is it too much to ask for a man who's interested in *my* garden?

I might be a princess, but I don't want 'suitable'.

I don't want 'proper'.

And as much as I love children, I don't want to be banished to a nursery. Not at the age of twenty-five, at least.

I want love.

I want lust.

I want to feel like a woman, not a royal womb to be bartered over.

If someone is going to control every aspect of my life, can it not be for my pleasure?

I'm no virgin, but the little experience I've had with men has been unfulfilling to say the least. Too formal. Too proper. Too staged. But I've read enough romance novels to know that there's more out there than that. And I refuse to settle for less. Even if I am a princess. *Especially* because I'm a princess.

Which is why I have no intention of being here when Lord Montgomery arrives. My parents would love nothing more than to trap me in Ireland permanently—far enough from the paparazzi's prying eyes but close enough to the Crown's influence. It's never going to happen. I miss London. I miss the hustle and bustle. I miss civilisation.

I slide my arms into my riding jacket, snatch up my leather gloves from the dresser, then slip down the spiral stone staircase and through the staff quarters. Pressing my back to the wall, I glance around, checking for my security team, but thankfully, there's no sign of them. Grant, my head of security, is Kat's boyfriend, and she often keeps him 'entertained' in order for me to slip out.

The eight royal guards stationed at Ardmore aren't exactly on high alert out here in the remote countryside. My parents and the staff are the only ones aware of my location. Not that the rest of the world would care—I'm a spare, not the heir— thank God for small mercies. My eldest sister, Princess Patricia, was married off to the Duke of Wellington's youngest son, Fredrick last year. It's an absolutely perfect match in our mother's eyes. Fredrick comes from an impeccable bloodline, he's obscenely wealthy, and dull enough not to cause any international incidents. Their lavish wedding was all over the papers as the "romance of the century," though romance had nothing to do with it. And there's no lust there either. Patricia confided that my new brother-in-law doesn't know what a clitoris is, let alone where to find one. I did suggest she take a lover, perhaps one of her burly bodyguards, but apparently she'd rather be loyal to an arrangement than experience true fulfilment.

Our other sister, Sabrina, faces the same pitiful fate. She recently accepted a proposal from the Crown Prince of Norway, Prince Harald. The wedding will take place in April at Westminster Abbey. Admittedly Prince Harald is rather handsome in a Viking-like way. I just hope his knowledge of vaginal anatomy is better than my other brother-in-law's, or I'll have two dissatisfied sisters.

I creep past the open kitchen doorway, the scent of freshly baked bread permeating my nostrils. Carbs have been my best friend since I got here last week. One of the cooks, Selina, is deeply engrossed in an animated conversation with Ardmore's chief housekeeper, and my mother's chief spy, Mrs

Medway. It shouldn't be too hard to slip by them and out the back door.

'Did you hear our elusive neighbour made Forbes' top ten eligible billionaires last month?' Selina fans herself. 'He's so dreamy. Have you seen him?'

My ears prick up as my feet come to an abrupt halt behind a large coat stand. I peer around the leather and wool, watching the women talk as they work.

'Sean Beckett?' Mrs Medway wipes her hands on her apron. 'I've seen him in the papers. He is rather handsome.'

'Oh my god, his eyes are so beautiful I could cheerfully drown in them.' Selina swoons, clutching her chest. I bite back a chuckle. 'I keep hoping I'll run into him one of these days.'

Pah. He can't be that good looking. Sean Beckett is head of Property Acquisition at Beckett Enterprises. Naturally, given the proximity of our estates, my family is aware of his. I assumed he was another typical billionaire in a suit, Forbes top ten or not—excuse me if I've had my fill of that.

'There's acres between his residence and the castle.' Mrs Medway reminds Selina, shaking her head.

'You know,' Selina pauses, lowering her voice, 'I heard he runs some sort of underground club at the edge of the mansion grounds.'

A club?

As in a nightclub?

My ears prick further. Eavesdropping isn't very ladylike, but if there's a remote chance of having some fun in this hell-hole, I'm going to find it.

'I'd need to be a millionaire to socialise in those circles, though.' Selina sighs.

'Billionaire, you mean.' Mrs Medway cocks an eyebrow. 'Now, enough of that, check that bread, it smells like it's done.'

I guess that's all the gossip I'm going to get, for now. Slowly and stealthily, I twist the buffed brass door handle and creep out into the cold January night. My breath fogs in front of my face as I dart towards the stables where my horse, Temptation, awaits. Riding is the only time I feel free. That, and when I have a paintbrush in my hand. I'm not allowed to express my feelings vocally, but no one can stop me expressing them creatively. My parents consider painting an awful waste of time. In all honesty, they consider anything other than securing myself a suitable husband an awful waste of time. I'd love to open my own gallery one day and prove them wrong, but naturally, they'd never permit it.

The nightclub thing is probably nonsense. Why would a billionaire open a nightclub all the way out here in the sticks? Still, we'll gallop that way to rule it out. The entire estate is lit with evenly spaced lanterns, but I'm new to the castle, so if I happen to accidentally cross the estate's boundary lines, who could blame me? I grin for the first time since I arrived in this hellhole.

The stable hand left Temptation tacked up and ready and waiting, as instructed. I swing into the saddle and give the horse a gentle kick. The cold air bites at my cheeks as Temptation's powerful stride eats up the frost-hardened ground. Each thundering hoofbeat matches my racing pulse as we navigate the moonlit landscape. For once, the Irish sky has decided to forgo its perpetual weeping, leaving a pristine canopy of stars overhead that makes me feel deliciously small and wonderfully insignificant.

A thrilling sense of satisfaction ripples through me as I trespass onto what has to be Sean Beckett's land. Doing something bad always makes me feel good—my silent F U to the stiff, solitary confines of the privilege I was born into. After thirty minutes of hard riding, finally, I spot a peculiar structure set against a hillside.

I slow Temptation to a walk as we approach. The building is modest by royal standards—black granite with subtle chrome detailing. There are no signs, no queues of people, nothing to suggest it's a club, although there are a small fleet of sleek, expensive cars parked nearby.

I squint through the trees as a man and a woman exit a Porsche. He's wearing a black suit. She's wearing some sort of mask and a long-belted coat. I watch as he ushers her in through the understated, mysterious tinted glass doorway. A split second before the door closes, they enter a lift. My eyes flick to the top of the granite structure. There's nowhere to go up, so they must be going down.

Maybe there *is* a nightclub below.

I rub my hand over Temptation's supple neck to pacify him as I watch two more couples enter the building, dressed in equally unusual, but sensual and elegant attire—both of the women are wearing intricate, elegant masks.

Is it a masquerade club?

How fun—and how convenient.

Excitement shivers down my spine.

I tug Temptation's reins, taking one final glance over my shoulder. I'll be back.

Next time, in an expensive little black dress and a mask.

Chapter Three

SEAN

'You coming to the club tonight?' Rian, my younger brother, pops his head in through my office doorway—my office in my 'day job' that is. Beckett Enterprises operates from a majestic Georgian building just off Grafton Street. My brothers and I each occupy a different floor with our different subsidiaries. James has the top floor because he's the eldest. Caelon has the fourth floor, Killian has the third, and I occupy the second. Rian occupies the ground floor—something which I know for a fact irritates the shit out of him.

I look up from the computer screen in front of me. I'm bidding on a site in Cork and trying to pass the time until tonight—Submissive Night. Property isn't the only thing I'll be acquiring today. It's been four days since the incident with my last sub, and the prospect of picking the next one brings out the beast in me.

'I can't tonight. I have plans.'

Rian snorts, leaning against the thick wooden doorframe. Like all of us Beckett boys, he has dark hair, dark eyes and a large physique—courtesy of our father. 'Like what? Watching *Pride and Prejudice* and having a wank?'

My brothers regard me as the 'proper' brother. I'm not proper, I'm private. They have no idea of my kinks, and that's the way I want it to stay. They're curious at my lack of interest in dating. James all but came out and asked if I was gay. Said it wouldn't change the way he, or any of my brothers, regarded me. It was a battle not to laugh in his face.

I'm not gay, I'm just guarded about my preferences.

But now James, Caelon and Killian are all loved up, they seem intent on seeing everyone settle down. It's never going to happen. I made peace years ago with the fact that my two worlds—above ground and below—must remain forever separate. Who I am in darkness and who I am in daylight don't mix.

'Or is it one of those fucking cooking shows that you love?' Rian tuts in disgust.

'Just because you can't even boil an egg.' I snort.

'Seriously, what are you up to? What's with the perpetual mystery?'

'No mystery, just none of your business.' My eyes flick back to the computer. Someone bid against me. I click to up my bid by a million. I want that site, and I always get what I want. 'Why don't you ask Anthony to go out with you instead?'

Anthony De Courcy is Rian's best friend, a banker—and a bit of a wanker—if you ask me, but he and Rian have been firm friends since they were in nappies. They attended the same school, the same college, and they behave like they never left, drinking themselves senseless most weekends. Even marriage didn't calm Anthony down. His wife, Rebekka, must have the patience of a saint.

A dark expression flickers over my brother's features. 'He's away.'

'With Rebekka?'

'No.' Rian shakes his head. Disapproval radiates from his every pore. 'With someone else.'

'The guy's an asshole.' I might have my kinks, but I'm not unfaithful. None of my brothers are—our mother brought us up better than that.

'Yeah, I'm starting to get that impression.' Rian glowers. It's not like him to be sullen. Out of all my brothers, he's usually the sunny one. The joker. The one who acquired a chain of bars and nightclubs just so he could party seven nights a week and tell our father he's "working".

I check my screen again. I won. Satisfaction sweeps through me. The auction is over. A smug smile lifts my lips as I close down my computer. Rian's staring into space in front of me. What is wrong with him?

'Come on, let's go for lunch.' I might have plans for tonight, but today, my workload is light. I stand, strut towards the door, grabbing my thick coat on the way. January in Ireland can be bitterly cold. James and Scarlett's wedding in St. Barth's a couple of months back feels like a lifetime ago.

'Fine, but you're buying.' Rian shoves his hands in his pockets, and stalks out the door in front of me.

'Tight bastard,' I give him a playful shove, following him out into the high wide corridor. I pause at the next open doorway where Michelle, my twenty-four-year-old, blonde PA, is typing furiously on her keyboard. 'I'm heading off for the afternoon. You should do the same. It's Friday, after all.'

Michelle's fingers halt their tapping, and she glances up with a smile. 'Thanks, Mr Beckett. I will do once I finish this report.'

'Have a good weekend.' I nod, then quicken my step to catch up with Rian, who's hovering by the elevator.

'You should tap that ass.' Rian gestures towards Michelle's office. 'I would.'

My eyes roll up to the expensive coving lining the double

height ceiling. 'Fuck's sake. Is that all you think about? Even if I wasn't concerned about a sexual harassment case, mixing business with pleasure is never a wise idea.'

'I don't know.' Rian smirks, hitting the button. 'It seems to work for James.'

Our oldest brother hired his now wife to work beside him the second she graduated from Trinity. His theory was clear. He didn't want some slippery CEO perving over his woman when he was perfectly capable of doing that himself.

As if to reinforce Rian's remarks, the lift doors slide open to reveal James and Scarlett in a somewhat compromising position. Her back is against the mirrored wall, her legs are wrapped around my brother's waist, and they're making out like horny fucking teenagers instead of the responsible parents of two toddlers.

James drags his lips from his wife's and fires a filthy look over his shoulder. She giggles, a blush creeping into her cheeks as he somewhat reluctantly slides her down the front of his body until her five-inch stilettos meet the floor.

'Don't stop on our behalf.' Rian's black eyes gleam. 'I was enjoying the show.'

'Careful, brother,' James growls, snaking a protective arm around Scarlett's waist.

'We're going for lunch, if you two want to join us?' I offer politely, trying to keep the peace as usual.

Rian snorts. 'I don't think Nobu serves what James wants to eat.'

'Shut up, dickhead,' James spits good naturedly. His lips curve upwards as he glances lovingly at his wife. They only got back from honeymoon a month ago, and I'd bet my life he put baby number three in her while they were away. It was an eventful Christmas, so none of us got to ask, but thankfully things are back on an even keel now.

'Thanks, but we're going home for lunch.' My sister-in-law smooths her pencil skirt over her thighs.

'As I suspected.' Rian smirks again as the elevator descends to the ground floor.

'You're just jealous.' James elbows him in the ribs, none too gently.

'I'm not even going to try to deny it.' Rian exhales heavily.

The doors glide open. I motion for Scarlett and James to exit in front of us. 'Have a great weekend.'

'We'll see you on Sunday, right?' Scarlett flicks her ebony hair from her shoulders.

Fuck. I forgot about Sunday. We've all been summoned for a family lunch at their place. Yep—definitely another pregnancy announcement.

'Absolutely.' I adjust my tie. 'Looking forward to it,' I lie. I had hoped to spend the day getting acquainted with my new sub. There are formalities to go over, and I'd hoped to get the paperwork done ASAP, but it looks like the only person climbing me will be my boisterous but beautiful nieces and nephew.

We stroll through the city to Nobu, where we're promptly taken to a booth table away from prying eyes. One benefit of being a Beckett— we can secure a table anywhere, anytime. Two neat Beckett's Gold and half a bottle of Gavi take the edge off my little brother as we dine at Dublin's finest Japanese restaurant.

Dublin's elite dine all around us. The sound of conversation and laughter floats through the opulent room. As the waiter clears away our dessert plates, I glance at my watch.

'You're not leaving already?' Rian cocks his head to the side.

'I told you, I have plans tonight.' I need to shower. I want to get to Reveal early and get some information from Larissa on the candidates and the agenda for the evening. It was her idea to make an entire production of it. I can't wait to see what that production entails.

Rian stares at me, his eyes boring into me like he can't quite work me out. 'Have you got a woman on the go? Or a man?'

A laugh rumbles in my throat. 'You'll never find out. Not all of us like to boast about our conquests.' I drain the remainder of the wine in my glass and signal the waiter for the bill.

'I will find out.' Rian raises a thick brow. 'If it's the last thing I do.'

It might just be the last thing he ever does, because if he were to stumble across my dark, kinky secret, there's no way my little brother could keep it to himself. And it's not just my secret to protect. Many of the members at Reveal are high profile faces, with connections—some of them dangerous ones. Case in point, my dear friend, Dominic Kincaid.

My reasons for keeping Rian away are for his own sake, as much as my own.

Chapter Four

LAYLA

'Where are you going, Princess?' Kat stops in her tracks at the sight of me at my dressing table, lining my eyes with a thick, coal pencil. She's carrying freshly laundered flannel pyjamas and a cup of camomile tea. Rock 'n' roll, right?

'Out,' I say simply. 'And I need you to cover for me.'

'Like that?' Alarm stretches across her features. 'If the Queen finds out…' she trails off.

Kat is well used to my antics—here and in London. Over her five years in service, she's hugged me, wiped my tears, and held my secrets along with her own. Oh, I have plenty of high society acquaintances—women who like to be seen with me, women who would have nothing to do with me if not for my title, but Kat—she's the real deal. She'd lie for me, probably even die for me if I asked her to. She's the only person who really understands the pristinely curated prison that's my life.

'She won't find out.' I place the eyeliner on the brass topped dresser and stare at my reflection.

'Where are you going? Is it safe?' Worry bleeds into her tone. 'Will you take Grant with you?'

'Relax. I'm only going to meet my neighbour.' It's not

entirely a lie. I spent the last few days googling Sean Beckett and his equally gorgeous billionaire brothers. They might be wealthy, but they've starred in too many scandals to ever be considered an appropriate match—even if they did have a title. Pity, because they have one hell of a gene pool. That's one match I wouldn't mind my interfering parents making. I would climb Sean Beckett like a tree.

'You've been here barely a week, and you have a date with Sean Beckett?' Kat's hand flies to her mouth and the pyjamas fall to the floor. I stand from the stool, pick them up and toss them onto the bed.

'Not exactly a date, more like a meet and greet. He runs some sort of secret, super exclusive nightclub, and I'm about to sign up as a member.' I shimmy my shoulders as excitement ripples over my spine.

I've been back to the entrance twice since the first, once with Temptation, and once in the Range Rover. Father insisted we learn to drive, even though we rarely get the chance to drive ourselves. Both nights the dress code was the same—sensual, formal; the men always wear suits, and the women often wear masks, which is why I ordered a bespoke Venetian half mask. It arrived this morning; thankfully I managed to snatch it up before it reached Mrs Medway's prying eyes. Crafted from the softest silk, it's enhanced with small, crushed diamonds which catch the light. Strategically placed cutouts enhance my eyes.

'You can't be serious?' Kat shakes her head and perches on the edge of the four-poster bed. 'We're in the literal back end of nowhere, and yet you still manage to find trouble.'

'It's not trouble; it's just a bit of fun.' My hands fly up in exasperation. 'I'll die if I have to stay holed up in here for the next few months.'

'Well, maybe you should have thought about that before standing up Lord Montgomery the other night. You could have pretended to be interested in him—he could have broken you out of the house for a few nice dinners or the theatre or something.'

'Pah. You know me better than that, Kat!' I swat the air in front of my face. 'I'm sick of "suitable suitors". Sick of putting on a façade all the time. Give me something raw. Something real. Something utterly inappropriate for once.'

Kat's eyes land on the dress hanging on the curtain rail. Its sheer ebony lace fabric is practically translucent. 'That's pretty inappropriate. The Queen would have a heart attack if she knew you were planning on leaving the estate in that.' The Queen is the most controlling, cold woman on the planet. She wouldn't give in to a heart attack. Poison probably wouldn't even take her out. To say my mother is strong willed is the understatement of the century.

'Good job she's not going to find out then, isn't it?' I shoot her my widest smile.

Kat stares at me for a long beat then exhales a weary sigh. 'If they lock me in the Tower of London, will you bail me out?'

'Oh don't be so dramatic, Kitty Kat!' I scoff. 'Besides, if they lock you in the Tower of London, it's because I'm there already.' I wink, and she shakes her head again, but I know she's got my back. She always does.

'Do you want me to accompany you?' she offers, stepping forward.

'Most certainly not! I need you to cover for me. Keep Grant entertained.' I wiggle my eyebrows. 'Ask him to order the rest of the staff to stay away from this floor. And I'm going to need your back door key in case Mrs M locks it before I sneak back in.'

'I'm worried about you.' A wariness bleeds into her tone.

'How much trouble can I get into out here in the sticks?'

She sighs, reaching into the pocket of her uniform and plucking the key out. 'If anyone asks, I *will* say you stole it.'

I prise it from her fingers before she changes her mind. 'No one would expect anything else.' Pivoting on my heels, I reach for the dress. It's a Valentino imported from Italy, cut with a low scooping back. Its luxurious fabric hugs my figure and skims just above the knee line. It's utterly unsuitable for a princess, and I love it.

'Do you have the right bra for that?' Kat stands, eager to help as always.

'No, which is why I'm going to forgo one.' I wouldn't get out of my bedroom in England without one, let alone the palace walls. God forbid the staff should spot the outline of a royal nipple.

Kat purses her lips, and I'm pretty sure she's suppressing a smile 'Why couldn't I have been assigned to Princess Patricia?' she teases, prising the dress from my hands and unzipping it at the side for me.

'She's a bore, trust me. I'm much more fun.' I shrug off my silk robe, and stand in just my black lace thong. Kat holds out the luxurious lace and motions for me to step into it.

'There's fun, then there's downright reckless.' She smooths the material over my hips and carefully zips it up. 'Please be careful, Princess,' she pleads.

'I will. I'll take the Range Rover.'

'Come into my room when you get back. Just to let me know you're safe.' She squeezes my arm as I slip my feet into a pair of black patent Christian Louboutins.

'I will, I promise.' I take her hand and squeeze it. 'Thank you.'

'Don't thank me, just be careful.'

————

Half an hour later, I park outside the discreet granite structure, with my heart pounding in my chest. Curiosity rises like a tidal wave. Glancing in the rearview mirror, I fasten my mask over the top half of my face and suck in a deep breath. A hard hit of adrenaline races through my blood. I love the sensation doing something forbidden supplies. I live for it, in fact. There's something so sublimely satisfying in rebelling against the role I was born into. Even if no one knows I'm doing it. In fact, it's better if they don't, then I can get away with it for longer.

I pluck my Charlotte Tilbury high gloss crimson lipstick from my handbag and touch up my lips, then feel around for the miniature brandy I slipped from the sideboard earlier. A bit of Dutch courage is just what the doctor ordered. I unscrew the cap, knock it back, and shove the empty bottle back into my bag. The burn makes my eyes water, but it offers me the ability to strut across the asphalt with the confidence of a woman who's meant to be here—because something inside me is convinced of exactly that. Whatever secret society is going on underground—I *need* to be a part of it. I need something to entertain me until I can get back to the buzz of London.

The cold wind whips around me, sending goosebumps scattering over my skin. There are more cars here tonight than I've seen before. Hopefully that'll make it easier to sneak in. At the entrance, the tinted glass doors open automatically. I step inside and into the lift like I've watched so many others do. My pulse pounds through my ears, but outwardly, I don't so much as tremble—a testament to six months in an exclusive Swiss finishing school.

The interior finish is expensive—chrome and black marble with tiny silver veins racing through it. Apparently, Sean Beckett and I have similar taste—impeccable—that is.

As I plummet underground into the unknown, the thought is oddly reassuring.

When the lift slows to a stop, I suck in a deep breath. The doors part to display one word painted on the black marble in elaborate silver italic font—*Reveal.* An interesting and evocatively sensual name for a nightclub. I like it. Excitement skitters over my spine.

The second I step out, two burly, suited bouncers pounce on me.

'I.D.' one demands gruffly.

I fumble with my tiny clutch, making a show of opening it and digging around past the cash, lipstick, and miniature brandy bottle like I might actually have some with me. I'm wracking my brain for a plausible excuse when a woman marches out from what looks like an office. 'Number three?' she barks, scrutinising me through thick-rimmed glasses. Her voice is as sharp as her haircut, a crimson-coloured bob that matches the frames of her spectacles.

'I...' This is my one opportunity.

The only chance I'm going to get.

I have no idea who number three is, but a voice inside my head screams at me to pretend to be her.

Saliva floods my tongue. 'Yes.' I nod vigorously. 'I'm... number three.'

'You're late. He's waiting for you.' Her beady gaze drinks up the Valentino dress with mild approval. 'In fact, everyone is waiting for you.' She might approve of my outfit, but disapproval radiates from her tone. 'We'll sort your credentials out later—when you're not holding up every single one of our one hundred and fifty members.'

My stomach somersaults. This is... weird.

Maybe I should go? Admit I lied—that I'm not number three and make a run for it.

But no.

My body doesn't get the warning screaming from my brain. I've come too far. If I walk out of here tonight, I'll never get another chance.

I step forward and wet my lips, trying to think of an appropriate excuse for my apparently poor timing, before deciding the less I say, the less chance I have of giving myself away. 'Sorry. It won't happen again.'

'You're damn right it won't. Mr Beckett doesn't like to be kept waiting.' She swats a long-painted fingernail at my dress. 'Take it off. I'll put it in your changing room for you. There's no time now.'

'Off?' I repeat like a moron. My jaw swings open. It's about an inch from hitting the gleaming marble floor.

Her eyes narrow. 'Is that a problem? You did read the contract? The dress code was clearly stated.'

What have I got myself into?

It's clearly something debauched. Degenerate. Decadent even. And something deep in my core begs me to go with it.

Taking my dress off in public would be the most rebellious, and oddly erotic thing I've ever done, or will ever do in my life. The idea thrills me, as much as it shocks me.

'I'm not wearing a bra,' I blurt.

The redhead tuts impatiently. 'Well, that will save you taking it off then, won't it?' She makes a rolling motion with her hand, signalling me to hurry up, then turns to the bouncers. 'Lock the doors. No one in or out until the show is over.'

Show?

What the hell is this place?

One thing's for sure—I'm about to find out.

I unzip my dress, and it slithers to the floor. My breasts, and the expensive lace nestled between my legs, are on full display to the bouncers and to this Madam, or whatever she is. I battle the urge to cup myself, instead flexing my fists at the side of my body like this entire depraved scenario is normal. My chin juts out, and I hold my head up high.

'Well, pick it fucking up then,' the redhead snaps, motioning to the Valentino. 'Who do you think you are? Some sort of fucking princess?'

Nervous hysteria threatens in my throat as I bend over and pick it up. She sticks out an upturned palm, and I hand it to her. Her sharp green eyes roam shamelessly over my bare breasts, examining them like I'm a prize pony. 'He'll like you. You're exactly his type,' she says after a long beat.

For some reason I can't even begin to fathom, her statement pleases me.

'Right, it's showtime. Follow me.' Her high heels click off the marble flooring as she marches down the corridor with my dress in her arms, stopping only when we reach another set of black tinted double doors, which are manned by two more bouncers with impeccable suits and earpieces. 'If you want this gig, do exactly as he says. If you please him, he will please you—more than you can ever imagine.'

This is the most surreal night of my life.

She waves a keycard over the chrome lock, and the doors glide open.

I take a deep breath and step inside.

Chapter Five

SEAN

Low, deep pulsing bass notes fill the air, adding to the anticipation in the room. The scent of high quality leather hangs in the air, mixed with subtle notes of cedarwood and amber. From my position on the red leather throne at the centre of the stage, I survey the two women on their knees before me, both kneeling on crimson velvet cushions. One blonde, one redhead— both have their hair secured back in a low ponytail. The blonde, sub number one, is wearing a leather corset, which stops below her nipples, revealing huge, large breasts. A matching leather triangle sheaths her pussy. She's barefoot and bereft of make-up.

The redhead, sub number two, has opted for a strappy leather body harness that crosses back and forth across her torso but covers absolutely nothing. She's also barefoot, face down, eyes to the ground, waiting.

I glance down at my own attire—black suit pants and a black fitted shirt. Despite my kinks, leather doesn't do a lot for me—unless it's leather restraints, that is. Hopefully number three will be wearing something slightly more imaginative.

Where is number three?

She's delaying everything.

The third cushion is ready and waiting.

The members are getting restless in their theatre-like seats overlooking the stage. Naturally, Larissa organised this evening's activities in the Observation Suite. The ceiling features a rotating installation of chrome spheres that catch and scatter light across the dark surfaces, creating the impression of stars against a night sky. Discreet servers move silently through the space, attending to the members' needs. I glance up at the familiar faces, friends, fellow doms—kinky, wealthy bastards, just like me. Some are dressed in suits and elegant dresses, while others have availed of the elaborate changing rooms and dressed in their preferred BDSM attire.

Finally, after what feels like hours rather than minutes, the black doors on the left side of the theatre open. As my eyes home in on candidate number three, my breath catches in my throat. She's naked, bar for a thin strip of lace covering her pussy.

Fuck. Me.

Her breasts are pert, full, round, and utterly perfect. Lustrous, glossy ebony hair falls in loose curls over her flawless skin. An exquisite, diamond encrusted mask conceals the top half of her face, but there's no concealing that she's stunning. Blood rushes to my cock as she struts into the room in black patent peep-toes—like she's goddam royalty.

I love women who ooze confidence. It makes it so much more satisfying when they submit. And this woman—she has it in spades. Mesmerising chocolate eyes gleam from behind two carefully cut out oval slits. The second they meet mine, an invisible charge courses between us. Furled nipples peak as she drinks me in. She wets her full, crimson lips, and I can't help but think how fucking perfect they'd look swollen around my dick.

I beckon her to the stage with a single finger, motioning to the remaining cushion. Something like surprise flashes through her eyes for a brief second. Her stilettos root to the spot. Long, toned legs tense, like she's contemplating making a run for it. The thought makes me want to laugh—mostly because I'd love nothing more than to chase her. And if I caught her? Well, she signed the paperwork... so she'd be mine to fuck whichever way I deem fit.

'I won't bite,' I call over the low, sensual music, 'yet.' A titter of anticipation ripples around the room from the members.

I watch the column of her throat bob as she swallows, then finally, she steps forward. Her eyes hold mine—a privilege that she won't necessarily be permitted in here if I choose her. Though the thought of watching those glittering eyes glaze as she comes on my cock has a certain appeal of its own.

I bet she'd be dynamite to fuck. She has a distinct look of defiance about her. And defiance isn't a good trait for a sub.

I don't like punishment.

I live for the toys, the power play, challenging boundaries and testing limitations, but I'm not a sadist. Yet, I have a feeling if I pick number three, she's going to need a little discipline. Perhaps I could clamp her nipples and fuck it out of her?

She crosses the room with that same regal confidence she entered with, then steps up onto the stage.

'Kneel,' I command, eyeing the empty cushion.

She hesitates for a split second—yep—defiant just like I predicted—then drops to her knees, gracefully assuming the same position as sub number one and sub number two. Her eyes focus on the floor in front of her.

Perhaps there's hope for her yet.

Dominic steps onto the stage and taps his microphone.

He looks formidable in a midnight black suit that emphasizes his powerful build. His white dress shirt is open at the collar to display the dark outline of a raven and skull tattoo. Behind black-framed glasses, his eyes hold a calculating intelligence that makes him utterly lethal. He's the only man I know who could charm a room full of strangers while simultaneously calculating how to eliminate every single one of them.

Someone lowers the music slightly. His lips graze the microphone as he speaks. 'Welcome, ladies and gentlemen, to our Submissive Night.'

A tiny gasp permeates the air, and for a split second, I think it comes from one of the potential subs, but I must be mistaken. Their contracts were crystal clear.

The members clap. Murmurs of anticipation and approval echo around the high ceiling.

'As you know, our leader is in the market for a new sub, and we thought you'd enjoy the audition process. We will require your input throughout the night. You'll find a remote control on the right arm of your chair to vote on how you would like Mr Beckett to test out his potential new submissive. I'll keep track and announce what you decide.' He clears his throat. 'Usual house rules are in order.' He swivels slowly on his heel until he's facing me. He offers a single clap as if he's opening a gladiator fight. The members burst into applause, the air buzzing with anticipation.

Dominic exits the stage, returning a minute later with two glasses of whiskey. Some sex clubs have a two-drink limit. Not this one. There's no need. Not with his men as security. No one would dare to get messy in here.

He hands one to me, then taps his glass against mine. 'Cheers.'

'It's not a bad life.' Willing women on their knees for me, and my favourite whiskey—I feel like a fucking king. Hell, down here, I *am* a fucking king. This power, this control, it's everything I crave.

I give the members another minute before motioning for them to simmer down. 'Let's get started.' I thrum my fingers thoughtfully on the arm of the throne as the room falls to a hushed silence.

'We're going to do this in numerical order.' My voice is low, calm and commanding. 'Number One.'

The blonde's face tilts up, and her blue eyes meet mine. They exude an eagerness to please—to obey. I can already tell she'd make an excellent sub, and she hasn't even opened her mouth.

'What are we going to do with you?' I muse, thrumming my fingers over my lips.

'Whatever pleases you, sir,' she says. I swear I hear a scoff from sub number three, but then she coughs.

I rise from my leather throne and stride slowly, deliberately, across the stage to eye the crowd. 'What do you think? Shall we start with spanking? Suspension? Both?'

Hushed murmurs of excitement fill the air.

'Time to vote. Press one for a spanking, two for suspension. You have two minutes to decide.'

All heads dip down to their remotes. I take the chance to stalk back to the throne and take another sip of my drink. Sub number one looks to the floor again, her thighs clench together in apprehension, and a small smile plays on her lips. Looks like she's fine with either option. Good to know.

'Which one takes your fancy?' Dominic whispers lowly. His eyes roam over the three candidates, lingering slightly longer on sub number three.

I take a long, deep drink and eye the women over my glass. All three are perfectly poised in position—stunning, naked and all ready to submit to me. If number three's arrival didn't do enough to stir my dick, the scene in front of me is lascivious enough to render it solid in seconds. Just like Dominic, my eyes keep straying to her though—number three. There's something intoxicating about her, something ethereal. Something I can't quite put my finger on. 'Three looks like she could be trouble.'

'I love trouble.' His eyes gleam as he watches the votes roll in on an iPad. Frenzied whispers circulate. 'You have voted.' His lips open in a wolfish grin. No wonder half the country is petrified of him. I probably would be too if I hadn't met him when he was a gangly teenager in one of the homeless shelters my family sponsor. 'Apparently, you'd like to watch sub number one get a spanking.'

A low round of applause follows as two of the staff carry a state-of-the-art black leather spanking bench onto the stage. A third follows with an extensive collection of floggers and riding crops mounted on a portable chrome stand.

I turn to Dominic. 'Let's organise some restraints in case our new girls attempt to escape when the pressure comes on.' It's all part of tonight's entertainment.

Another ripple of approval sounds from the members above as more staff carry out a selection of restraints in a glass display unit.

'Rise,' I instruct the blonde, and she immediately obeys. 'Yes, sir.'

I beckon her towards the bench. 'Bend over. Face down, ass up.' She arches over the luxurious leather and sticks her ass out as instructed. I turn my back to her, running my fingers over the selection of restraints. Leather bound hand-cuffs. Cold chrome chains. Collars. Elaborate selections of rope. Leather arm binders. Ankle cuffs.

I make a point of drawing it out. This life is about delayed gratification. Not just physical restraint, but mental restraint too. Exercising control in every aspect.

Finally, I settle on an adjustable spreader bar with ankle

cuffs, and Italian leather wrist cuffs. I'll save the real show for later. It's no coincidence that that will involve sub number three.

I turn back to sub number one, who's still bent obediently over the bench. A string of black leather nestles beneath her peachy ass cheeks. I lean in closer, so only she can hear me. 'You comfortable with this?' I double check as I cuff her wrists to the bench, even though spanking and restraint were both clearly stated in the contract.

'More than comfortable with it, sir,' she glances at me over her shoulder, then catches herself, and reverts her eyes to the floor.

I fasten a cuff around one of her ankles, adjusting the chrome bar to spread her legs wider, then cuff the other one. 'And your safeword is?'

'Mercy.'

I like it.

I stalk towards the extensive array of floggers and whips and run my hands thoughtfully over each delicately crafted piece contemplatively before settling on a round leather paddle.

'How about this one?' I brandish it above my head, and I'm met with a quick burst of applause.

'I'll take that as approval.' I stride slowly across the stage, rolling up my shirt sleeves as I go. It's not about inflicting pain. It's about testing limitations, teetering on the pain/plea-sure border.

I turn to sub numbers two and three. Number two's head remains down, number three's hair is swishing like she'd just jolted her face back down. Oh, I'm going to enjoy testing her limits shortly.

'Number two,' I bark. 'Get over here.'

What's better than playing with one potential new submissive?

Playing with two.

She rises and walks towards me, keeping her eyes firmly trained on the floor like a good girl. When she reaches me, she kneels at my feet. I push the round leather paddle into her hands. 'I want to watch you with number one.'

Excited 'oohs' echo around the room. Group play is popular at Reveal. Dominic and I often share women.

'Yes, sir.' She rises and struts seductively towards sub number one, stopping behind her. She looks at me once again, seeking permission. I nod, and a split second later she cracks the paddle across the blonde's backside. The satisfying thwack of leather on skin pierces the air, followed by low rumbles of appreciation.

I turn to sub number three, who isn't even pretending to look at the floor now.

Her rosy nipples are peaked on her chest, and I'd bet my life the lace between her legs is soaked. Time to see what she's really made of.

Our eyes lock, and that invisible chemistry pulses through the air between us. I beckon her over with a single finger. 'Crawl to me.'

Chapter Six

LAYLA

Oh. My. Fucking. God.

I'm equally appalled and aroused at the scene unfolding in front of me. If I had any idea what I was getting into, would I still have done it?

Yes—I would.

No one's so much as laid a finger on me, yet I've never been as wet in my entire life. Sitting here almost naked, while an entire theatre full of people are champing at the bit to watch whatever Sean Beckett decides to do with us feels so wrong, but yet at the same time so undeniably right.

Selina wasn't exaggerating. He is unequivocally the most attractive man I've ever laid eyes on. Aside from the shockingly sharp bone structure, strong square jawline, and the physique of a Roman God, his big black eyes exude a dominance that no one could deny. He radiates a raw power I've only ever read about. With his shirt sleeves rolled up, and his tanned powerful forearms on display, the man means business. Kinky business. He's the single most sexual creature I've ever seen.

My parents would literally kill me if they found out I'd

stumbled into some sort of underground BDSM club. The Tower of London isn't looking so unlikely after all. But fuck it, if the glint in Mr Beckett's eye, and the promising bulge in his crotch is anything to go by, it would be worth it.

'I said crawl.' His low, deep voice exudes confidence, authority, and a tiny flicker of impatience.

I swallow thickly, eyeing the array of equipment on the stage, contemplating what he might do to me, and why I'm salivating at the prospect of it. Cuffs could be sexy, if he's the one wielding the weapon. Would he actually hurt me? My knowledge of BDSM is limited to sneakily reading a copy of *Fifty Shades of Grey*—or that 'disgusting atrocity' as my mother called it, before tossing it onto the fire. Thank God for the Kindle.

'Crawl,' he demands for the third time. 'If I have to ask you again, you're out of here.'

The paddle cracks against the blonde's bare ass cheeks again, and she moans like she's in her element. My core clenches. I can deny it all I like, but I want some of that. Need it even. My entire life, I've been treated like this fragile royal object. I wanted real. I wanted raw. I wanted inappropriate. Careful what you wish for, right?

What would it feel like to be whipped and chained and fucked like I'm a nobody?

Maybe if I crawl to him, I'll find out.

It should be degrading, disgusting, but the entire scenario is deliciously decadent.

I inch forward, shuffling one knee in front of the other until I reach his immaculately polished shoes. I keep my eyes on his the entire time, which if his expression is anything to go by, he appears to find confronting.

'Eyes to the floor,' he demands. I obey as a thrilling jolt of electricity fires between my legs. No man has ever dared to boss me around in the bedroom—which has made for very passive, boring lovers. But there's nothing passive about Sean Beckett. I bet he'd fuck me into next year.

'What am I supposed to do with this one?' His raised voice tells me he's asking the audience, who reply with an outburst of indecipherable suggestions.

Another pair of polished feet approaches. The guy with the microphone, intimidating presence, and expensive suit. 'I think you should take her straight to the Saint Andrews Cross.'

My eyes widen. Saint Andrews Cross? I've never actually seen one, but the prospect of being tied spread legged to one while this gorgeous creature does unspeakable things to my body sends a fresh burst of arousal between my legs.

'No, let's draw this out a bit.' Sean Beckett shoots the idea down in flames. 'How about we start with some clamps?' His tone oozes devilment. 'Clamps or chokehold chains?'

Fuck.

The man with the microphone addresses the crowd. 'Press one for clamps, two for chokehold chains. You have two minutes to decide.' My stomach churns; a ball of nerves, anticipation, and excitement as I watch his feet disappear out of view. The bass thrums through the stage flooring and up over my spine.

Sean Beckett sits back into his leather throne, a king surveying his kingdom. If he had any idea he was entertaining actual royalty tonight, he'd probably combust. Hysteria threatens my throat. 'Come closer,' he barks, and I shuffle forward on my knees without looking up. The scent of raw masculinity combined with his expensive cologne floods my lungs.

'What's your safeword?' A hint of devilment taints his tone. 'I suspect you may need it.'

'I...' I wet my lips and blurt the first word that comes to mind, 'Freedom.' Because despite being ordered to crawl to him, and the possibility of being cuffed and bound, that's exactly what this feels like—freedom.

'Interesting choice,' he muses. The thwack of the paddle slapping the blonde again momentarily steals his attention away.

'That's enough.' I sneak a peek from beneath my eyelashes to see him raise a palm. 'Now, kiss her better.'

I suck in a breath.

I've never been curious about other women, but the urge to watch the scene behind me burns like an itch I can't scratch. Is she kissing her *there*? I'm vibrating with the need to steal a look, but I'm already on my last warning. From the approving grunts and hums from the crowd, I gather the redhead is doing an impressive job.

'Good girls,' Sean's slick deep voice slides over my spine, along with a sharp stab of something else in my sternum— jealousy.

What the fuck? It takes me a good thirty seconds to process that *I* want his approval. *I want* to please him enough that he'll call *me* a good girl.

This is utterly insane. I've been here barely twenty minutes and I'm discovering kinks I never discovered in my entire twenties.

The stern woman's words whirl back through my mind like a cyclone. *'If you please him, he will please you—more than you can ever imagine.'*

I want to please him, and *need* him to please me—even just once. I wrack my brains for any hint of BDSM etiquette. I heard the other women calling him sir. Might be a safe place to start.

I don't dare look up, yet I feel his eyes on me. Feel the burn of them on my bare back. 'Rise.' His low voice is gruff. 'Let me get a proper look at you.'

I raise my face first, grateful for the chance to drink him

in again, desperate to commit every moment of this night to memory. 'Yes, sir.'

He quirks one thick, dark eyebrow at me as I stand. In this position, with him sprawled languidly in his red leather throne, his face is in direct line with the little lingerie that I'm wearing. That proximity alone has me squirming. His eyes meet mine, and that same sense of chemistry I felt when I walked into the room swirls thickly between us.

Does he feel it?

Or is it all in my head?

His gaze drifts to my lips, lingering for a minute before dropping to my breasts, then shifts lower over my stomach to the black translucent lace between my legs.

'Are you wet?' he asks in a low conversational tone.

'Excuse me?' No one has ever spoken to me like this in my entire life. Hearing those words from a man's lips is almost as shocking as the scene behind me.

'I said, are you wet?' He brushes a thoughtful thumb over his chin. 'Does this turn you on?' He motions to the crowd surrounding us.

'Yes.' The word rushes from my lips.

'Show me.' He beckons me closer with one finger. My gaze remains firmly locked on him, on his liquid molten eyes, on full, plump lips that I can't stop imagining between my legs. I have never felt so alive.

'You want me to take off my lingerie?' My nipples tighten further at the prospect, and a dull ache throbs between my legs. 'Sir,' I add as an afterthought.

Fire dances in his irises as his eyes snap back to mine. 'No. Pull them down at the front, show me your pretty pussy. If I'm going to commit to a three-month contract, I want to see what I'm getting.'

Three months?

I could have three months of kinky sex games with the billionaire next door?

Sign. Me. Up.

I don't even hesitate. I slip my fingers inside the front of my waistband and show him my bare pussy. Going full Hollywood was yet another act of rebellion against my royal role, and tonight, I'm beyond grateful for it.

His eyes blaze. 'Open your legs.'

I widen my stance; the weight of his attention has me practically writhing.

'Touch yourself. Show me you're dripping for this.'

I have never touched myself in front of a man—ever. There are about a hundred other people in this room. My cheeks flame, but I want this. I want him, so I swipe a finger lower, and fuck, the friction feels so good. This is already the best sexual experience of my life, and he hasn't even touched me. I swear if he were to spank me there even once with that paddle thing I'd come on the spot.

He tuts playfully, as a slight frown creases his forehead. 'You haven't earned it.'

Clearly, I'm going to have to work on my poker face.

'Show me how wet your finger is.'

I sigh, yank my glistening finger away and hold it in front of his face. He eyes it with a satisfied smirk. 'You're different,' he muses. 'Is it inexperience?' He strokes his chin thoughtfully. 'Or defiance? Do you *want* to be punished?'

I don't know what I want. I haven't got a clue about this life. About pain and punishment and whips and chains, but one thing's for sure—I will die if I don't find out.

'No, sir.' I suck on my lip and lower my eyes to the ground, hoping it'll buy me some brownie points.

He reaches forward and tugs the lace back up to cover me. Disappointment drills into my chest. Wherever that three-month contract is, I'll sign it this second—in my own blood if I can't find a pen.

'Kneel,' he commands, and I obey. Even I'm impressed with my ability to do as I'm told for once. 'Take the mask off. I want to see your face.'

Shit.

Shit.

And a royal fucking shit.

If I take my mask off, it'll all be over.

Then again, if I don't, it'll probably be over too.

Fuck.

'Remove it,' he commands, stronger this time. 'If you have any hope of being my submissive for the next three months, I'm going to need to see your face.'

'Promise you won't let it put you off, sir?' I whisper, acutely aware that our two-minute reprieve is almost up.

Something like sympathy flashes across his face. He probably thinks I'm scarred or something. I am, but not on the outside, on the inside. Scarred from a lifetime of duties and royal obligations. From shit sex and men who are frightened to touch me in case they break me. From men who view me like a trophy instead of a woman.

He stares at me thoughtfully for a long beat. 'I promise I won't judge you on your face.'

'Do I have to show everyone? Or just you?'

'Just me.'

I reach up and tug the silk ties at the back of my head. The mask slips, revealing the face that's been regularly plastered over every British tabloid since the day I was born.

His mouth drops open, and his expression of sheer horror would be comical if it weren't so damning.

Chapter Seven

SEAN

Princess Layla Sinclair, the third daughter of the King of fucking England, is in my club.

And I made her *kneel* for me.

I made her *crawl* across the fucking floor to me.

I made her pull her pants down and show me her glorious royal fucking cunt.

Fuck. Fuck. Fuck. Fuck. Fuck.

I literally feel the blood draining from my face.

Dominic chooses this exact moment to return to the stage, but most of the members are so focused on the redhead eating the blonde out from behind, they haven't noticed. He stalks across the stage towards me, addressing the members. 'The votes are in,' he booms in the same psycho show voice I've heard him use a hundred times before.

This can't be happening.

It's like a bad movie playing out in front of my eyes, and somehow, somewhere along the line, I was cast as one of the clueless main characters. 'You opted for...clamps.'

'Put that back on immediately.' I motion to the mask. 'Don't even think about taking it off until you're far, far away from here.' Leaping from the throne, I throw myself between the princess and the path Dominic is paving across the stage to us. 'Change of plan.' I lean to whisper in his ear. 'I need you to take over with sub one and two. Play with them. Spank them. Fuck them. Do whatever you have to do to entertain this lot, but as of this second, number three unequivocally cannot be a part of Submissive Night anymore.'

A wondrous smile splits open Dominic's face. He cocks his head in a curious expression. 'Don't you want to share her? Is it possible I'm looking at the next Mrs Beckett?' he teases in a hushed tone. Dominic—unlike me—believes that he will lock down a wife who's into this life and they're going to live happily and kinkily ever after.

'Not a fucking chance.'

His smile falters as he registers my grim expression. 'What is it?'

'I'll explain later. In the meantime, you're going to have to appease this lot.' I motion towards the seating area over-looking us. 'Entertain them. Or there will be a riot.'

Where the fuck is Larissa when I need her?

'The things I have to do for you,' he shrugs with faux reluctance. Dominic might be obsessed with a woman he can never have, but he's also obsessed with distracting himself from her too—his favourite distraction being group activities. He'll be in his element.

I turn back to the princess, whose mask is now firmly back in position. No wonder she strutted in here like royalty. She *is* royalty. How did I not recognise her? What the fuck is she doing in my club? And more importantly? How the fuck did she get in? 'We're leaving. Now.' I put my mouth beside her lips and add, 'princess'.

I'm so fucking mad at her for putting me in this position.

But mostly, I'm mad at myself.

'Crawl to me.'

'Touch yourself, show me you're dripping for this.'

Fucking hell.

I take her by the wrist and guide her off the stage.

'Where are we going?' Her voice even carries that unmistakable royal cadence, each syllable precisely enunciated as if consonants are valuable currency not to be wasted. How did I not notice? It was obvious the woman was from a different class to the others, but royalty? Fuck.

'Anywhere but here.' I step off the stage first and then help her down, willing my eyes away from her fantastically fuckable princess tits.

What on earth was she thinking coming here? I mean, obviously I'm aware her mother's ancestral home is the estate next door—hell, it was one of the reasons I bought it. There's rarely anyone here, and when there is, they require as much privacy and security as I do. But what on earth is a woman of her status doing applying for a position as my submissive? There's no way I could dominate her for the next three months. Jesus—one wrong move and she'd probably have her father alert the army. The fact that Dominic and my brother, Killian, each have one of their own is irrelevant. Who in their right mind would go up against the Royal Circus?

She steps tentatively off the stage in those ridiculously sexy stilettos and I force my eyes away from the shapely curve of her calves, from inch after inch of taut, flawless flesh on display. From the tiny bit of lace sheathing the pussy, which I know for a fact is dripping for my touch.

For fuck's sake.

Not helpful. Nothing about this entire fucked up scenario is helpful.

I march her across the marble back to the black sliding glass doors she came in through a mere half an hour ago. Amazing how quickly the shit can hit the fan.

'I don't want to go.' She drags her feet like the spoilt

princess she probably is. I should put her over my knee for her insolence. If she were anyone else, I would.

'For once in your privileged life, this isn't about what *you* want.' I snap, placing my finger on the recognition pad to open the doors. They slide open at what feels like a ridiculously slow pace. Despite Dominic's voice booming behind us, the members are still unsettled by our early exit. Fuck them. If they don't play by my rules, their memberships simply won't be renewed.

'You know nothing about my "privileged life",' she makes air quotes with her free hand.

'Whatever. Go cry to your therapist. Or better yet, join a BDSM club and work out your issues that way—oh wait— you just tried that.'

Finally, the doors open wide enough for me to shove her through. As we step out into the softly illuminated hallway, I breathe a small sigh of relief. If any of the men in there had any idea they had a princess in their midst, she'd never have gotten out of the building. Not in one piece at least. Role play is a big part of this life for some members. They'd be clawing each other's eyes out to spend some one-on-one time with Britain's wildest royal. Oh, I've seen the tabloids. Princess Layla brings drama—everywhere she goes. But not here. Not in my club.

'I don't have issues—other than the one in my lingerie that is.' She eyes me steadily through the slits in her mask. 'Things were just getting interesting.'

'Go find a duke's dick to sit on or something—just not here.' I'm pretty certain that's not the formal way to address royalty, but then there's been nothing formal about our exchanges to this point, so why start now? 'Where are your clothes? Did you avail of the changing rooms?' My fingers are still wrapped tight around her wrist, tight enough to feel her pulse racing. She's pumping adrenaline, fight or flight, but given that she's digging her heels into the floor and refusing to take another step, it's clear she has no intention of fleeing.

'You promised me you wouldn't judge me on my face.' She shakes herself free from my grip. Given that she's nearly naked, one would imagine she might cross her arms over her chest—but no—she places one on her hip and thrusts her chest out, drawing my attention once again to her beautiful, bewitching body.

'I'm not judging you on your face. I'm judging you on your family. If they had any idea I let you into my club, that I made you...' I scrub my hand through my hair. It doesn't bear thinking about.

'Technically, I snuck in, and you didn't *make* me do anything. I wanted to.' Her voice softens slightly. 'I slipped out, away from my guards, and crossed into your estate specifically because I *wanted* to be here.'

'You can't be here, Princess.' I glance over my shoulder, double checking the corridor behind us but it's empty. 'It's not worth the risk.' My eyes fall to her lips. It's a damn fucking shame she is who she is because the second she walked into that theatre, I knew instinctively that out of the three, she was the one I'd pick.

'Why not? You're the only person who knows who I am.'

'And now I know, there's no way I could...' Images of her beautiful body strapped to the Saint Andrews Cross assault my brain. Of her spread legged and begging for me to let her come. Of her screaming my name and exploding on my cock when I finally let her. Fuck. It can never happen.

She blows out an exasperated breath. 'That privilege you mentioned?' There's a hint of hysteria in her tone. 'It's nothing but a prison. Protocols. Duties. Charity functions. Photoshoots. Every minute of my life is mapped out for me. I've been banished here to consider my options—the truth is,

I don't have any. And I never will. So please let me at least have this.'

Her words stir something in my chest. 'I get it.' I soften my tone. 'Believe me, I get it. My life is much the same—minus the title. My future was planned out for me from the day I was born. College. Masters. Which section of the business I'd manage. Which bullshit ball I have to show up and "network" at. Which is why I exercise complete control down here. It's my own sexual sanctuary. I can't risk you ruining that. Imagine if your guards followed you? They could be outside the front entrance right now.'

'They didn't, and they're not,' she says matter of factly.

Still, I'll be happier when I get her out of here. Then I can check the cameras, find out how she actually managed to get into the building, and bollock Larissa, and every other one of my security staff for landing me in this predicament.

'You've had your fun.' I motion for her to start walking again.

'Actually, I haven't.' Her voice is low and husky as her steps match mine. 'Maybe we could...'

'Not going to happen.' No matter how much my dick is screaming at me. We reach the door to my office. I pull her in, flick on the light and close the door behind me. 'Stay here. I'll find your clothes, and I'll personally escort you back to Ardmore Castle.'

She sashays her hips across the room, stopping when she reaches my desk, running a long slim finger across the dark glass top. 'The thing is, Mr Beckett, now I've seen what you've got going on down here, I want—need to be a part of it.'

'You have no idea what you're asking for,' I prowl closer. 'What you experienced tonight wasn't even the tip of the iceberg. You can't even imagine what I would have done to you on that stage in front of all of those people. What I would have made you do to me.' Blood rushes to my cock at the mere idea of it. 'Thank fuck I didn't.'

She turns so her pert backside is resting on my desk, then hoists herself back on to it, slowly and seductively parting her legs. Holy fuck. Princess Layla has a reputation for being wild, but fucking hell, no one ever mentioned how sexual she is. How, in person, her body exudes pheromones that scream *'fuck me until I can't fucking walk'.*

The image of her bare pussy will be forever burned into my brain.

Her hands rest on her thighs. 'I want you to show me. Teach me. Educate me on this life.'

'Why?' I still don't get it.

'Because I learnt more about what turns me on in twenty minutes than I've learnt in my entire twenties. Because I'm sick of being treated like a fragile flower, whose sole purpose is to look good, or to make my family look good. I'm sick of boring sex with "suitable suitors". I want something real, raw...before I'm married off into a life of diplomatic dinners and breeding royal fucking robots to carry on the lineage.' There's that defiance again. It's in the straightening of her spine, the way she holds herself. She knows who she is. She knows what she wants. But she has no idea of the ways I would test her limits.

'It's not going to happen, Princess.' I unhook my coat from the chrome hook on the back of my door and hold it out to her. She swats it out of my hands, and it falls to the floor.

'Quite the secret society you've got going on down here.' The threat in her tone is unmistakable. Her chin juts out as her eyes lock with mine.

'Are you threatening me?' Un-fucking-believable.

'Not exactly,' she purrs, leaning into whisper in my ear, like we're not the only two people in the room. The scent of her perfume wafts into my nostrils. I inhale sharply as it hits me with unexpected force. It's nothing like the predictably pretty fragrances I'm accustomed to. This is something altogether more complex. She smells like danger and temptation in equal measure.

If she were my submissive, I'd tie her to this desk and fuck her hard enough to remind her who's in charge around here—and she'd love every fucking second of it. But she's not mine. And she can never be.

'I'm just saying it would be a shame if knowledge of this establishment were to get back to your family, or perhaps even the press.' She makes a show of examining her nails, like she didn't just threaten to blow my world apart.

'And what about your own reputation? How would it look if I were the one to go to your family, or the press?'

She laughs then, pressing one hand to her bare chest. 'Do you read the papers? The Queen is hell bent on setting me up with someone—anyone—with the right title. I've been trying to ruin my own reputation for years in order to avoid being married off to some boring, balding heir to a throne—not a leather one either.' Our eyes meet again, and the air short circuits between us. The chemistry is palpable. She's threatening me, and yet I still can't stop thinking about fucking her. 'Do it—I dare you.'

'You're seriously blackmailing me?' I shake my head. 'What is it that you want, exactly?'

'I want to be your submissive. Grant me access to your club for three months. Educate me on this way of life,' she cocks her head to the side, 'and I won't say a word about it to anyone—ever.'

'And if I don't?'

'Then you'll be on the front page of every tabloid ever printed before the sun even comes up.'

The little witch.

Chapter Eight

LAYLA

Blackmail isn't in my nature, but then again, up until half an hour ago, neither was getting turned on by crawling across the stage in an audition to be a billionaire's submissive. What I saw tonight, what I experienced, made me feel more alive than I've felt in my entire life. There's no way in hell I can scurry on back to Ardmore Castle and pretend it didn't happen. Not when it's the most exciting—and oddly liberating— thing to happen to me, given that I'd be surrendering all control—.

Silence stretches between us. If looks could kill, I'd be bleeding out on the floor right now. That strong square jaw ticks. He folds his arms across his broad chest. 'I still don't think you understand what you're asking for.' The resentment in his tone is real. It doesn't faze me. I'm used to being resented by my parents—for the very same reason—I want to live as I choose–experience exciting new things.

'I do.' My eyes fall to his lips. His perfect cupid's bow. The full bottom lip that his perfect white teeth are digging into. 'I want to be your submissive. And I want you to treat me how you treat every other submissive.'

'Did you read the contract?'

'No. I didn't get one. I arrived, was mistaken for "number three" by a cross-looking woman with red hair, and saw an opportunity, and took it.' I shrug, thrumming my nails on the desk behind me. 'Look, you have a position to fill, and I'm looking to explore. I can keep the mask on anytime we're in there. I'll be summoned back to London in a couple of months anyway. What's the problem?'

'The problem is you're attempting to blackmail me into doing unspeakable things to you.' He flexes his fingers.

My core clenches. 'Unspeakable sounds unparalleled.'

'It can be,' he concedes. 'Look, we both got a shock tonight. Let's not rush into anything drastic.' He changes tack, flashing a tight smile that doesn't reach his eyes. I can read him like an open book. Mr Beckett believes he can negotiate with me. It would be funny if it weren't so insulting. I was raised by the Queen of England—who also happens to be the Queen of Manipulation. I learned to spot a deflection before I learned to curtsy.

'I'll get you a copy of the contract. You can take it back to Ardmore. Spend a few days going through it, and then we can discuss this again when you fully understand what you're signing up for.'

I roll my eyes. 'You mean, the second you get me out of the front door, I haven't got a hope in hell of getting back in?'

'I have a better suggestion.' His face dips closer to mine, temptingly close. 'Come to my place for dinner. That way we can discuss things properly. Away from prying eyes.'

My curiosity piques. I'd love nothing more than to access his personal space. I bet it's dark and brooding and masculine, like him.

It's the best offer I've got since I arrived in this perpetually damp, windy country, but I make a show of thinking about it anyway. 'Fine.'

'I'll give you my card, and we can arrange something for next week.'

'We'll arrange something now. And if you try anything sneaky between now and then, like cancelling on me, I *will* go to your family. And to the press. I heard your parents are very traditional. Apparently, they insisted your brother James find a wife after his last scandal. It was on a yacht, I believe?' Of course, I came prepared. My Google search history is over-flowing with Beckett scandals.

A vein thrums at his temple, and he blows out a breath. He stares at me for a long beat like he's part horrified yet reluctantly impressed. I bet my life a man like him doesn't like taking orders, which is why he does what he does down here. If he'd just agree to let me try this, I'd take orders from him day and night—especially if they involved taking his body inside mine.

'What do you think they'd ask of the son they discovered running a kinky sex club?' I push my mask up on top of my head and arch a single eyebrow. 'That you join the priesthood?'

'You're very bossy for a woman who is supposed to be auditioning for a submissive role.'

'Don't worry, sir,' I salute him. 'I can take orders as well as I can give them.'

'I guess we'll find out.' He shoots me a hard glance, like he's contemplating all the ways he's going to punish me for this.

Bring it on.

'Dinner at my place on Sunday, seven o'clock sharp. I'll go get the paperwork, and your clothes.'

'Are you sure you don't want to start the initiation process right now?' Tension swirls in the air between us. The ache between my legs is practically painful.

'I won't lay a finger on you until you sign the contract.'

His eyes darken to almost black. 'And so help you when you do.'

———

An hour later, after checking in with Kat—who I categorically didn't mention any of tonight's erotic events to —I get into my bed with a glass of cold, crisp Sancerre and a contract the size of a peace treaty. Sean Beckett's shiny black business card is pinned at the top with a paperclip. I run my fingers over the glossy thick card, slide it out from under the metal and turn it over in my hands.

You don't have to do this is scrawled across it in an Italic font.

Oh, but that's where you're wrong, Mr Beckett.

I categorically *do* have to do this. Or my body will never forgive me, and my brain will never let me forget. I take a huge mouthful of wine and open the contract.

DOMINANCE & SUBMISSION AGREEMENT

BETWEEN SEAN BECKETT AND LAYLA SINCLAIR

This document, drafted on the _____ day of _____, 2025, represents a consensual power exchange relationship between the undersigned parties.

1. PARTIES

Dominant: Sean Beckett, hereafter referred to as "the Dominant"

Submissive: Princess Layla Sinclair, hereafter referred to as "Submissive"

2. PREAMBLE

This agreement is entered into with the understanding that both parties are consenting adults of sound mind and body, participating of their own free will. This agreement serves to outline expectations, boundaries, and commitments between the parties but is not intended to be legally binding. Either party maintains the right to terminate this agreement at any time for any reason.

The foundation of this relationship is mutual respect, absolute consent, and transparent communication. Both parties acknowledge that true submission is a gift freely given, not a right to be taken.

3. TERM

This agreement shall commence upon signing and remain in effect for a period of three (3) months.

4. FUNDAMENTAL PRINCIPLES

4.1 **CONSENT:** All activities undertaken shall be consensual. Consent may be withdrawn at any time by either party without blame, judgment, or repercussions.

4.2 **CONFIDENTIALITY:** Both parties agree to maintain absolute discretion regarding this relationship. No details shall be shared with third parties without mutual consent. The Dominant specifically acknowledges the Submissive's public position and agrees to extraordinary measures to protect her privacy and reputation and vice versa.

4.3 **EXCLUSIVITY:** For the duration of this agreement, the Submissive agrees not to enter into similar dynamics with other Dominants. The Dominant agrees not to take other Submissives.

4.4 **LOCATION BOUNDARIES:** All activities shall take place exclusively within the private confines of Reveal. No activities, communications, or interactions shall occur outside the club's premises. The arrangement exists only within Reveal's walls.

5. SAFETY PROTOCOLS

5.1 **SAFEWORDS:**

The Submissive shall use the following safewords:

- "OBSIDIAN" - All is well, continue
- "CHROME" - Approaching a limit, adjust but continue
- "SOVEREIGN" - Stop immediately
- "FREEDOM" - Emergency stop, end scene and agreement immediately

5.2 **CHECK-INS:**

The Dominant shall conduct regular check-ins during all scenes and activities. The Submissive agrees to respond honestly to all check-ins.

5.3 **AFTER-CARE:**

After-care shall be provided following all scenes. The Dominant will arrange physical comfort, hydration, and support as needed.

6. SCOPE OF SUBMISSION

6.1 **TIME PARAMETERS:**

The Submissive agrees to submit to the Dominant for the following time periods:

- Two scheduled evenings per week, to be determined at the beginning of each week
- All activities shall take place exclusively within the confines of Reveal

Outside these designated times and locations, no contact or fraternisation shall occur between the parties. The Dominant shall respect the Submissive's royal duties and public responsibilities, and both parties agree to maintain complete separation outside of Reveal.

6.2 **DOMAINS OF CONTROL:**

The Dominant's authority extends to the following domains:

- Physical positioning and movement during designated scenes
- Manner of dress within private scenes
- Sexual activities as outlined in the Acceptable Activities section
- Speech and behaviour during scenes
- Rewards and corrections

The Dominant shall have no authority over:

- The Submissive's professional duties, friendships, or family relationships
- Financial matters
- Personal appearance outside of scenes
- Public behaviour and statements

7. ACCEPTABLE ACTIVITIES

The following activities are acceptable to both parties:

- Bondage (rope, leather restraints, cuffs)
- Sensory deprivation (blindfolds, earphones)
- Sensation play (feathers, ice, wax, Wartenberg wheel)
- Impact play (hand, paddle, crop, flogger) - moderate intensity only
- Orgasm control
- Verbal commands and directed speech
- Light discipline and correction
- Role-play scenarios (negotiated in advance)
- Exhibitionism (within Reveal only, to pre-approved audiences)
- Anal play

All activities shall occur exclusively within designated areas of Reveal and nowhere else.

8. HARD LIMITS

The following activities are explicitly prohibited:

- Permanent marking or scarring
- Heavy pain or extreme impact
- Public exposure or identification
- Photography or recording of any kind
- Kissing on the mouth
- Intercourse without protection

9. HEALTH AND WELLBEING

9.1 Both parties agree to disclose any health conditions that may affect play. 9.2 Both parties agree to regular sexual health screening. 9.3 The Dominant shall not engage in activities when judgment may be impaired by alcohol or medication. 9.4 The Submissive agrees to maintain adequate rest and nutrition to support safe play.

10. COMMUNICATION PROTOCOLS

10.1 Pre-session check-in discussions shall take place in a designated private room at Reveal, outside of power exchange dynamics. 10.2 The Submissive may communicate concerns, desires, or feedback during these check-ins without fear of disappointment or correction. 10.3 A secure messaging system administered through Reveal's management shall be established for scheduling confirmation only. 10.4 All communications shall be conducted through secure, encrypted channels and limited strictly to scheduling arrangements. 10.5 No

personal, social, or casual communications shall occur outside
of Reveal.

11. DISCRETION AND SECURITY

11.1 The Dominant shall provide security during the
Submissive's time at Reveal. 11.2 Minimal staff at Reveal shall
know the Submissive's true identity. 11.3 The Submissive shall
have a cover identity and story for any necessary explana-
tions. 11.4 The Dominant shall maintain security systems and
personnel to ensure absolute privacy. 11.5 All written records
of this agreement shall be stored in the Dominant's secure
office safe.

12. TERMINATION

12.1 Either party may terminate this agreement at any
time without judgment or penalty. 12.2 Upon termination, all
physical records of the agreement shall be destroyed. 12.3 The
confidentiality clause shall remain in effect indefinitely. 12.4 A
formal closure conversation shall take place within 14 days of
termination, if desired by either party.

13. SIGNATURES

We, the undersigned, enter into this agreement freely and
with full understanding of its contents. We acknowledge that
this document represents our mutual desires and boundaries
and commit to honouring them for the duration of our relationship.

Sean Beckett, Dominant

Princess Layla of the House of Sinclair, Submissive

Date

· · ·

This document exists solely between the signatories and shall not be shared with any third party without explicit mutual consent.

By the time I've finished reading about bondage, orgasm control, discipline and exhibitionism, I'm wetter that I was in Reveal. One hard limit isn't sitting well with me though, but that can be negotiated. I drain the remainder of my wine, then reach between my legs with Sean Beckett's blazing black eyes at the forefront of my brain.

Roll on Sunday.

Chapter Nine

SEAN

Thankfully, James and Scarlett are less frisky at Sunday lunch than they were in the lift on Friday. Like the rest of the house, the dining room drips with old money, but since Scarlett moved in, James's pristine bachelor pad has evolved into a proper family home. Personal touches line every surface now —fresh hydrangeas in crystal vases, family photographs, kids' drawings are framed and displayed like an expensive art collection. There's an ambience of comfortable chaos that comes with toddlers and genuine happiness.

My mother, Vivienne, perches on the edge of her chair, perfectly groomed and talking incessantly as usual. My father, Alexander, sits beside her, suited and booted, holding her hand atop the table. They're still sickeningly in love after forty years.

Caelon has one arm draped over his fiancée Ivy, her massive diamond catching the firelight as she leans into him. Their children, Orla and Owen, systematically dismantle an antique chess set in the corner.

Killian is practically devouring his new girlfriend, Avery, with his eyes. They've been inseparable all afternoon, his hand permanently attached to her back like she might be kidnapped before his eyes—again. Last month's Christmas festivities were beyond dramatic—even by Beckett standards. They're utterly enamoured with each other. I don't know if I'll ever get used to seeing Killian with a woman.

Rian occupies the seat to my left, my sister, Zara, is to my right, both squabbling about whose car is faster, his midnight blue Porsche 911 Turbo S or her candy red Jaguar F-Type R. They're leaning across me as if I'm not even here. Rosa, James's housekeeper, glides between us with practiced efficiency.

'More wine?' Rosa asks, already tilting a bottle of Château Beckett Cuvée Private Reserve toward my glass—a robust Bordeaux blend from our family vineyards in Provence.

'No, thank you.' I place my hand over the top of the glass.

Orla runs across the floor and launches herself into my lap. 'Uncle Sean, why don't you have a girlfriend?' She wraps her little arms around my neck and stares at me in that curious way that only children can get away with.

'Oh, he's not into women, honey.' Rian answers for me, firing a wink at her.

'What does that mean?' Orla looks from me, to Rian, to Caelon, then back to me.

'Some of us have better things to do than pursue the next conquest.' I glare at Rian over Orla's head.

'What's a conquest?' Her little palms land on my cheeks, angling my face to look at hers.

'Go ask your Uncle James. He conquered plenty before he met Scarlett.' Rian snorts.

Orla hops off my lap and rounds the table to where James is sitting, but thankfully, before she can open her mouth, Scarlett appears with a bottle of Beckett's Black Label champagne. She hands James the bottle to open. 'So...we have an announcement,' she says, her hand reaching for his as they beam at each other like love-struck teenagers. 'We're expecting again.'

It's official. My oldest brother cannot leave his wife alone.

The room erupts appropriately. My mother dabs the corners of her eyes with her knuckles. My father claps James's shoulder with dynastic pride, while my nieces, Harper and Halle, remain blissfully unaware their reign as family princesses will soon face a new screaming, but no doubt adorable, challenge.

'Congratulations,' I offer, raising my glass in a toast that, for some reason, feels a little hollow. James grins with the smugness of a man ticking another box on life's grand checklist.

I shake my brother's hand, offer my sister-in-law a perfunctory kiss, then take my seat again, watching this tableau of domestic perfection. Of the six Beckett children, only Rian, Zara, and I remain unattached. Zara's too young to even consider settling down. And God help the man to take her on. With five older, formidable brothers, I don't envy him. As for Rian, he simply flits between models, actresses, and influencers with a butterfly's attention span.

And me. Well...The things that satisfy me exist in a reality disconnected from this butter-coloured bubble of conventional success. Like I said, I accepted long ago that the chasm between my underground existence and my surface life could never be bridged.

As the excited chatter subsides, my mother catches my eye. 'Sean, darling, Majella Wellington's daughter is back from Paris. She's a lovely girl.'

The relentless matchmaking machine powers up again.

'I'm sure she's wonderful,' I respond with a practiced smile; the deflection is automatic at this stage.

'Does she have a brother?' Rian pipes up gleefully, elbowing me. Dickhead.

I'm tempted to show him the Saint Andrew's cross in my underground club. The toys. The restraints. The sounds I can extract from a woman with nothing more than a modulated command. But my preferences are private.

And that's the way I want it to stay.

Which is why I'm having dinner with a ball-breaking British princess tonight.

'Shut your mouth, Rian,' Killian growls. He could uncover my club in a matter of minutes, should he choose to. As CEO of Europe's largest security empire, he has access to all the resources he needs, but unlike my littlest brother, Killian respects my privacy—thank fuck.

My father ignores the squabbling, eyeing each of us in turn like he's surveying his expanding dynasty with satisfaction—six children, four grandchildren, and now another one on the way.

Could I ever have this?

Will I ever want to?

The question surfaces from nowhere as I watch Scarlett's protective hand resting over her still-flat stomach.

'You'll be next,' James claps my shoulder with brotherly presumption.

I offer another polite smile because it's expected, but despite this perpetual exposure to familial bliss, I'm a dominant, not a domestic, and I wouldn't trade my cultivated darkness for all the golden-hued family portraits in Ireland.

Which is why I need to excuse myself to prepare for tonight's meeting. I'm the Dom, yet that little royal witch wields more power than me—the power to reveal me. Though, after reading through the contract, Princess Layla Sinclair might not be quite as cocky as she was the first time we met. Words like orgasm control and sensory deprivation tend to have that effect on a lot of women. Which is why I keep my sex life completely separate from my social life. If the princess doesn't cancel, or simply fail to show up tonight, I'd bet my ass she'll want to negotiate things down.

I spent the last few days researching her, and from the reports in the tabloids, she wasn't exaggerating about trying to ruin her own reputation. Her latest antics just before Christmas certainly ruined her chances with her last suitor. Tipping a drink over a man's head has that effect. The article made me laugh out loud. She's got spirit, I'll give her that. Despite her attempts to blackmail me, part of me admires her.

Attending a kinky sex club might feel like her best rebellion against her royal restraints yet. Once her rebellion doesn't start a war, I wouldn't be entirely averse to getting behind her—literally and figuratively—providing our arrangement never gets out. The chemistry between us was explosive. Now the shock has worn off, I've thought about Friday night more times than I can count—mostly with utter want.

Larissa was distraught when I caught up with her. She offered her resignation immediately. I couldn't accept it. The truth is, I couldn't manage Reveal without her.

I drain the rest of my wine, then rise from my seat.

'Where are you going?' Scarlett calls across the table where Harper and Halle are hanging off her like a climbing frame. 'We haven't even had dessert yet.'

'Sorry,' I force an apologetic tone. 'I'm meeting someone.'

My mother's head snaps up hard enough to give her whiplash. 'A woman?'

'Yes. But don't get your hopes up. It's not like that.'

'That's how these things start,' Caelon says, looking at Ivy with huge puppy dog eyes. Their own wedding is only a few months away.

'It's just business. Talk soon.' I shake hands with the men, kiss the women's cheeks and make my way out into the damp, drizzling evening where my driver, Ben, awaits. He's one of

Killian's men—a lethally trained bodyguard, but he's also my friend, sparring partner and confidant. When we spend so much time together, there's no other option.

All Becketts have security detail. My estate is littered with cameras and armed security guards, but they know to stay away from the west side. They're under strict instructions to turn a blind eye to the comings and goings. Dominic's guys police Reveal. The two never usually cross over. Wealth welcomes enemies in this world, and we have plenty. Which is why I'm determined not to add the British royals to that list.

Half of me hopes the princess will cancel.

The other half is still imagining her spread out like an all you can eat buffet on my Saint Andrew's cross.

'You ready for your royal guest tonight?' Ben teases as he drives me home to Blackstone House. I had no option but to confess what happened on Friday night. If the princess is anywhere near my place, it's his job to protect her in addition to protecting me. He can't do that if he's unaware of her presence.

'I have a sinking suspicion no one could be ready for Princess Layla Sinclair.' I thrum my fingers over my chin.

'You like her.' He glances in the rearview mirror to squint at me through the moonlight.

'Don't be so ridiculous.' I tut, hitting the button to slide up the partition separating the back of the Bentley from the front. The last thing I hear before it closes completely is the sound of his smug laughter.

He drops me off at the house's pillared entrance then heads to his own private quarters to check the CCTV and then the estate's perimeters. Given the princess's high profile, we need to be vigilant, unlike her own security. She'll enter and leave my property with the same level of protection she'd receive at a diplomatic function. No one will touch her under my watch—no one but me, that is.

Bar the security team, no one is here. I gave all my staff the night off, including my elderly housekeeper, Mrs Walsh, with strict instructions not to return until morning. Her raised eyebrow said everything about the unusual nature of my request, but twenty-six years of service to first my mother, then to me, has taught her not to ask questions. She left a lamb marinating as I requested and laid out the vegetables for me to prepare. I asked her to leave scallops in the fridge to serve as a starter. I'm a surprisingly good cook, even if I do say so myself. I actually like cooking. Like the routine of following recipes. It's oddly therapeutic.

I ditch my coat and make my way to the kitchen. It gleams with the same precision as my office—custom Gaggenau appliances in brushed steel imported directly from Germany, forty-foot Calacatta marble countertops sourced from the same quarries in Carrara the renaissance masters used when crafting the Vatican, and not a single item out of place beneath the handblown Venetian glass pendant lights. It was designed by the same architect who renovated Gordon Ramsay's flagship restaurant, with floor-to-ceiling windows framing the meticulously landscaped gardens.

I methodically arrange my mise en place on the hand-crafted walnut chopping block, each ingredient precisely measured in small crystal bowls and positioned within arm's reach. There's comfort in the familiar ritual— unlike whatever the fuck is about to unfold with Princess Layla Sinclair.

The image of her crawling across the stage with heat and hunger in her eyes has taunted me every hour of every day since. Not helpful, given I'm about to be alone with her.

I check my watch and select a bottle of Beckett's Black Label from the cellar, the same exceptional vintage champagne from our family's vineyards that Scarlett brought through earlier. Champagne is my favourite aperitif. I select a bottle of red to accompany the lamb, open it, and leave it to breathe on the counter.

The intercom from the main gate buzzes. I pull up the feed on my mobile phone. The princess is at the main gate in a nondescript black Range Rover with heavily tinted windows. She's surprisingly punctual. I'd half-expected her to arrive fashionably late, some petty assertion of royal privilege. More surprising still: she's actually turned up. Few people truly understand what they're asking for when they seek this life. But then again, fewer people still have the audacity to blackmail their way into it either.

I press the button to grant her access, then ease the scallops into the smoking pan, quietly contemplating how to broach the conversation ahead. Larissa normally does this part for me, but given the princess' status, and her threat to expose me, it's imperative I handle this personally. Plus, I can't deny the part of me that is desperate to see her again—to explore if that raw, primal chemistry between us was as real as it felt in the club. I've never felt anything like it in my life.

The doorbell chimes. I lower the heat, wipe my hands on a towel, and straighten my cuffs. I opted for black suit pants and a black shirt. Maybe my outfit will reflect the darkness of what she's asking for.

I stride through the double height hall and open the door.

Fuck me.

My throat tightens as I fight the urge to gulp her in.

She was stunning on Friday night in a scrap of lace.

Tonight, she's a knockout in a belted cashmere black coat, which suggests quiet money rather than royal ostentation. She clutches a thick brown envelope in her hand like a lifeline. Her thick lustrous hair is tied back in a poker straight pony tail that my hands are itching to wrap around. Did she do that on purpose? Did she notice the other subs' style and copy it?

Flawless makeup dusts her high, prominent cheekbones. She's wearing that shiny scarlet lipstick again. Thick black lashes frame her deep chocolate eyes. They sweep downward as she takes me all in. When she finally tips her head back to meet my eye, that same lethal electricity pulses in the air between us.

'I did wonder if you'd come.' I recover, stepping aside and beckoning her in.

'I wondered the same thing.' The small smirk that touches her lips tells me she's referring to something else entirely.

Will she cry out my name as she shatters on my cock?

My dick jerks in my pants at the prospect. For fuck's sake. This isn't what tonight's supposed to be about.

'What's the proper form of address? Your Highness or Princess? Forgive my ignorance, I've never had the pleasure of dining with royalty before.' Though I've dined with plenty of women who thought they were princesses.

'Princess is fine.' She breezes into my house, eyeing the décor with what looks like appreciation. 'That way, when we're in the club, it'll sound like a form of endearment.' Her perfume—that same intoxicating, complex scent I'd noticed on Friday night—seeps into my nostrils, crawling its way into my lungs.

'We haven't signed anything yet,' I remind her, closing the door.

'I have.' Her eyes gleam boldly back at me as she waves the envelope under my nose.

'Keen, aren't you?' I motion for her to head on through to the kitchen. 'I've prepared dinner. I thought we might discuss terms after we've gotten to know each other a bit better.'

She glances around my entrance hall, taking in the

portraits lining my walls with interest. 'You have an impressive art collection*, and* you can cook?'

'Is that so surprising?'

As she shrugs out of her coat, she keeps a tight hold on the contract. My jaw almost hits the floor at her attire. A strapless fitted black lace bodice sculpts her breasts, then nips in her tiny waist, before disappearing into leather fitted pants which hug her thighs in a way that can only be described as overtly sexual.

I changed my mind about leather—on her, it's fucking irresistible.

She's dressed for war.

Let's hope we don't start one.

I take her coat and try not to stare at her as she gazes so intently at the abstract art lining my walls.

'The former—no, given you're a billionaire. The latter—yes.' She shrugs. 'Again, given you're a billionaire.'

'My friend Jaxon has an art gallery. He makes sure I get first dibs on the best pieces.' I shrug, running my eyes over her feminine frame again. 'I like beautiful things.' I hang up her coat, then point her towards the kitchen, watching her pert ass sashay as her red heeled patent shoes click precisely over the polished wooden flooring. 'And as for cooking— it relaxes me. It's all about nailing the control and timing—'

'Much like your other recreational activities?' She raises an eyebrow, dropping the envelope onto the gleaming kitchen counter.

I ignore her comment and turn my attention back to the pan. It's safer that way. 'Make yourself comfortable. There's wine breathing on the counter and a bottle of champagne in the cooling bucket.'

The princess pours herself a glass of champagne, then perches on one of the high leather bar stools at the kitchen island. Her eyes burn into my back as I work. 'Surely it would be more appropriate to discuss the contract in one of your sex dungeons, not over dinner.'

I flip the scallops with practiced precision. 'There's nothing appropriate about any of this, but if you're referring to my club, dinner isn't typically served there.' I twist my head to drink her in again. 'The only thing we eat down there is each other.'

Our eyes lock. Hers flash with heat and hunger as she bites back a smirk. Let's see how funny she thinks this arrangement is when her wrists are bound so tightly she'll have rope burns for a week. That chemistry thrums between us again. The air is charged with illicit possibilities. I've never felt it so acutely with a submissive before. Previously, it was the agreement between us that turned me on, not necessarily the submissive herself. But I can't stop wondering what the princess's pretty little cunt tastes like. Wondering if she'll scream when she shatters on my tongue. The thought has my dick solid in seconds.

'Sign me up.' Her perfect white teeth bite into her lower lip.

'That's what you're here to discuss—after we've gotten to know each other a bit better.'

I never wanted to get to know a sub before. The only thing I was interested in before was her body. But the princess is different. She's intriguing. Ethereal. Sexy as fuck. And so off limits, it doesn't bear contemplating, which if I'm honest, only adds to the appeal.

She takes a sip of her champagne, and her eyes travel to the label with surprising attentiveness. 'Beckett's Black Label. Your family's vineyards?'

'I see your research extended to my family's subsidiaries as well as our scandals.' I cock my head. 'It was my brother James's idea to acquire the original vineyards in Provence—a lucrative one at that.' I plate the scallops, adding a drizzle of brown butter and herbs. 'We've acquired several more over the past year.'

I can't wait to wipe that smirk off her face. Preferably with my dick. Blackmailing a Beckett has serious consequences. In her case—those consequences will be sexual. The thought alone is sending me feral. It's taking every modicum of willpower in me not to bend her over the table this second.

'I hope you're not vegetarian.'

'No, sir.' Her full lips part in another sexy smile, and her eyes drop to my crotch. Oh, she's good.

I shake her deliberately planted salacious thoughts from my brain and slide a plate towards her.

She accepts it with a quiet thank you. 'You sent your staff away. Don't you trust them?'

I pour wine for us both, measuring her reaction. She's remarkably at ease for someone about to discuss whether she's happy for me to gag her while I fuck her in the ass. Either she's an excellent actress—entirely possible given her royal training—or the contract genuinely didn't disturb her.

'I prefer to keep certain aspects of my life separate,' I admit.

'Like keeping your family from your club?' she spears a bit of scallop, and I watch as she pops it between her crimson lips.

I freeze, my wine glass halfway to my lips. 'What is the obsession with my family?'

'You're interesting. All of you. All the different subsidiaries of Beckett Enterprises. There isn't a pie one of you doesn't have a finger in. Nice little acquisition you picked up in Cork on Friday.' She says this casually, as if reciting a weather report. 'I did my homework, Mr. Beckett. Just as I'm sure you've done yours on me.'

'I don't need to do my homework. Your family is plastered all over the media. You especially. Quite the stunt with Lord

Harrington. What did the press call it again? Oh, yes.' I click my fingers. 'The Royal Splash.'

'Lord Harrington was a chauvinistic, presumptuous, sexist twat.'

I bite back the laughter rising in my chest. This woman, this royal creature, is sassy, sexy, sharp and sensual—absolutely nothing like I expected. 'Don't hold back.'

'I never do.' She arches a perfectly plucked dark eyebrow and pops the fork full of food into her mouth. I watch as her lips move, and an appreciative moan slips out. My blood heats in my veins. 'This is so good.' She points a perfectly manicured red glossy nail at her plate. 'Practically orgasmic,' she says in a voice that dares me to challenge her.

'And you are so bad. Look at you. All you can think about is sex.'

'So punish me.' Fire dances in irises as she gives a shimmy of her shoulders that shakes her breasts. She knows exactly what she's doing to me. My fingers itch to put her over my knee and spank her, but I can't—not here. I've never had relations with a sub, or potential sub in this case, outside of Reveal.

'Don't tempt me.' Given the direction this conversation has taken already, we may as well get to the point. 'What did you think of the contract?'

She swallows her food, reaches for the crisp white linen napkin in front of her, and dabs her mouth. Her lipstick doesn't budge. Would it come off on my cock? I'd love to find out.

Fuck's sake, Sean. Get a grip.

She reaches for her champagne again. 'There are a couple of points I'd like to negotiate.'

I knew it. Which point was too much for her? My guess is on the anal play. Shame, I was looking forward to fucking her tight little ass.

'Go on.' I eye her over the top of my glass and bite back the smug smile that is threatening my lips.

'Firstly, section 6.1 Time parameters. I want four nights in the club, not two.'

I scoff. 'You have no idea what you're asking for. Your body will be sore. You'll be exhausted, physically and mentally.' I don't add that my usual submissives are at my beck and call five nights a week. But the less time she spends in my club, the less chance she has of getting caught there by her security detail. They seem pretty fucking useless, given the ease at which she can sneak about, but it's still a considerable risk.

'It's for three months. I think I can handle it.'

'You have no idea what you can handle.' I hold her eye. 'Yet.'

She stares back with that unwavering defiance again.

'Fine, we'll up it to three nights per week.'

'With a review to moving it to four after a month's settling-in period.' Her gaze drops to my mouth, then back to meet my eye again.

'Fine.' When I get started, she could be clawing at the door to escape on the first night anyway. 'What else?'

'Hard limits.'

Satisfaction flickers in my chest. I knew it. 'What would you like to add to it?'

'Nothing.'

'So you're okay with anal?'

She splutters, then catches herself. 'I *think* so.'

'You've never tried it before?' For some reason the thought I'm going to be the first man to go there makes me fucking feral.

'No.' She looks to the floor. 'But I'd like to... with you.'

Something stirs in my chest as my imagination runs riot with all the things I want to do to her. I bite my tongue to stop it from saying something stupid like, 'Let's start right this second.'

'Which hard limit is troubling you?'

She eyes me for a long beat, then her gaze flicks to my lips. 'Kissing on the mouth.'

'No.' I shake my head. 'That's a hard limit for a reason.'

'The reason being?' She inclines her head.

'It's too intimate.'

Her laughter swirls through the air like a song. 'More intimate than having your cock inside my ass? I don't think so. What's the real reason?'

I exhale heavily. 'It gives the wrong impression. This isn't a romantic relationship we're entering into. It's a sexual arrangement.'

Understanding dawns slowly across her features. 'It's to stop women from falling in love with you.' She laughs again. 'Don't worry, Mr Beckett. I can categorically assure you I will not fall in love with you.'

That I believe.

She's like no one I've met before. And it has nothing to do with her title or her position in society. It's the way she holds herself. The way she radiates confidence. Class. Elegance. She seems untouchable. That combined with her curiosity and unashamed desire to explore her own sexuality makes her easily the most attractive, intriguing woman I've ever met.

Which is why I irrevocably cannot kiss her. For the first time in my life, it could be me who catches feelings.

I take a sip of wine and place my glass on the table, eyeing her levelly. 'It's non-negotiable. Besides, you'll find it hard to kiss anything when I have a ball gag in your mouth.'

Chapter Eleven

LAYLA

I inhale a ragged breath.

What I wouldn't give to drop to my knees for him right now. To service him any way he directs. To surrender my body to him to do as he wills with. But the contract was very clear; all activities, all types of fraternisation are to take place at Reveal. Technically we shouldn't even be having dinner together tonight, but judging by his expression, he wasn't even expecting me to turn up, let alone make my own sexual demands.

'What about group activities?'

His eyes flare with surprise. 'They're a regular occurrence at Reveal.'

I don't particularly want to fuck anyone but him, but after what I witnessed the other night, I wouldn't mind an audience for certain activities.

Silence stretches between us. He lifts his wine glass to his full lips, and I watch his thick masculine throat as he swallows. 'Are you asking for a threesome?'

A hot jolt of electricity strikes between my legs. 'I'm not averse to the idea, provided you're involved.' He is the hottest part of every fantasy for me now I've seen him sprawled out in that leather throne barking out orders.

'That goes without saying,' he snaps. 'If we do this, your body will be mine. And I'll have no problem demonstrating that in front of every single member of my club.'

We're only having a conversation, and I'm already soaked for him. For this. 'Yes, sir.'

'If you keep calling me sir, I'll have you on your knees again before you can say freedom.'

He remembered my safeword.

'If you make promises like that, then you leave me no choice,' I meet his eyes. They flame with a hunger that mirrors my own, 'Sir.'

A low growl rumbles in his throat. 'You're officially the worst submissive I've ever had. Not only are you blackmailing me for this position, therefore stripping me of my power, but you seem determined to test me. I am supposed to be testing *your* limits. Not the other way around.'

I push back my stool and stand, slowly.

'I didn't strip you of any power. You had full control of me the second I stepped into your club. And we both know it. The same way we both know you would have picked me anyway.' I take a tentative step towards him. The air crackles between us as his pupils bore into mine. 'I told you, I already signed the contract. That will be the last thing I do without your say so... should *you* sign, sir.'

I tear my eyes from his, forcing them to the ground, then slowly lower myself to my knees beside his stool. I want this more than I've ever wanted anything in my life. I want him to take me to the dark side. I want to bathe in it with him as my guide. I want him to make me feel alive, free, and like a woman to be enjoyed, not a royal object to be admired from afar. I want to be touched, teased and tested. And I want to start now.

He rises from his stool. In my peripheral vision, I see his handmade Italian oxfords cross the room to where I left the contract. I don't dare look up. Not when I hear the impatient tear of the envelope. And not when I hear the slide of a drawer opening. I'm acutely aware I'm holding my breath. When he struts back towards me, then takes his seat again, I hear him reach for his wine glass, hear him lift it to his lips, hear how they smack together as he swallows.

Why is being on the floor on my knees for him so hot?

Why is the prospect of pleasing him so fucking arousing?

Why am I silently willing him to open his buckle and make me work for that signature?

It's on the tip of my tongue to offer him anything he wants for it, but I bite my lip and keep my mouth shut. I'm not the one in control here and, paradoxically, it's the most liberating feeling in the universe.

He skims the pages painfully slowly. Is he drawing this out deliberately? Of course he is.

'I can't sign this,' he says darkly, and I hear the paper flutter to the island.

I say nothing, certain it's a test. I don't look up. Don't dare to move even a muscle.

'Because if I do, you will officially be my submissive.' I hear the base of his wine glass dragging across the marble countertop as he drags it towards him.

Still, I say nothing. I hear him swallow as he takes another drink. 'And touching my submissive outside of Reveal is strictly forbidden.'

I suck in a breath. What's he proposing? The anticipation is killing me. It's also ruining the lining of my bodysuit.

'You know, you never did get a proper trial,' he muses, and I get an idea of where this is going. 'Would you like the opportunity to show me what a good girl you can be?'

'Yes, sir.' Still, I don't dare look up.

'I'm going to give you a tiny taste of this life, right now, right here in this kitchen. And when I'm finished with you, if you still want to sign up, I'll sign the contract.'

'Thank you, Sir.'

'Don't thank me. This is entirely for my benefit, not yours. Take your clothes off,' he demands. His gravelly tone sends shivers skating over my spine.

'Yes, sir.' I slip out of my patent Louboutin peep-toes and line them neatly beside me, wiggle the leather Victoria Beckham pants down over the curve of my hips, then my thighs. I feel the burn of his stare, but I don't look up. Instead, I revel in the knowledge that I have his undivided attention. Having an audience was thrilling on Friday, but this is next level. When I'm free of the leather, I fold the trousers and place them on top of my shoes, before unclipping the lace bodysuit.

He says nothing, but I don't miss his sharp inhale as I pull the lace over my head, revealing myself to him. I toss the bodysuit on the pile and kneel before him again. I'm so aroused I'm ruining his expensive flooring, but I'm too turned on to even care. My nipples are furled little buds, begging to be touched, my blood is molten lava pumping through my veins, and the throbbing sensation between my legs is practically painful.

'How does it feel being on your knees for me? Knowing you've relinquished your power—submitted to me.' His voice oozes raw masculinity, confidence, and control. His patience is remarkable. If he took his clothes off in front of me, I'd have climbed him like a telegraph pole.

I wet my lips. 'It feels... oddly empowering.'

'That's the thing most people don't get. Choosing to submit *is* empowering. Surrendering your needs is empowering. As your dom, I'll take care of those needs. You just have to trust me.' His fingers reach to cup my chin, and he tilts my face upward until our eyes lock. Electricity pulses between us. 'Do you trust me?'

'Yes, sir.' I nod to reinforce it.

'Good girl,' he purrs in a throaty tone. My insides melt. 'Now, let's get started. Get up on the table and lie face down. I'll be back in a minute.'

I glance at the thick, dark wood polished table across the room, and I'm crawling towards it before I've had the chance to even think about it. The anticipation of what he might do to me has me salivating. I hoist myself up as gracefully as I can manage and lie as he instructed, with my head in the middle of the table and my feet dangling over the edge. The wood is cold against my breasts, but it does nothing to quell the fire licking every inch of my skin. I press my cheek down and face away from the door he just walked out of and wait for him to return.

Thirty seconds later, the soft thud of his approaching shoes rings through my ears. A shiver of anticipation ripples over my spine. Tonight, I'm not 'your majesty', 'your highness', or 'your' anything. Tonight, I'm just me. And I'm his for the taking.

He prowls around the table, taking in the scene in front of him. I watch out of the corner of my eye as he wraps his fingers around my wrist, lifts my hand, and places it in a loop made of rope, then tightens it to the point it tugs.

'How does that feel?' he demands darkly, yanking on it as he lowers himself to a crouching position on the floor beside the table. His hands disappear, and it takes me a minute to realise he's tying the rope to one of the sturdy table legs.

I sneak a peek at his face while he's engrossed in securing the rope. 'It feels... utterly depraved. I love it.' A flash of approval lights his eyes as he moves around the table and reaches for my other wrist. He binds it equally tight, tugging once again to make sure it's secure. It is. I couldn't move if I wanted to, which obviously, I don't.

He prowls around the table to my feet. I let out a shriek as he grabs both ankles and yanks my legs open. 'Your cunt is dripping for me, Princess.'

I can't even try to deny it.

His hand reaches for my backside, mapping it and squeezing, then releasing. 'Let's see if it's still dripping for me after this.' It's the only warning I get before his palm cracks against my bare ass. The sound is almost as shocking as the sting. It wasn't hard, but still, my skin burns—in a way that I never knew could feel so good. Instinctively I pull against the restraints. The reminder that I can't get away—that he has me tied and trapped to his table and only serves to soak me further. I've never felt more alive.

'How did that feel?' He stalks around the table then circles back on himself.

'It feels like more,' I admit.

'It feels like more, *please, sir*.' He corrects me, as his palm connects with my ass again. Fuck, there's something so wanton about writhing naked on his table while he slaps my backside like I'm a naughty girl caught with her hand somewhere it shouldn't have been.

'It feels like more, please, sir,' I pant, pulling at the rope again, purely because I love the sensation.

'Greedy girl.' He tsks, as he does it again. And again, and again. Each slap gets slightly lower. Slightly closer to the junction between my legs.

'You're making a mess all over my table,' he muses. 'I should make you clean it up.' His hand lands on my ass again, but this time it's with gentle, soothing strokes. 'With your tongue,' he adds. 'But I've been wondering what your pretty, royal cunt tastes like since you auditioned for me.'

My heart hammers in my chest as I squirm with need,

yanking against the restraints. I need him to touch me there. His palms continue to smooth over the globes of my cheeks in maddening circles that skirt close to my centre, but nowhere near close enough.

He tears his hands away from me, and a whimper leaves my lips. 'Please, sir.'

'I see you're not above begging.' He pauses for a long beat as I hold my breath, waiting. 'I like that.'

Without warning, he thrusts two thick fingers deep into my core, and I cry out. That deliciously decadent full feeling is short lived, and he glides them out again, slowly. A sucking sound fills the air, followed by a deep moan of appreciation.

'You taste positively fucking regal. I'm going to need more of that.'

There is a god, there is a god, there is a god.

The table shakes slightly as he climbs onto it. Thick, strong shoulders nudge my thighs wider, demanding access as he positions himself between my legs.

His tongue swipes my entrance, and my back arches at the sublime sensation. I cry out as he sinks it into my core. It's gone again all too soon. 'Since you showed me this bare pussy, I've been dreaming about licking it, fucking it, fisting it.'

No one has ever spoken to me like this before. I could come just from his filthy mouth.

'Please, sir.' There I go begging again. I'm so fucking desperate for his touch, I can't even bring myself to feel ashamed.

'Please what?'

'Lick it. Fuck it. Fist it.' I can't believe the words leaving my lips. They're both shocking and thrilling in equal measure.

His low laugh tickles the junction between my legs, but he doesn't touch me there again. A begrudging groan is out of my mouth before I can stop it. I am officially the worst sub ever.

His teeth sink into my ass cheek, and I yelp at the sensation. 'If I sign that contract. You are mine for three months. Mine to bite. Mine to spank. Mine to suck. Mine to fuck anyway I please. Are you sure that's what you want?'

I don't even hesitate. 'I want it more than I've wanted anything in my life.'

'Good girl.' He offers me a long, languid lick. 'You were right, you know,' he mutters between strokes of his tongue. 'I was always going to pick you.' He rolls his tongue higher to sweep over my clit. It's so good. Too good. I'm so close to coming. It was always going to be quick. I was ready to blow the second I saw him again.

'You radiate a defiance that I can't wait to fuck out of you.' As if to demonstrate, he thrusts his tongue deep into my centre. It's too much. My core combusts, shuddering and rippling through the most intense release of my life. White hot stars burst behind my eyelids. Pure ecstasy rips through me as my sex pulses on his tongue.

Chapter Twelve

SEAN

So much for being a good cook. I burned dinner. It's the first time I *ever* burned anything. And not only did I burn dinner, I blew my load in my own fucking pants as Princess Layla Sinclair came on my face.

Thankfully, that's one fact she's not in possession of.

So much for being in control. That regal creature is going to be the undoing of me.

After the table incident, as I'm referring to it as, I ran the bath for her—an excuse to go clean myself up in the process and collect my thoughts. I've never come like that in my life. Never. Mind you, I've never tied a woman to my kitchen table before and lapped at her like a starving dog before either. I've never had a submissive in my house. Never run a bath for one. Never cooked—burned—dinner for one.

But Layla does something to me.

She's not some random sub.

She's a fucking princess, and while we're entering this arrangement together, I'd do well to remember it. It's one thing carrying on like that in the secure confines of one of the private rooms in my club, but not on my kitchen table.

What if she'd been followed by one of her guards?

What if my own security team were watching through the window?

What the fuck was I thinking?

Thank God, I'd had the sense to send the rest of the staff home, because the second she got on her knees, the ending was inevitable.

I dump the burnt lamb into the bin and pull out two fillet steaks from the fridge.

'Mr Beckett?' That majestic British accent floats from upstairs. 'Could I have a towel, please?'

Oh shit. I meant to leave one up there, but I'm so fucking distracted I can't seem to get anything right tonight. I'm supposed to be the dom. In control. Unfazed. But we both know deep down that no matter how much she submits to me, she will always hold the true power because of who she is. And she just so happens to be sexual and sultry and so damn fucking eager to learn about this life—the life I've hidden from every woman who ever wanted to know me outside of the club. No wonder I'm acting irrationally. It's confronting. I need to get my shit together ASAP.

'Coming,' I call, tossing the steaks beside the cooker. She came for dinner, she's going to get dinner if it kills me. I refuse to be found lacking—in any department.

I jog up the stairs, grab a thick, white fluffy towel from the press and hover outside the bathroom door for a second. Should I knock, given there's a princess in my clawfoot bathtub? Or do I just enter, given she's signed a contract to be my submissive? We haven't even officially entered our agreement, and it's already greyer than the Irish Sea on a bleak, bleary day.

I opt for the latter, given I've seen every royal inch of her —intimately—and place the towel on the edge of the porcelain bathtub.

'Thank you, sir.' Her head remains bowed, and she doesn't even try to make eye contact.

'Don't call me that. Not here. In the club, if you want.' I rake my fingers over my scalp. 'Here it...does things to me it shouldn't. Things I shouldn't feel in the real world. Call me Sean.'

Her red lips twitch. The little witch. She knows exactly what it does to me, and she's milking it for all it's worth.

'And look at me, will you? You came here for dinner. It'll be ready in ten minutes.' I stalk out of the room before I ruin another pair of suit pants.

Downstairs, I take a giant slug of wine, then get to work on the steaks, sealing them on a high heat before placing them in the oven. Thankfully, the potatoes aren't spoiled. I drizzle oil over the vegetables and place them in with the meat.

'Why did you invite me over for dinner?' Layla enters the kitchen, dressed in the bodysuit and leather pants again. Her outfit wouldn't look out of place in a trendy wine bar, but it looked better on my floor.

'Honestly, I've been asking myself the same thing since you dropped to your knees for me.' I snatch up the champagne bottle and fill up her glass. 'Truth is, I wanted you out of my club, and you wouldn't leave without arranging another meeting. This seemed like a safe place.' How wrong I was. I suck in a breath and reach for my own glass of wine. 'The contract was supposed to terrify you.'

She steps closer. 'The only terrifying thing about it is the idea that you might not sign it.'

I glance at the thick wad of papers on the island, stride towards it, plucking a pen from a kitchen drawer on my way. Before I can overthink it, I scrawl my signature across the bottom and toss the pen down. 'Happy now?'

'Yes, si—'

'Don't even think about it, Princess.' I hold my hand up, and she grins. 'No activities outside the club. In fact, this is the last time we'll see each other out of Reveal.' I don't add that it's safer that way for both of us. 'Make sure you're not followed. If any one of your security detail so much as suspects you're in a sex club, your family will come down on mine like a ton of bricks.'

'Don't worry. I'm good at sneaking around.' She waggles her eyebrows.

'I noticed,' I mutter, shaking my head.

I hate that she's put me in this position. But what I hate more is how much I'm going to enjoy being the man who gets to fuck her for three months. Who gets to educate her about my way of life. Who gets to test her limits and turn her on in ways that she can't even imagine.

'Sit.' I motion to the island.

'Are we not eating at the table, s—?' she sniggers, actually sniggers.

'I already ate at the table tonight.'

'But I didn't.' Her gaze drops pointedly at my crotch.

'And you won't.' Even though the thought of her pretty crimson lips around my cock is one to behold.

She pouts playfully, but her disappointment is obvious.

'You came here for a discussion,' I remind her.

'I came here for your dick, *sir*.'

I tut. 'Like I said, you're the worst sub I ever had.' I shake my head and turn back to the oven to check the food. 'Part of this life is taking care of your body. That involves eating well, drinking little, and working out.' It's a relief to move on to safer subjects. 'Do you work out?'

Mischief flares in her chocolate-coloured irises. 'I like to ride.'

My cock twitches in my pants—just like she intended. Fuck. My. Life. What did I do to deserve this? I like the simple life. An experienced sub, and somehow, I've just taken on the most inexperienced, defiant, daring minx ever to grace my club.

But like I said, deep down, dominating the defiant ones is so much more satisfying. The ones who *need* to be fucked into next week to know who's really in control. And Princess Layla Sinclair is the most defiant of all. She might test me. Not like Samantha did, but in other ways. But I'm going to test her in ways she can't even imagine.

And I'm going to enjoy every second of it.

'Cheers.' I raise my glass and clink it against hers.

Her eyes meet mine, and that invisible charge surges forcefully between us again.

'Cheers,' she says. 'To us.'

'There is no us.' It comes out sterner than I intended, but it's imperative she knows this isn't a romance. It's an endurance test—for both of us.

Her face falls for a split second, then she catches herself. 'To our arrangement.'

I nod my approval. 'To our arrangement. May it fulfil your every fantasy.'

'It already is,' she replies coyly.

Chapter Thirteen

LAYLA

The north-facing room I've claimed as my studio is the only space at Ardmore Castle where I can breathe freely. There are no stern-faced ancestors glowering down from gilded frames, no reminders of duty or bloodline or expectation— just blank walls, copious amounts of natural light, and the rich scent of oil paint and turpentine that means freedom to me.

I've been holed up in here since dawn, completely absorbed in the canvas before me. Deep crimsons bleed into charcoal blacks, creating forms that suggest shadows and secrets, curves that could be construed as architecture—but I know to be flesh. There's something sensual and mysterious emerging from the paint—my way of processing everything I witnessed at Reveal last week. And everything that happed at Sean's place.

The painting is unlike anything I've ever created before. I might even be bold enough to say it's my best piece yet. Where my usual work tends toward landscapes and portraits —this piece pulses with dark mystery and promising intensity.

Carnal images from the club spin around my brain like a carousel: elegant restraints that collared those women like jewellery, the controlled power in Sean's every movement, the assertive masculine dominance that radiated from him. I can't believe I'm his, and he's mine—for the next three months anyway.

I study the picture again. No wonder I'm feeling so inspired. It's been four days since he signed the contract. The memory makes my pulse quicken. I'm still trying to process it all before tonight's session at his club, and words—even if I had someone to speak them aloud to, which I don't—can't explain what I'm trying to capture.

I add another layer of deep red, letting the paint flow like silk across the canvas. Anticipation thrums beneath my skin like electricity as I try to imagine where he'll start with me tonight. What he might do to me. And the not knowing, the imagining, has me in a permanent state of arousal.

Why does doing something so wrong feel so right?

I've always been naturally inclined to rebel, but this is on another level. And since I stepped inside the club, since I witnessed the sheer carnality of what occurs down there, worryingly, I don't actually think the need to rebel is the driving force here. Sean is. And of course the need to explore sexually, which is confronting because... well, what if I like what I find?

I catch myself and shake my head. As usual, I've taken one step forward, then let my mind run ahead fifty more.

A gentle knock interrupts my overanalysing. 'Your Highness?' Kat's voice carries that particular apologetic note that usually brings unwelcome news from the real world.

'Come in,' I call, reluctantly setting down my brush. Kat knows this is my only escape. She wouldn't disturb me when I'm burrowed away in here unless it was essential.

'Sorry,' she says, slipping into the room with her usual

quiet efficiency. The wince on her face tells me all I need to know. 'Her Majesty is on the phone. She's rather... persistent.' She holds up her own personal mobile, which suggests how badly the queen desires my attention, when she's resorted to calling my lady-in-waiting.

It was inevitable, I suppose. I've been avoiding her calls since I rebuffed Lord Montgomery last week. I wasn't ready for another patronising lecture then, and I'm not ready for one now.

What am I supposed to say to her when my head is full of tonight's possibilities and my hands are covered in paint that feels like direct evidence of all the forbidden things I've seen and done?

Kat holds the phone out, her expression openly sympathetic.

'Did you tell her I was painting?' I'm stalling. And we both know it. Kat knows my mother considers painting to be a frivolous waste of time. I'd love to prove her wrong one day. But it would mean nothing if someone bought them because of who I am, not because of their beauty.

'Yes.' Kat's slight smile tells me she tried to buy me time. 'She said it wasn't a request.'

I sigh, pulling off my paint-stained apron. I suppose I can't avoid her forever. Knowing my luck, she's probably decided to summon me back to London just when things are getting interesting. 'Wish me luck.'

I take the phone and inhale deeply. Kat hovers near the door—close enough for moral support, far enough away to maintain plausible deniability about overhearing royal conversations.

'Hello, Mother.'

'Ah, I was beginning to wonder if you'd eloped with one of the stable hands.' My mother's voice drips with disapproval.

'There's no need to be dramatic, Mother. We're merely

having casual sex twice a day.' I glance down at my paint-stained hands and wait for the onslaught. 'He is rather charming, though.'

Her disapproval smothers me from across the Irish Sea. 'How you can jest about such vulgarity is beyond me.'

Yes, because obviously my sisters and I were immaculately conceived. Or did she just lie back and think of England?

'Relax, Mother, you know I live to torment you.'

'Indeed,' she sniffs. 'How are you? Has your migraine finally passed?' The way she drags out the word migraine assures me she didn't buy the excuse Kat offered Lord Finegan Montgomery for my absence.

'Just about. Dreadful things. You know I seem to get one every month at *that time.*'

Kat coughs out a little laugh from the doorway, all too aware that my mother considers the female menstrual cycle yet another utterly inappropriate topic for discussion.

'Ah yes, well,' my mother stumbles as she recovers herself. So backwards. If I ever have children—and that's a big if—I will normalise all healthy bodily functions. 'I trust you're feeling better now.'

'Yes, thank you, Mother.' I roll my eyes. I wish she'd get to the point because you can bet your arse there is one.

'Good, because Lord Montogomery has asked if he could call again this evening. I assured him you would be there, given the nature of your visit to Ardmore Castle is limited to the estate because of the circumstances you left under.'

Fuck. Fuck. And Royal Fuck.

Kat's eyes widen. Apparently, she can hear my mother's majestic voice as clearly as I can, even from the door. She has no idea that I signed a contract to be Sean Beckett's submissive for three months, but she does know I signed up to his "nightclub" and that I'm supposed to be meeting him there tonight. Naturally, she demanded details of our dinner. While

I told her Sean had an exceptionally impressive skillset for a billionaire bachelor, I didn't include his ability to tie me to his table with an elaborate knot and make me come so hard I saw not only a myriad of stars, but the moon, and the entire fucking galaxy.

She promised to cover for me tonight, as long as I promised not to leave Sean's estate.

'And Lord Caspian Ashworth is in Dublin next month. He's invited you to join him at the Annual Formal Ball for the Wicklow Hunt Club.'

'Who?'

'Lord Caspian Ashworth. His father and your father go way back. You might remember him from Patricia's wedding. He's a handsome fellow. Tall. Auburn hair. Piercing green eyes.'

Could this get any worse? 'Can't say it rings a bell.' I twist my ponytail around my fingers. So much for being sent to consider my options. My parents are just pimping me out to a different set of suitors. Even exile is exhausting.

I need to come up with an excuse, and quickly.

'I suppose there were over six hundred guests in attendance, so that's understandable, but I assure you Lord Ashworth would also be a wonderful match for you.'

By me, she means her—this family.

She's delusional enough to think setting me up with two 'suitable suitors' is allowing me to choose. In reality, it's like choosing between an alligator and a bear. She drones on utterly oblivious to my horror. 'The ball's being hosted at The Shelbourne. Randomly, it's a Wednesday. Black tie, of course.'

'I thought I was on house arrest.' I have no interest in being set up, but I could be persuaded to drink champagne on a Wednesday night in a nice hotel, given it won't clash with my sessions at Reveal. It's not like Sean's ever going to take me out.

For a split second, that realisation stings.

I shake it off.

It's an arrangement.

One that has already provided me with more pleasure than I've ever experienced. That's all it can ever be.

Would he care if he knew I was out with another man?

Probably not.

The contract clearly states that whom I see outside of Reveal is none of his business. I doubt Lord Ashworth is a dom. I'd never be that lucky. Despite my mother's glowing description of him, he's probably another ancient bore.

'You're not on house arrest. I cancelled all of your royal engagements and sent you to the countryside in order to give you time to contemplate your future. And if you can form an allegiance with either Lord Ashworth or Lord Montgomery, you may just have one.'

'Tonight isn't convenient, Mother.'

'Why ever not? It's not like you could have any other plans, is it?' Her tone dares me to challenge her.

I scramble around for an excuse in my head. Kat waves her hand at me and flutters her fingers. Bingo.

'I've been out of civilisation for two weeks. Kat arranged for a beautician to call at Ardmore. And goodness, if I'm going to been seen at the Shelbourne soon, I could do with a little TLC.'

'Can't you rearrange?'

'Do you want Lord Montgomery to see me in this state? If he and Lord Ashworth are as suitable as you claim they are, I think it's essential that I'm better... groomed.' The only grooming I want is from a six-foot-four, dark-haired dom, but I'm not about to admit that to my mother.

I can practically hear the cogs whizzing in her brain. 'Very well,' she concedes. 'I'll ask Lord Montgomery to call next Friday instead.'

'Could you push it out for a few weeks, please? I don't wish to appear too available either, even if that is the case.'

Unless it's available to spend every Friday night getting fucked senseless—and not by some boring Lord who'd need a map, a torch, and six full months to find what Sean found in less than three seconds the other night.

'And arrange for Lord Montgomery to visit during the afternoon.' I insist. 'Isn't it more appropriate to have tea first?'

'True,' she says thoughtfully. 'Perhaps that Irish air is doing you some good after all.'

I exhale the breath I'd been holding. 'It's actually rather refreshing,' I admit. Though no way will I elaborate how or why.

'Good. But don't become too accustomed to it.' She pauses to add weight to the punchline she's undoubtably about to deliver. 'Because if things don't look promising with either of the Lords in the next few weeks, I *will* bring you home. You're not getting any younger. It's essential you're engaged before your next birthday. And you must have a respectable date for Sabrina's wedding.'

Shit.

It's like she has this innate ability to sense me having fun wherever I am in the world.

'Let's not rush things, Mother.' I adopt an air of calmness I don't necessarily feel. 'I'll attend the ball with Ashworth and entertain Lord Montgomery in the following weeks, and we'll take it from there.'

I'll date all the suitable bores in the world in public if it means I can have Sean Beckett in private for the next three months.

'I expect a full update.' Her warning rings clearly in my ears.

'Absolutely.' I'm eager to change the subject. 'How is Father?'

'He's currently out shooting pheasants with Sir Patrick Donnelly. Or trying to, at least. We both know his aim is as accurate as a blindfolded three-year-old.'

I chuckle. 'He does try, Mother.'

'Yes, he's very trying.' Her dig at my father isn't lost on me. My parents' marriage, like my sister's, was not one born of love. Another reason why I don't relish the idea of being fobbed off to someone with an appropriate title. Life is too short to be miserable. 'Call me next week. If I have to resort to getting my lady-in-waiting to call yours again, I'll visit in person to acquire an update.'

I shudder at the thought. There would be no sneaking out the back door with Queen Hawk Eyes in the castle.

'I will do. The ball will give me something to look forward to.' Liar. Any second now my pants will catch fire. But if I don't convince my mother I'm serious, she could well send the family plane for me. She's done it before. I don't doubt she'd do it again.

'Good.' For once, it's approval echoing through the phone. 'We'll talk again soon.' She hangs up without further ado. Long, drawn-out emotional goodbyes aren't the Queen's style.

I hold Kat's phone back out to her. 'I take it you got that.'

She nods glumly. 'What are you going to do?'

'I'm going to do whatever it takes in order to spend the next few months at Ardmore. Even if it means entertaining that monstrous bore Montgomery. There's something about Sean Beckett that I'm compelled to explore. I need time.'

Kat slips the phone back into the pocket of her crisp navy uniform. 'I know he's rakishly gorgeous, but, Princess, whatever you do, don't fall in love with him. He might be rich, but he doesn't have a title. And you know your parents would never permit that union.'

'Relax. It's just a bit of fun.'

Am I trying to convince her?

Or myself?

Because I've only met the man twice but if it was a choice between marrying him, or marrying Lord Montgomery, I wouldn't even think twice.

Chapter Fourteen

SEAN

Friday night is the club's busiest night. I glance around the main lounge. There's a famous politician currently eating out his submissive on one of the benches. Several other members are watching intently. I'm perched at one of the high, red leather bar stools, sipping a whiskey as I await the arrival of my own new submissive. Unlike at our last meeting, when I wasn't sure if she'd actually show—tonight, I'm in no doubt.

What happened in my kitchen has played through my mind on repeat all damn week. It's all I can think about. The way her body responded to my touch. How quickly she fell into her role. How well she took the strokes of my palm across her backside. How wet she was for it—for me. My dick's been rock hard ever since. While I still haven't forgiven the princess's attempt to blackmail me, I can't bring myself to regret the night she managed to sneak into my club.

Dominic and Larissa are the only two people in the club aware of the princess's identity. Dominic is at the front door waiting for her arrival. I instructed him to bring her directly to me. She'll wear the mask she wore last week for her own protection, and for mine. No matter how many NDAs the staff and other members sign, having royalty partaking at Reveal is a hot topic for discussion. One that even Dominic's men might not be able to keep quiet. I need those lips to stay tight—not just for security reasons, but for personal reasons too. I need these three months with Layla to scratch an itch I didn't know I had. My previous subs were all professionals in this way of life. Layla's innocence in this world is part of the attraction. The prospect of teaching someone so proper such improper things brings out the beast in me.

I raise my glass to my lips and take a drink, feeling the burn as the liquor slides down my throat. A sharp sense of awareness prickles my skin. The air around me shifts. Instinctively, my body knows hers is near. I straighten my spine, pretend I'm not as ridiculously eager to restrain her and fuck her fifty ways to next Friday, then slowly incline my head towards the black double doors.

In a black lace bodysuit and those black patent peep-toes, the princess looks every bit the part. Long, exposed legs. Inch after inch of flawless taut skin on display. Her perfect, pert breasts are covered, bar a hint of cleavage. Huge chocolate-coloured eyes peer out from behind her mask, gleaming with excitement and a hint of uncertainty. When they lock with mine, that intense, all-consuming electricity crackles between us, powerful enough to fuel a fucking city.

Why couldn't I have had this with *any* of my other subs?

Dominic flanks her side, escorting her across the marble floor. He leans closer to murmur something into her ear, brushing his arm against hers in the process. For some reason that small touch sets a flicker of irritation running through me. We've shared women before. It's never been a problem. But for reasons I refuse to analyse, I'm ridiculously possessive of my new sub.

She tears her eyes from mine and bows her head as they approach. Good girl. Perhaps there's hope for her yet.

Because while she holds all the power outside of the club, down here, I'm in charge.

'Good evening, sir,' she purrs, then drops to her knees at my feet.

'Leave us,' I snap at Dominic. The slight smirk that twitches his lips assures me he caught my ridiculous wave of jealousy. Knowing him like I do, he probably touched her on purpose to test me. He and his daft romantic notions.

Layla's glossy, lustrous hair is tied back in a sleek ponytail that shows off her long, elegant neck. I have a pretty little present waiting for that neck in the Surrender Suite. All my subs wear a custom-made collar, but I had something exquisite made for the princess this week. I've never bought a woman a diamond before, but there was no way Princess Layla was going to get anything less. The need to impress her is something I am categorically not analysing.

'Good evening, princess.' I reach out and brush my fingers over her cheekbones. 'Are you ready to play?'

'Yes, sir.' Her voice exudes confidence, but I don't miss the shallow, ragged breath she draws in. Naturally, she's nervous. Alcohol will help her relax into the role.

'How about a drink first?' I run my finger lower, cup her chin and tilt her face up to meet mine. I don't need her to kneel or look at the floor right now. We both know who's in control tonight.

She sucks in her lower lip. 'Thank you, sir.'

I slide my palm over her shoulders, along the back of her arm to take her hand. Satisfaction sweeps through me as goosebumps blaze over her skin. I help her up and pat the stool beside me, motioning for the server behind the bar to bring over another whiskey and a glass of champagne.

She slides into the chair and crosses her long legs. I can't wait to tie them open and slide between them. The spreader bar might be a nice option for tonight.

I lean forward to brush my lips over her ear and swivel her chair to face me. My fingers skim over her knees, part her legs, and position them either side of mine. 'Are you nervous?'

'No.' Her breath hitches. Liar.

'You should be.' I lean closer. 'Because I've been contemplating what I'm going to do to you all week.'

'Me too.' Her eyes meet mine again. 'It's all I can think about.'

I glide my hand up over her bare thigh, tracing small circles over her smooth flesh with my finger. 'Are you wet for me?'

She reaches for the champagne placed in front of her. 'Yes, sir.'

'You don't have to call me that.' Her thighs tense as I inch my fingers higher. I'm dying to slip them inside that lace and find out exactly how wet she is, but delayed gratification is all part of the experience. By the time I finish with her, I want her begging for her release, screaming my name, and coming so hard she's dazed for days.

'I like calling you sir,' she admits. Either she's been reading up on this life, or she's naturally submissive. 'It makes me feel...' her eyelids flutter closed for a second, 'subversively sinful.'

'Happy to help your rebellion.' I slide my fingers higher again. 'How was your week?'

She glances around, checking if anyone is watching. Her eyes land on the show the politician is putting on, and her mouth pops open. Her thighs flex again. She's practically squirming. Good.

'We're in a sex club and you're asking about my week?' She wets her lip, then turns her attention from the lascivious scene behind her, and back to me. Dilated pupils stare back from behind her jewelled mask, burning with heat and hunger.

'I guess I am.' In the three months Samantha was with me, I don't think I ever asked about her week. Or ever asked her anything, in fact. But the princess intrigues me. Several times, I considered inviting her over under some pretence or other, but that would be in breach of our contract. The rules are there for a reason. I learnt the hard way that it's imperative everyone knows where they stand. And no one mistakes this for something that it's not. Not that she would. She made that abundantly clear the other night. She's fucking royalty. There's no way in hell she'd fall for me. That's one thing I don't have to worry about. Which is why I don't mind the eye contact. Besides, watching the way her pupils burn when she's turned on makes me harder than steel.

Unable to help myself, I brush my fingers higher, skimming over the lace sheathing her pussy. Her breath hitches in her throat. The material is soaked through.

'Well? How was your week?' I continue stroking her, teasing her.

'It was...' Her eyes flutter closed behind the mask.

'Eyes on me, princess.' They fly open as I take my hand away.

'It was long.'

'What did you do to pass the time?' And more importantly, why do I care? I should quit the small talk, but for some reason, the little details of her life are big details to me.

'I painted.' There's that defiance in her tone again. Like even painting is a form of rebellion. Maybe it is where she comes from.

My curiosity peaks. A flashback of her examining the art lining my walls springs to the forefront of my mind. 'What do you paint?'

'Anything and everything. I used to favour landscapes. Sometimes portraits.' She hesitates for a second. 'This week's pieces are rather different.' Her eyes fall to my hand, and she licks her lips. 'Forgive me, Sir,' she smirks. 'But do you seriously want to discuss art now?'

'I want to discuss *your* art. I want to know you more.' The admission slips out before I can stop it. What the fuck is wrong with me? 'How are this week's pieces different?'

Her head snaps up until our eyes meet. 'They're more sensual.'

I can only imagine. My hand gravitates to her thigh again. The urge to touch her, taste her again is utterly consuming.

'I like your hands on my body,' she whispers.

'Good, because my hands are going to be all over you—sooner, rather than later.' I push her legs further apart, taking a minute to appreciate the view. My lips skim over her jawline, then down over her neck. Her nipples tighten against the lace over her chest.

'Are you trying to make me combust?'

'Quite the opposite, in fact.' The familiar scent of her perfume surrounds me. It's feminine and erotic and utterly fucking intoxicating. My fingers brush over her sex again, and she hisses out a breath.

'Are you certain of that, Mr Beckett?'

'Absolutely. Now, be a good girl and finish your drink. We have a date in one of the Surrender Suites.' I can't hold off any longer.

'The Surrender Suite,' she repeats, her voice thick with desire.

'It's one of several. We're starting in the smaller one. Do you trust me?' Our eyes lock again. 'For this to work, it's imperative that you do.'

Her throat bobs as she swallows. She nods once.

I brush my hand over her cheek, staring at her with intent. 'I will never hurt you. This is about pleasure. Testing your limits. You have your safeword. Trust me to take care of you. Your body wants this.' I stroke her pussy again. 'Surrender to me, and I'll show you pleasure beyond anything you've ever imagined.'

She reaches for her champagne glass again, brings it to her mouth and drains the contents in three mouthfuls. From the way she winces, I gather she didn't enjoy it as much as my family's private reserve. I make a mental note to get a supply here for tomorrow.

'I'm ready.'

'Good girl.' I finish my whiskey, and stand from the stool, holding a hand out to take hers. She eyes it for a long beat, then places hers in mine. It feels small and feminine and slightly clammy as I lead her through the club.

Chapter Fifteen

LAYLA

My heart hammers in my chest as Sean leads me through the dark, rope-lit corridors. We pass an open door, and I get a glimpse of the huge, imposing Saint Andrew's Cross. The polished ebony frame must be at least seven feet high. It gleams, ominous yet tempting, beneath the low seductive lighting. My feet falter as my eyes scramble around the room, trying to take it all in.

'One step at a time, Princess. I want to savour breaking you in.' Sean's breath tickles my neck as he leans in to murmur into my ear.

He tugs my arm, and we press on further until we reach another heavy, dark wooden door. My eyes widen further as he opens the door with a key card. The vast, opulent space stretches before us, but the weight of my want fills every corner. Polished black concrete walls soar fifteen feet overhead. Chrome suspension points gleam like stars against the dark ceiling.

The centrepiece dominates everything: an elevated platform of black leather stretched over sleek chrome framework.

Dramatic lighting throws precise pools of illumination into strategic corners. Shadows claim the rest. One wall is comprised entirely of a tinted black mirror. The scent of leather and Sean's expensive cologne floods my senses. Underneath that—anticipation. Raw want. Hypnotic sensual music floats from discreetly positioned speakers, low enough to allow conversation—or, more importantly, to hear a submissive's safeword.

Sean's hand slides up over my wrist, gripping it like he's frightened I'm going to turn and run. His thumb traces over my pulse point, soothing strokes steady the blood racing through every vein and artery. I swallow thickly, my eyes drinking in every detail.

This is nothing like I imagined. Every elegant surface speaks of control, precision, beauty that makes my pulse quicken. My eyes home in on an enormous glass cabinet showcasing an array of toys—some tame, some which look frankly terrifying.

'Last chance to leave, Princess.' He drops my wrist and reaches for the open door.

I step further inside, spinning round to take it all in. Excitement and anticipation duel for dominance in my stomach. This is more decadent than anything I could have dreamed up, even in my wildest fantasies. 'I'm not going anywhere.'

'Thank fuck.' He pushes the door closed and twists the lock with a definitive click. 'For a minute there I thought I'd have to chase you down–fuck you in the main lounge in front of everyone.'

A hot jolt of lust strikes my core.

'Take your mask off. I want to see every single one of your expressions in here. I want to see when you're flirting with the edge of oblivion. And I *need* to watch when you fall spectacularly over it.'

I reach up and untie the silk strings at the back of my head. The mask falls to the floor. He inhales sharply.

'Lose the bodysuit. I need you naked for what I have in mind.'

I pop the buttons between my legs and pull the lace up over my head. His low appreciative hiss chases away any niggling trace of doubt. His eyes rake over my breasts as my nipples tighten to two hard buds, begging for his attention. I go to slip out of my heels, but he stops me. 'Leave them on.'

A dull ache throbs between my legs as I watch him cross the room to the leather bench. A black square velvet box rests in the centre. He picks it up and turns to face me. 'When you're in my club, I want you to wear this.' He snaps the box open to reveal some sort of necklace. Cartier, from the look of it. He beckons me closer with a single finger.

My breath catches as I realise exactly what it is.

A collar.

Platinum nestles against black velvet, so beautiful it could grace any red carpet or state dinner. It gleams under the suite's dramatic lighting. Tiny diamonds—perfectly matched brilliant cuts—are embedded along its length, catching and throwing light. At the centre sits a larger stone. Two carats, maybe more. Flawless. Stunning.

I reach for it, lifting it from its velvet bed. It's heavier than it looks, substantial against my palms. I run my thumb over the diamonds, each one perfectly placed. As I turn it over, examining the exquisite craftsmanship, my fingers find something unexpected at the clasp. A tiny chrome ring. Hidden. Deliberate. The kind that gets chained to the bed, or worse.

My stomach flips as I realise exactly how much power I'm surrendering.

I look up at Sean, the collar still cradled in my hands, my pulse hammering against my throat.

'On your knees, Princess.' He motions to the crushed velvet pillow strategically placed on the floor. I don't hesitate. He prises the collar from my fingers and carefully clips it around my neck. It's tight and heavy. The weight of it is a lot to bear— an uncanny reflection of how I feel about my life.

'Now, you belong to me. And everyone in this club will know that. No one touches you unless I say so.'

My fingers reach for it, stroking over the jewels. 'Yes, sir.'

'While you are mine, I will ruin you, whichever way I see fit. I will take care of every single one of your needs. I will pleasure you in ways you can't even begin to imagine.' He cups my chin, angling my face up until our eyes meet. The air crackles between us. 'On your feet.'

I do as I'm told, watching as he rolls the sleeves of his black fitted shirt up with an intent that makes my insides melt. He strides across the room to open the tinted glass display cabinet. His fingers brush over several objects: black leather studded restraints, a long chrome chain, then finally, a chrome bar with leather cuffs either side. He turns to me with a wolfish expression, removes the bar and stalks towards the leather bench. A fresh ripple of anticipation swoops over my spine.

'Come here,' he commands, and I do as I'm told.

He motions for me to lie on the bench. 'On your back, Princess.' This isn't the man I had dinner with the other night, the man who cooked steaks for me, asked me about growing up at the palace. No, this is the man I first met at submissive night. The man who ordered me to crawl to him. And I am here for it.

I drop onto the leather—it's soft and cushioned beneath my backside—then slowly lower myself until I'm flat for him. Anticipation thrums like a drum beneath my skin. My bare breasts beg to be touched. He twists the chrome bar, and I recognise it for what it's for—to spread my legs open—and keep them that way. The prospect sets a fresh wave of arousal flooding my core.

I crane my head up to watch his long powerful strides eat up the distance between us. 'Do you trust me, Princess?' He asks again.

'Yes.' And oddly, I do. I barely know the man, but instinctively, I know he'll take care of me. He doesn't care who my parents are. He's not looking for a family allegiance. He's here claiming a different type of power over me—and it is hot as hell. He cuffs the restraints around my left ankle, then my right, clipping each side so it's secure, but not tight to the point of pain.

He twists the bar, and I watch in open fascination as he pulls my legs wide apart, baring my sex to him. His pupils devour his irises as they drink in the sight. 'Look at your pretty pink cunt glistening with need. So fucking beautiful.' A low guttural noise sounds from the back of his throat.

No other man in this world would dare speak to me this explicitly.

No other man would dare to cuff me.

No other man would dare to use my body like this.

I swallow my nerves as he lifts the bar higher, raising my legs to inspect every inch of me like he's committing it to memory.

It's utterly erotic.

This is what I've been craving.

He lowers the bar again so my feet are resting flat but my knees are raised. He circles me thoughtfully, like a predator eyeing its next meal. I've never been more acutely aroused. I need him to touch me. Somewhere. Anywhere. 'Sir.' The plea slips from my lips.

'Yes?' He slows to a stop at my head. I tilt my head back to meet his eyes; they're burning with a heat that promises pleasure. He reaches for my wrists, wraps his fingers tightly around them and places them above my head.

'I need...' I don't know what I need, but I need something.

'Patience, princess. The night is young.' He licks his lips. 'Keep your hands here, or I'll cuff them.' He releases my wrists, sliding his huge, hot hands over my forearms and then onto my chest. The relief of his touch has my lower back arching off the bench. He starts tracing those damn circles on my breasts, circling my nipples, which are silently screaming for his attention. Finally, his fingers flick over them. The moan from my mouth is like no sound I've ever made before.

His lips lift into a wicked smirk as he takes them away again. I'm about to cry out my objection until I see where he's going—the other end of the bench. He grabs my ankles and spreads the bar another few inches wider. 'I could watch you writhing on here all day and all fucking night, princess. Knowing you're spread open and dripping for me has my cock harder than steel.' My eyes fall to his suit pants. There's no missing the bulge straining against the material.

'Give it to me.' The words are out of my mouth before I can stop them.

'That's not how this works.' His fingers brush up over my knees, slowly teasing my inner thighs, inching higher and higher, closer and closer, before he draws them down again. The man is trying to kill me, I swear. My frustrated sigh draws out a laugh from him. Instinctively I try to move my legs; the pressure of the restraint tightens on my ankles, and I swear I could almost come on the spot. Almost. Our eyes lock. Without breaking our stare, he resumes stroking my thigh again. This time, when he reaches my sex, he doesn't stop. As his thumb brushes over my clit, my hips jerk upwards.

'Stay still like a good girl and I'll make you come so hard

you'll forget your own name.' His dark eyes gleam and he sinks two fingers into my centre. 'I can't wait to fuck this tight little cunt.'

'Do it.' I beg, temporarily forgetting I have no say in where and when he does what to me.

'I need to make sure you're ready.' His fingers thrust in and out of me, working me until my legs are violently shaking. Fire licks over every inch of my skin.

'I was born ready for this.' My release shimmers on the horizon. I'm so close. He watches intently, like he's getting as much pleasure out of this as I am. Just when I'm about to erupt, he stops.

'Fuck.' I pant, bereft. Disappointment and raw need flood my body. I've never felt so empty.

He angles himself over the bar between my ankles, lowers his face to my sex and offers me one long languid lick. 'When I let you come, it'll be on my tongue. Since I tasted your pretty pussy last week, it's all I can fucking think about.'

'You're driving me crazy.' I'm vibrating with the need to come.

'You're driving *me* crazy.' He brushes his lips over my clit, and the sensation is sublime. 'You came crashing into my club, and then into my house looking like this. I haven't been able to get you out of my fucking head ever since. I've never wanted to fuck a submissive as much as I want to fuck you...' he takes a deep breath, inhaling my scent with an appreciative moan.

The entire world as I know it ceases to exist, replaced by pure primal pleasure as he circles my entrance teasingly with his tongue then thrusts it into my core. Over and over and over again. Every cell in my body is wound tight, ready to blow. I squeeze my eyes shut as heat dances deliciously over every inch of my body.

'Eyes on me, Princess.' It's not a request.

Our eyes collide. His look is as feral as I feel, as his talented tongue sweeps upwards over my clit, once, twice, and I explode, shattering on his face. 'God. God. God. God.'

When he finally finishes, he lifts his head up. 'God has fuck all to do with this. It's just you and me, princess. You pray to me, and me alone. But down here, there will be no mercy.'

He backs off the bench and reaches for the buckle on his belt.

Chapter Sixteen

SEAN

Seeing Princess Layla spread out for me like a fucking banquet wearing nothing but those heels and the collar I put on her neck is something I've been imagining all week. Which is why I beat myself off twice before leaving the house tonight. No fucking way was I risking a repeat of the other night. That was a first—and last.

Her cheeks are flushed with arousal, her eyes huge and dazed. Her chest rises and falls as she struggles to catch her breath. I'm not going to give her the chance. I unzip my suit trousers, and my cock bursts free. Her eyes fall to it, wide and wanting.

I reach for the spreader bar and yank her down the leather bench until her ass is balancing at the edge. She squeals as her back slides over the smooth leather and her nipples tighten again. 'How are your legs?'

'Shaking like a newborn fawn.'

I unfasten the cuffs at each ankle and place the bar on the floor. I need to feel her legs wrap around me the first time. Need to feel her dig her heels into my backside when she comes on my cock. And I need to watch her face when she does. It's her innocence to this world again. The prospect of decadently defiling something so polished. The fact that she's trusting me so implicitly to do exactly that is fucking beautiful.

She goes to sit up, but I hold her down. 'The angle is better this way. Trust me.' I smooth my hands off her thighs and down the taut curves of her calves and massage her ankles for a minute over the faint indentations on her skin where the cuffs bit in.

Her gaze flicks between my dick, my hands, and my lips.

I pluck a condom from my pocket. I know she's clean. Her latest medical examination results arrived via email during the week, but I always use protection. It's not just the pregnancy risk—that rubber barrier prevents people from getting more of me than I'm willing to give. The same as kissing on the mouth—it's just too personal.

She licks her lips as I tear it open with my teeth, then roll it over my length. I nudge her legs wider and step between her open thighs, resting the tip of my cock at her entrance. My eyes hold hers. 'Are you okay, princess?'

I watch her throat bob as she swallows and nods. 'Yes, sir.' Her hips arch upwards in an open invitation, and I glide in, inch by glorious inch, stretching her tight little channel until she's absolutely full of me.

Her hands reach for my hips as I slam into her, over and over and over again. Her legs wrap around my waist, locking me in. Like I'd ever dream of leaving. Huge, wild eyes catch mine, mesmerised, like she's never been fucked before. She probably hasn't—not like this anyway. I lower myself over her torso, grab her wrists and pin her hands above her head, then take one of her tight little nipples into my mouth and suck to the point she squeals. Her core clenches around my cock and fuck me—it's practically a religious experience.

'This body belongs to me.' I switch to the other breast.

'Yes,' she pants. I feel the tiny pulses of her climax building again. She's close. Thank fuck, because so am I.

I spread a hand over both of hers above her head and reach for her clit with the free one, circling it with my thumb while I continue to rock into her, again and again and again.

'Sean,' she shrieks as she shatters on my dick, pulsing and squeezing me, dragging me into my own decadent explosion. We buck and claw our way through an orgasm intense enough to surpass the Richter scale. She writhes beneath me, riding out the last of her release with her eyes fastened on me like I'm some sort of god. Truth is, it's her who's ethereal.

I've never had a more attractive woman under me.

A more responsive one.

And a more unavailable one.

I release her hands and drag my dick out of her, even though it's screaming at me to stay, to go again.

'Let's get you cleaned up.' Who even am I? I don't do aftercare, yet sending her out of here to let someone else take care of her isn't an option. Who knows who she might see out there. Or more importantly, who might see her. I'm not worried about her cover being blown. No, I'm concerned they'll want a piece of her, because she's easily the most extraordinary woman to grace this club.

And the most extraordinary thing about her?

She has no idea.

I tie the condom, toss it in the discreetly placed bin and stalk towards the tinted mirror, getting a glimpse of myself in the process. My face is flushed. But it's my eyes that I don't recognise. They're wild with a fresh bout of want. Not helpful.

I push gently on the glass, and it swings open to reveal a hot tub big enough to fit ten, which it has done on occasion. I turn the taps on, add some muscle soothing salts, and grab a wash cloth. Layla is still lying flat on her back on the bench. She's staring blankly at the ceiling.

Did I push her too hard with the spreader bar?

'Are you okay?' I offer her the cloth.

She stares at me for a long beat like she's not sure what to do with it, so I place it between her legs and clean her up.

It's official.

The woman has me doing things I've never done before, and it's only the first night. Yet something about her makes me want to take care of her. Maybe because she's not from this life. Maybe because she's too good for it. I don't know, and I don't want to spend too long thinking about it.

She watches as I clean her up. 'I'm...' she pauses like she's struggling to find the right word. 'I don't know if I'll ever be alright again.' She rolls her lips like she's biting back a smile. 'That was incredible. The way you commanded my body. The rush when you finally gave me what I needed. Is it always like that?'

Our eyes meet again. Hers are earnest and full of wonder, like a child seeing Christmas lights for the first time. Something stabs my sternum. I contemplate lying to her, but it'd probably be written all over my face.

I pause for a long beat.

I can't admit the truth—that I've never felt anything close to this.

I offer her my hand. She takes it, and I help her upright, and for some reason, I can't let it go. 'That was mild compared to most of what I've done down here, but it was easily the most... gratifying.'

I'm putting it down to her innocence of this life, and rare luxury of looking at my sub while I fuck her—safe in the knowledge that she won't fall for me. But fuck, I didn't give any consideration to the unthinkable—that I could be the one to fall.

I shake my head.

No Sean.

Don't be so fucking stupid.

It's just the high of doing something so forbidden. Banging a princess has to be the most forbidden thing I've ever done. I have money by the bucketload, land, connections. I come from a prominent family—one which has been unfortunately shrouded in scandal over the years. Between our public feud with the O'Connors, James's sex scandal on a yacht, Killian's glamour model girlfriend and the stalker who set her house on fire, the tabloids definitely wouldn't convince anyone I'm an appropriate match. Plus, I don't have a title, and even though it's not mandatory, it hasn't escaped my attention that every man the princess has been pictured with over the years possesses one—yes, I spent all week doing my own online stalking. I'd bet everything I own that the Queen would never allow her baby girl to date a commoner, which makes any sort of relationship between us forbidden— even without the BDSM element.

I catch myself again. Relationship. Like I told Layla over dinner, it's an arrangement. What the fuck has got into me tonight?

Silence stretches between us as the full meaning of my admission weaves between us; understanding flares in her eyes.

I drop her hand, hearing the sound of running water overflowing. 'Shit. The hot tub!'

Her laughter floats through the air as I rush to turn the taps off. I did mention aftercare isn't my forte.

'Get in. The salts will help your muscles.'

'Are you getting in?' She appears behind me with a hopeful expression on her features.

'No.' I don't do that. 'Put your mask back on. I'll send two of the masseuses in with your things. They'll take care of you.'

Disappointment flickers in those huge chocolate eyes, and I feel like a massive twat, but I can't stay here with her. I need to process. I assumed it would be her who would be reeling after tonight, but turns out it's me. I need to get out of here. I need to get myself together. I hate leaving already, but I can't stay. It feels too intimate. Too much.

I do something I never do—press a fleeting kiss to her temple. 'I'll see you tomorrow, okay?' I run a thumb over the back of her arm before backing away.

'Yes, sir.' Her tone is laced with a defiance that I don't know what to do with. We both know what we signed up for, and it wasn't romance. Her fingers reach for the collar and unclip it. I shoot forward again, halting her hands. 'Leave it on until you get out of here.' The prospect of anyone else thinking she's free and touching her is enough to set me feral.

'Yes, sir.' A small smirk of satisfaction touches her lips.

The first night with her and I'm fucking obsessed with her—and now she knows it.

Fuck.

Chapter Seventeen

SEAN

I slam my office door behind me, grab the bottle of Beckett's Gold from my desk, and pour a generous measure into a crystal tumbler. I knock it back and pour another. A sharp knock raps on the door, and Dominic's head appears, followed by his big burly shoulders.

'How did she do?' His focus falls on the glass I'm clutching. My fingertips are white.

'She was fucking phenomenal,' I spit, shaking my head, draining my glass again.

My friend steps in, closing the door, but before he can shut it properly, Larissa darts through. 'Oh no you don't! I need details.' She struts across the room and pours three more whiskeys.

I have no words.

'Well?' Larissa nudges me impatiently. 'What happened? Don't tell me you scared her off already?'

Nope. The only person running scared is me.

'It was...' I roll my lips. 'She was...'

'Spit it out.' Larissa makes a circling motion with her hands.

'It was fucking transcendent.' I take a sip of my drink. Over the rim of my glass, I watch as Larissa and Dominic exchange a look that tells me what I already know—I'm fucked.

'She's a natural. So responsive. I swear she's made to be a sub.'

'That's good.' Larissa's tone isn't convincing any of us. 'Where is she now?'

'I left her in the hot tub off of Surrender Suite Two.'

'You bailed on her?' Larissa's eyes narrow.

'Not exactly. I filled it for her and buzzed two masseuses to go to her.' I am a massive twat. She deserves better. But I had to get out of there. I've never felt so... connected to a sub before. And this connection isn't one that I can ever let develop. It needs to be severed immediately, before the King of England finds out and decides my head needs to be severed too.

'That's more than you normally do.' Dominic tilts his head to the side. The smirk on his face tells me he's enjoying seeing this new side of me.

'If it was that good, why did you bail on her?' Larissa throws her crimson painted fingers in the air. 'It's her first night in here; she probably feels like shit.'

'I bailed because this isn't a fucking romance movie.' I blow out a breath. I need to just spit it out. Dominic and Larissa are two of my oldest friends. They'll get it. Even if I don't get it myself. 'I don't do aftercare... but something about her made me want to. And it scared the shit out of me.'

Dominic's booming laughter fills the air. 'Finally.' For someone who built an empire on instilling fear, he finds humour with almost unsettling ease. Shame it's at my expense tonight.

I shoot him a glare.

'I knew it was only a matter of time before you found a

sub you truly connected with. Next, you'll be sending her flowers, taking her out to fancy restaurants.'

'Don't be so ridiculous.' I snap, pacing the floor. 'You know I don't believe in that crap. And even if I did, there's the tiny, insignificant matter of her being a princess. I'd never be what she needs in the real world. It can never be more than what it is.'

'As long as you know that,' Larissa says darkly. 'I know you've never believed you could have a real relationship and maintain this life, but you know Dominic and I have always disagreed. In other circumstances, I'd tell you to face your fears and open your mind to the possibility this could be something more, but you can't—not with her anyway.' Sympathy washes over her face.

'I know.' My gaze falls to the floor.

'Enjoy the arrangement for what it is, but whatever you do, don't get attached.' Larissa pushes her glasses higher on her nose, peering at me like I've grown two heads.

Dominic's laughter echoes through the air as he stalks across the room to plonk his gloating ass into my chair. 'Too late. He already did. You should have seen the look he gave me when my arm accidentally brushed hers. I thought he was going to slit my throat.'

Larissa clicks her tongue. 'How will she get the full Reveal experience if you're going to lock her up and keep her to yourself?'

'I was not considering slitting anyone's throat.' I lie, pinching the bridge of my nose. 'You know I've never been possessive with my subs before.'

'So, you wouldn't mind if we doubled up on her?' An evil glint sparks in Dominic's eyes.

It's a reasonable suggestion. As I said, it's not the first time we've shared, but this feels different. Rage flares in my chest at the mere prospect, despite third party involvement being included in the contract.

'A hundred grand says he can't do it.' Larissa swirls the whiskey around in her glass. I get the feeling she's enjoying this as much as Dominic. Who needs enemies when I have friends like these?

A hundred grand is pocket change for me, but for some reason, I'm compelled to prove them wrong. To prove to myself that I'm not as attached as I fear.

'Make it two hundred, and you have a bet.'

'I'll make it three, if you share her in the main lounge. The voyeurs will go feral for it.' Larissa knocks back her drink and slams the glass on the desk.

'You just want in on the action too.' I shake my head.

'Damn right I do.' The cackle that leaves her lips sounds almost evil.

'When?' Dominic is determined to nail down a date to get a piece of the princess. I can't say I blame him. If she was his sub, I'd want a bit of the action too. The idea of him touching her turns my stomach. Which reinforces exactly why I need to do this.

'Tomorrow night.' Larissa says, rubbing her palms together. 'Let's strike while the iron's hot.'

'No. Not this week. I want to get acquainted with her first.' I'm stalling, and we all know it. The thought of anyone else taking her makes me murderous, which is why I need to try. I have to get over it. This isn't a relationship.

'Better do it soon before that attachment gets any deeper.' Dominic points his index finger at my chest.

'Give me some credit. I'm a professional.'

'A professional what though?' Dominic teases.

'Shut up and pour us another drink.' I roll my eyes at him.

'Fine, next weekend,' Larissa taps a long fingernail against her glass.

'I can hardly wait,' Dominic rubs his palms together gleefully.

Twat.

I'll have her to myself tomorrow night and Sunday night. Surely, that'll help burn off some of that mad attraction between us. And I'll have all of next week to get my head around sharing her.

I can do it.

Because if I can't, I'm even more fucked than I thought.

Chapter Eighteen

LAYLA

I spent the week answering my sister Sabrina's WhatsApp messages. Unlike Patricia, Sabrina's dreamed of a big white wedding her entire life, which is probably why she sent me a hundred photos of potential floral arrangements for the tables, two hundred potential upstyles for her hair, and three thousand links to potential first dance songs on YouTube.

You want to know the worst bit about listening to love songs all week?

The person that keeps popping into my mind is Sean—and as he said, this isn't a relationship. It's an arrangement, but it's weird adjusting to our roles. I was prepared physically for what might happen between us, but I wasn't prepared for the whiplash of feelings.

My first three sessions at Reveal were transcendent, but each time we finished, he literally bolted out the door.

The contract covered hard limits, but it said nothing about the hollow ache I'd experience each time he left me in one of the club's suites.

I know it's what I signed up for, but while I'm discovering kinks I never knew I had, I'm also discovering the hard way that my vagina is somewhat tethered to my heart—well, it seems to be where he's concerned anyway.

Every time one of Sabrina's messages pinged in, I stupidly hoped it would be Sean. Obviously, it wasn't. We're contractually forbidden from speaking outside the club, but for some inexplicable reason, I'm still slightly pissed off with him for not at least trying to contact me during the week.

As I stride into Reveal's lift, I try to shake the disappointment and focus on what's to come—pleasure. Tonight, I picked out a lace baby doll slip that barely covers my ass cheeks, a matching lace thong, and holdups. I chose the patent Louboutins again, seeing as he had liked them enough to leave on last week. My black cashmere coat hangs over my forearm. The diamond encrusted collar is clipped tightly around my neck, and my mask is firmly in position.

Dominic meets me with a grin as the doors slide open. 'Princess.' His gaze roams over my outfit, or lack of it, I should say. In a black shirt and suit pants, he's every bit as commanding as Sean. If he hadn't been so kind to me last weekend, I'd be intimidated by his sheer size and physique. Both he and the woman I met on Submissive Night, Larissa, made a point to introduce themselves to me on my first night, Dominic at the start of the evening, Larissa as I left. She escorted me out to the Range Rover, apologising for the "Do you think you're some sort of princess" remark the week before. Her horror was actually kind of amusing.

'Good evening.' Dominic takes my coat and hands it to a pretty blonde who's manning the reception desk tonight. Sultry electronic music pulses from the lounge beyond, its hypnotic rhythm promising a million decadent possibilities.

'He's waiting for you.' Dominic fires me a conspicuous smile as his gaze falls to the collar clipped around my throat. 'To be honest, I think he's been waiting a long time for you.'

What's that supposed to mean?

Before I can ask, the lift doors open again and a couple dressed in matching leather outfits step out. Dominic halts them from coming any closer, motions for two suited security guards to sign them in with the receptionist, then guides me through to the main lounge where the bar is. He swipes a keycard over the security panel, and the black tinted glass parts like the Red Sea.

My stomach flips at the sight of Sean sitting on one of the high-backed stools by the long, wide bar. Images of him have taunted me all week, but my memory failed to do him justice. His huge shoulders are encased in his usual black fitted shirt. Black suit pants sculpt his perfectly carved ass. Power and masculinity pulse from him. He spins slowly, like he senses my arrival, and when our eyes meet, I swear the ground shakes with the intensity of it. He drags his tongue over his lower lip as I stride towards him, with Dominic as my escort.

I'm acutely aware that his mouth has mapped out my entire body, but it hasn't yet touched my lips. Damn his hard limits.

There are about fifty people scattered throughout the lounge. A woman is bent over one of the tables getting railed by a shirtless guy. They've attracted quite the audience. Desire slams low into my belly like a physical blow.

When I drag my eyes back to Sean, he's glowering. Huh. You'd swear I was the one who kept running out on him after the best sexual experiences of his life.

I don't kneel when I reach him.

Instead, I stare him straight in the eye.

'Worst submissive ever.' He mutters, but his hand darts directly between my legs, cupping my pussy like he's claiming it as his own.

Dominic's eyes flick between us, and his deep rumbling laughter attracts the attention of several members of the club.

'That will be all for now, Dom.' Sean says, without taking his eyes from me.

'I thought…'

'Later,' Sean snaps. Maybe it's not me he's glowering at. Maybe he and Dominic had a disagreement. If they did, it clearly isn't bothering Dominic; the sound of his carefree laughter floats across the room as he strides to the other side of the bar.

'Why aren't you kneeling for me?' Sean growls, unashamedly slipping his hand inside the lace triangle sheathing my pussy. His eyes flare when his fingers meet the proof of my arousal.

'I don't feel like making things easy for you tonight.' Despite the way my body reacts to his proximity, the urge to tell him how I feel eats at me. If we're going to do this for three months, I'm going to need more out of this arrangement.

'Why?'

'Because I'm annoyed with you.' I've never been one to hold back.

'Why?' He slides a finger into my core, and it's a battle to remember.

'Because I spent the entire week checking my phone, stupidly hoping to hear from you.'

'You know the rules.' He tuts. 'The contract clearly states that no activities, communications, or interactions shall occur outside the club's premises.' He adds another finger. 'Doesn't mean I didn't think about you though,' he admits gruffly. 'More than is healthy.'

My gaze falls to his full lips. 'Speaking of health, the contract also clearly states aftercare, shall be provided following all scenes.'

'Were the masseuses no good? I specifically asked them to

take exceptional care of you.' His fingers slow to a stop; there's genuine confusion on his face.

'Point 5.3 states the Dominant will arrange physical comfort, hydration, and support *as needed*. I want *you* to support me instead of running out on me. While I was sort of prepared for what you might do to me physically, I had no idea you would hijack my head.'

His dark eyes smoulder. 'If it's any consolation, your head wasn't the only head that has been hijacked.'

'It's no consolation. While I signed up for you to use my body, I also signed up for you to take care of it. That includes mentally.' My fingers instinctively brush over the collar around my neck.

His hand reaches for my cheek. Understanding flickers through his eyes. 'I'm sorry. You're new to this life. I should have checked in on you this week. What can I do to make things better?'

'Running out on me right after we're done isn't an option anymore.'

His eyes darken as his hand falls from my face. 'There's a reason I don't hang around.'

'You're not still worried I'm going to fall in love with you?'

'No, princess,' he swallows thickly. 'I've spent all fucking week counting down the seconds until I see you again. Until I get to see you again. To touch you again. Taste you again. So no, I'm not worried you're going to fall in love with me. I'm worried you're going to fucking ruin me.'

My mouth pops open. 'Ruin you how?'

'I don't think about my sub. I don't beat myself off imagining my hand is hers in the shower. And I don't fucking stab myself in the eye with my fork at breakfast,' he points to a mark above his right eye, 'because I'm fantasising about eating her out on the dining room table—again.'

His admission is a balm to my bruised ego. Or is it my heart?

'The only thing that's ruined is my lingerie. Now can we play?'

He tears his eyes away from mine and glares at Dominic. 'Yes, we can play.'

I glance around the room. Being watched is up there in my top ten fantasies, all of which just so happen to include my new dom. Would he do it? Take me, right here in front of everyone?

He leans closer, and the rich scent of expensive whiskey surrounds me. 'How about a glass of champagne to wet your tastebuds?' He motions to one of the serving staff to fetch me a drink.

'They're pretty wet already,' I bite my lip.

'So I see.' He fucks me with his fingers, working my core, slowly, deliberately. It feels so good, even more so because we're in a room full of people. More and more eyes begin to land on us with interest, and unconcealed hunger.

He snatches up the glass of champagne from the bar with his free hand and holds it up to my lips. I part them, and he tips in a small mouthful. The bubbles explode on my tongue. It's Beckett's Black Label, his family's own brand. Way nicer than whatever I had in here last week. A coincidence? Or did he bring it in especially for me?

He tilts the glass and drizzles a little over the hollow of my neck. The drops roll in slow motion, trickling over my chest. His head dips, and he licks the liquid from my skin. The strangled little moan that escapes my mouth is positively feral. He traces his tongue upwards over my clavicle, and up along the column of my throat, then my jawline, carefully avoiding my mouth.

'Tell me want you want.' His voice is low and commanding. His black eyes daring me.

'I want you.' I blurt.

His lips curl upwards into a wolfish smile. 'In here?' He places the champagne flute down and glances around, where more curious eyes are homing in on us. 'In front of all these people?'

My eyes frantically scan our rapidly growing audience. My pulse races. Stomach flutters. If any of them so much as suspect who was behind the mask, I would be in so much trouble. Naturally, that only adds to the appeal.

'Yes.'

He slides his hand out of my lingerie, resting both palms on my hips. With one swift, sudden movement, he lifts me, carrying me like I'm a rag doll, and stalks towards a free table near the centre of the room. I hold my breath as he lays me out across it, pushing me backwards until I'm flat on my back, then pulling my knees apart until I'm spread wide for him, right here in front of everyone.

'You want everyone to watch while I claim you? You want them to watch as I taste you? Does that turn you on?' His eyes blaze.

'Yes.'

I wriggle, rocking up onto my elbows to watch him.

'Lie down, princess. Or I'll get someone to hold you down.' His pupils flare with pure devilment as fire ignites between my thighs, quick and consuming.

My mouth drops open in shock. Dominic appears beside Sean again; my eyes dart between the two of them. 'Do you remember your safeword?' Sean says. His eyes are wild, feral. He's totally getting off on the thought of fucking me in front of all these people.

I nod again, unable to form actual words. So much for savouring me, breaking me in slowly. He's claiming me. Owning me. Marking me as his. My stomach clenches in anticipation.

Dominic rounds the table to stand at my head, his eye gleam as they roam over my torso. 'She's wearing too many clothes. I think we should take some off.' He pushes the baby doll dress up until my breasts are exposed. My nipples are preening for attention.

'That's enough.' Sean growls, slapping Dominic's hand away.

Dominic smirks.

'What do you think of my new submissive?' Sean glances around at the members as they begin to congregate around us. 'Stunning, isn't she? Sorry we ran out on you the other night. We're going to make it up to you tonight, though, aren't we, sweetheart?'

I nod and murmurs of appreciation flood the air. I've worn dresses that cost millions of pounds. I've been gifted rare and precious stones. I've had suitors vying for my attention my entire life. Yet, I have never felt so sexy, so desired— and so utterly insignificant. I'm no one to these people, but I have their undivided attention. It's utterly intoxicating.

'We certainly are,' Dominic says, with a mischievous smirk.

Sean glowers at him. I get the impression they're having an entire conversation with just their eyes. There's some sort of silent power struggle going on here. I don't understand.

Dominic reaches for my breasts, but Sean's hand shoots up in a halting motion. 'Stop,' his command is low, lethal— and utterly unquestionable. His expression is positively murderous. The two men stare at each other for a long, painful beat before Dominic's low psychotic laughter fills the air again.

Finally, Sean speaks, eyeing every man in the room in turn before landing on Dominic again. 'Watch, by all means, but not one of you lays a fucking hand on her. Or I'll rip it from your wrists.'

Dominic's answering grin is somehow victorious, but I don't have time to ponder it.

Approving titters fill the air, but I only have eyes for Sean. He cocks an eyebrow. 'Ready?'

'Yes.'

'Good. Because you're not leaving this room until you come twice. Once on my face, and once on my cock. Call it your official initiation. Welcome to the club.'

I suck in a ragged breath. Oh. My. Fucking. God.

Chapter Nineteen

SEAN

I thought I could share her. But now we're here in the club, I can't. The mere prospect makes me homicidal. It's one thing to let the entire club watch, but the thought of anyone in my place, between her legs, is an absolute hard limit. It's official. I'm ruined.

I spent all week mentally preparing for this, but now we're here, I can't go through with it. I can't fucking do it. It's not even an option. Coughing up three hundred grand is a piece of piss compared to watching Dominic put his mouth, hands or dick on what is mine. Fuck the money. Fuck the bet. The urge to mark my territory is all-consuming.

I push the lace sheathing her pussy to the side and drop into the leather seat at the bottom of the table. My mouth gravitates to her sex, inhaling her scent. She watches me intently with heat and need in her eyes. I glide my tongue over her clit, and the noise she makes is primal. Every man and woman in the vicinity is entranced by her mews and the way her hips jerk in response—especially me.

I work her with my mouth, good and slowly at first,

licking and sucking, teasing and devouring, revelling in the fact that I'm the only person in the room who gets to do this to her. And that every other person in here would trade an arm to be in my position.

I spread her legs wider, just because I can, and sink two fingers into her centre. She's so wet. So tight. So responsive. Those hooded eyes never leave mine. Even though the room is full of people, she only has eyes for me. That alone makes me hard enough to hurt.

I pump and flick and lick and suck until she's on the brink of blowing. Every writhe, every squirm, every little mew and moan marks her as mine—single me out as the man who knows what her body wants and needs. The man who gets to give it to her.

'Come for me, princess.' I demand, sliding a third finger into her tight, slippery channel.

'Sean,' she cries as she shatters—hard—riding out her release, bucking against my face. My name on her lips is a balm to my jealous soul. I smile against her sex, licking every drop of her pleasure because I can. Because it's mine.

I'm so fucked. And the expressions on Dominic and Larissa's faces as they lock eyes across the room only accentuates that fact. I can't deal with that now. I unbuckle my suit pants and pluck a condom from my pocket. I've fucked subs in here before—loads of times—but never with such intent. The need to claim her is primal.

I sink myself into her slippery centre, her core still pulsing from her release. She stares up at me with those huge eyes overflowing with wonder and want. 'You feel so fucking good.' I reach for her breasts now, ripping her clothes from her body. A chorus of approving murmurs circle the room, but I don't look, and neither does she. It's like we're the only two people in the world. I pinch and roll her nipples. Her hands reach round to my backside, her fingernails sinking into my ass cheeks as she propels me harder into her core like she can't get enough. I rut into her, again, and again and again until I'm nearly blind with the sheer number of hot white stars threatening the backs of my eyelids.

She cries out, convulsing around me a split second before my own release rips through me like wildfire, burning and consuming everything in its wake. I spill myself into her, burying my face into her neck as pure primal pleasure devours me.

I need to get her out of here.

Get her all to myself.

When we both finally stop shaking, and the crowd around us finally disperses, I drag myself out of her soft centre, dispose of the condom in a strategically placed bin beneath the table and button up my suit trousers. Another couple are already going hard at it two tables up from us.

I offer her a hand up. 'Let's go, princess.'

She stares at me like I'm some sort of god, yet it's her who's ethereal. She places her hand in mine, and I hoist her up, then lift her beautiful body up onto my chest, cradling her limp frame against me. The urge to protect her, provide for her, and keep her with me forever beats in my chest like a caveman. As I carry her out of the lounge, I ignore the warning look Larissa shoots my way. I don't need her on my case. I already know I'm fucked.

'That was incredible,' she mumbles, nuzzling into my neck. She's clearly wrecked, but I am nowhere near finished with her, but I think we've both suffered enough intensity tonight.

'You were incredible.' Whether we have days, weeks or months left in our arrangement, I need to make sure I satiate every single one of her needs myself—including aftercare. Because it's clear. I can't share her.

If I had any sense, I'd terminate this arrangement with immediate effect. Every fibre of my brain is silently screaming this isn't going to end well. It *can't* end well. Yet every bone in my body begs me to go with it. I have...feelings for this regal creature. Big feelings. Feelings that scare the ever living shit out of me, because the last time I caught feelings for a woman—it didn't end well.

I take a left and head towards the Sanctuary Suite, still carrying her against my chest like a groom carrying his bride over the threshold.

Three masseuses rush to greet us. 'Mr Beckett, we'll take care of her for you.'

'No, I'll do it myself.' If this doesn't tell me I'm fucked—I don't know what does. 'Organise some clothes. Leave them outside the rainforest showers.'

I leave my staff with their jaws on the floor and open the door to the rainforest shower suite, an enormous room comprised of black marble and glass. The air is infused with eucalyptus and bergamot. There's a changing area to the left, showers to the right. I lock the door behind us and turn on the multiple overhead rain heads. They cascade from the ceiling, while side jets create a cocoon of warm mist.

I set the princess down on one of the heated stone benches lining the wall.

'How did you get into this life?' She asks, her legs still trembling in the aftermath of our performance.

I swallow thickly, debating on how much to tell her. 'A woman. We met at a party. We'd had a lot to drink. She brought me to a club similar to this one.'

'And you liked it.' It's not a question.

'I liked that I had something of my own, something that I could control, something I chose for myself that wasn't marked out for me. A secret identity that separated me from my brothers. To a lot of people, I'm just one of the "Becketts"—sometimes it's suffocating.'

'I get it, believe me, I get it.' She sweeps a hand in front of her face. 'How long were you two...?'

'A year.' I swallow. 'We didn't have a formal contract.' My jaw ticks. 'It didn't occur to me that we'd need one.'

She stares at me for a long beat. 'But you did?'

I shake my head. Even years later the memories still stir a dull ache in my chest. 'I assumed our arrangement was exclusive, and I fell for her—hard.'

Realisation dawns in her eyes. 'Oh.'

I blow out a breath. 'To me, it was a real relationship. We kissed. We fucked. We played, mostly inside the club, but sometimes at her place too. I didn't realise it was just sex to her. It kind of fucked me up for relationships after that. Truth is—I'm broken.'

'You're not broken,' she says, touching her fingers to my lips. 'You're beautiful.' Her earnest eyes bore into mine.

That might be the nicest thing anyone has ever said to me. But she's wrong. I am broken. Because when it comes to choosing between this, what I have at the club, and what my brothers have—real relationships—love, I choose this. Because this is safer.

I take her hand gently in mine and move it from my mouth. 'Come on. Let's get you cleaned up.'

I strip her slowly, starting with her mask. 'Just so you know,' She stares at me, silently contemplating. 'I know this isn't a relationship or whatever— but contract or no contract— I'd never do that to you.'

'I'd hope not.' Especially because I'm catching feelings way bigger than the ones I held for Hannah.

She places a finger beneath my chin and tilts my face to meet hers. 'Apart from common decency, there's not a man on this planet who could hold a candle to you.' She drinks in my torso as I unbutton my shirt. Her eyes widen and fill with a fresh appreciation.

'If you keep looking at me like that, Princess, I'm going to take you again, right here in this shower.'

'If you keep looking at me like that, I might just let you,' her voice is low and full of wonder as she devours my naked body with her eyes.

I step under the steaming jets, reach for the bottle of shampoo and beckon her under the water with me. She stands, shakily, keeping one hand on the wall for support. Her vulnerability is my undoing. The urge to kiss her pouty lips is all-consuming. But I can't. I won't.

'Turn around.' I motion for her to face the wall. She rests both palms flat against the marble, and the jets bounce off her back.

Her hair is silk between my fingers as I work the shampoo through the strands, taking my time, letting the warm water carry away the bubbles. She tips her head back, eyes closed, completely surrendering to my care. The trust in that simple gesture undoes me further. What is this woman doing to me?

I squirt the body wash into my hands and lather it over her shoulders. She moans as my hands glide down her back, over the curve of her hips and then round to her stomach. I find myself memorizing every curve, every small mark on her skin. She's pliant, leaning into my touch. Something in my chest tightens.

A soft sigh escapes her lips as my fingers skim higher until they reach her breasts. My dick is rock solid again, straining against her back.

'Sean,' she whispers.

'Yes, Princess.'

'I need you.' She opens her eyes, and the heat in them hits me like a physical blow.

I scan the room. Why are there no condoms in here?

'I'm clean.' She grinds back against me. 'You've seen my medical report.'

I hiss. If only she knew what I'm truly terrified of catching—feelings. Truthfully, it's too late, I caught them the second she crawled across my stage. 'I'm supposed to be testing your limits, Layla, but so far, you're testing every single one of mine.'

She pauses. 'Sorry, Sir.' She knows exactly what she's doing to me. And, dom or not, I'm powerless to prevent it. She backs onto me, her arousal coating the tip of my dick, and I surrender to the inevitable, sinking bareback into her slickness, inch by glorious naked inch. The sensation is sublime.

Her head rolls back as she grinds herself against me. 'You are the worst submissive I've ever had.' My hands grip her hips, guiding her as she rocks against me, taking me in, one life affirming inch at a time.

'So you keep saying.'

For the second time tonight, I do something I've never done with a sub. I thrust into her slowly, gently, with a tenderness that I never knew I was capable of. Her back arches and fuck, I forgot how beautiful bareback sex was. I place my hands on top of hers, pinning her against the wall as I slam into her again and again and again. The sensation of sinking into her flesh is transcendent.

Her core contracts around my cock, pulsing and squeezing, dragging me into oblivion with her. Knowing my cum is inside her, marking her from the inside out makes it all the sweeter. Reluctantly, I pull out, watching as my mess drips from between her legs. It's almost as satisfying as the sex itself.

This wasn't part of the plan.

'So hot,' she murmurs, looking down as it streaks the inside of her thighs. Looks like I'm not the one who's completely fucked here.

'Please tell me you're on birth control.'

'I am.' She bites her lower lip, and the urge to kiss it better consumes me, but that's the one mistake I haven't made.

Yet.

Chapter Twenty

LAYLA

This week's paintings are as colourful and expressive as last week's. The things that Sean Beckett knows how to do to a woman is mind-blowing. Friday night was intense, both what we did in the main lounge and then in the showers afterward. Saturday was different again—more playful. And Sunday night was equally erotically gratifying as the first two.

Nipple clamps.

Toys.

Ice cubes.

Blindfolds. Even when I'm blindfolded, he's opening my eyes. I've never experienced pleasure like it.

It's all consuming.

Addictive.

Temptation and I have galloped past Sean's estate more times than I can count this week, and it's only Tuesday. I'm like a schoolgirl with a crush. The urge to see him again is eating me alive. Not just sexually, either. I want to be with him. To know him more. To learn more about the man outside of the club. The man who was hurt before. The man who looks like a god, but is every bit as human as me beneath his hard exterior.

What woman in their right mind would cheat on Sean Beckett?

I couldn't even contemplate looking at another man–not when he's all I see at the forefront of my mind all damn day, every day.

He was right about one thing though–I'm tired. My muscles were in agony yesterday, not from the toys or restraints but from being tight and taut with the prospect of inexplicable pleasure. And don't get me started on the mental fatigue. Who knew surrendering entirely could be so exhausting?

I stand back to survey my handiwork—another bold, bright explosion of colour. I could start an entire collection the way I'm banging them out at the moment.

A knock sounds on the door. It can only be Kat.

'Sorry to interrupt,' she enters cautiously, carrying a tray laden with afternoon tea. 'It's just you've been in here all day. You have to eat, princess. I brought you tea and scones.'

'The time ran away with me.' I wipe my paint covered hands across my overalls and turn to her. 'Will you join me?'

Without Kat, the days at Ardmore would be unbearable.

She pops her head out into the corridor and looks both ways before closing the door. 'I've got one eye on your laundry.' She winks. 'Can't have the rest of the staff seeing your new collection of lingerie.'

I bite back a smile. 'It'll give them something to talk about at least.' The custom-made bodysuits imported from Italy are racier than anything they've ever laundered here before. They're racier than anything I've ever left the estate in too, yet when I get to Reveal, I'm still overdressed.

'Trust me, Princess, that's the last thing we want to do.' Kat places the tray down on the mahogany table overlooking the castle's pristine grounds. Even in winter, they're glowing green and perfectly maintained.

She pulls a chair out for me, and I sit, motioning for her to take the seat opposite me. 'What's the gossip among the staff today?'

Kat usually regales snippets of information about who's arguing with whom, or who's sneaking around with whom. Some days it's like listening to a soap opera. Fraternising among the staff is a sackable offence. I keep Kat's secrets, just like she keeps mine. I'd hate to lose her, but if she and Grant ever decide to get married, one of them will have to resign. The prospect doesn't bear thinking about.

'Never mind that.' She swats a hand in front of her face. 'I want details from the weekend. You were out with him three nights in a row and you've barely given me anything.' She hunches over the table, setting her blonde ponytail swishing. 'What's the billionaire like in bed?'

'Katerina Magdalena Smith!' I clutch my chest in mock horror. 'Are you implying your princess is easy?'

She giggles and reaches for the teapot, pouring into two delicate china cups. 'Oh, princess, I've seen your outfits. Don't be coy with me now, Your Highness.' She rolls her hand in a mocking gesture.

I splutter, then waft my hand in front of my face. 'If you want details, don't bring me tea! Bring me wine, Kitty Kat! And not that awful dessert stuff my parents favour.'

In truth, I'm dying to talk to her about Sean, but given the NDA, I need to be very careful. I trust Kat with my life. She's covered for me more times than I can count, but there's no way I could admit what we've been up to. Besides, it's not just my secrets I'd be revealing.

She reaches into her apron and pulls out a hip flask, waving it under my nose. 'I had a feeling you might say that!' Her blue eyes glint with mischief. 'It's not wine. It's whiskey.'

'Better again.' Every day of my life for the past five years, I've thanked the universe for this gorgeous creature opposite me. She's held my hand before royal events, wiped my tears, and laid beside me when I've felt I had nobody. My sisters are amazing, but they have their own pressures from our parents.

'Details first—then you can have a sip.' She arches an eyebrow.

'Trust me, we'll both need a drink for what I have to say.' I motion for her to take a sip and then pass the flask to me. She hesitates for a split second, glances at the closed door, then brings the hip flask to her lips, spluttering as it hits the back of her throat. Laughter bursts from my lips.

'Christ, that's strong.' She hands over the whiskey, then dabs the corner of her eyes.

'It's not nearly strong enough, trust me.' I take two large gulps; the liquid burns its way through my body. 'Don't tell me... Beckett's Gold?' I hold up the flask. When I haven't been galloping past Sean's place, hoping to glimpse him, I've been doing some serious googling. Beckett's Gold is his family's most expensive whiskey. After tasting it, I can see why.

'Absolutely! It seemed appropriate given the circumstances. Now tell me, Princess, what else did you taste at "Mr Beckett's club" last weekend?' Kat squeals.

I bite my lip. 'Enough to know that I've been missing out my entire life. And if my mother gets her way, I'll miss out for the rest of my life.'

'Was it that good?' Kat's eyes widen.

'It was better.' I take another sip of whiskey. 'It's hard to explain, but you know better than anyone, I've been treated like a royal vessel ready to be traded to the right family for my entire life. Sean, well, he treats me differently.'

'Princess.' Kat's eyebrows crease into a frown. 'That sounds... dangerous.'

She has no idea. How will I ever go back to London? To a

normal boring life now my eyes have been opened? And my legs.

'It's dangerously sexy.' I pass the flask back over. 'But don't worry. I know what it is. What it can only ever be. Which is why I'm determined to make the most of the next couple of months.' Am I telling her that? Or myself? Because every hour I spend with Sean Beckett, I can appreciate how easy it would be to fall for a man like him. I already feel a bond with him that I've never felt with any other man.

Finally, I can appreciate why kissing on the mouth is a hard limit. Still, I bet he kisses like he fucks—passionately. The need to go there, where he doesn't go with other women, is gnawing at me. I want to be different. Special. I want him to trust me, like I have to trust him. And I don't want him to treat me like a princess—worryingly, it's way worse—I want to be his Queen. But thoughts like that have the potential to burn down my world.

'Just be careful, okay. I'm all for you having a bit of fun, but if the Queen ever found out...' she trails off. There's no need to finish that sentence. We both feel the weight of the implication. 'You have the ball at The Shelbourne with Lord Ashworth next month. I was talking to Judy, the Queen's lady-in-waiting. She has high hopes for this one.'

I roll my eyes and take the flask back. 'She has high hopes for any bore with a title. But if it means I get to stay here for a couple more months, I'll play along.'

'Who knew when we got here that you'd grow so fond of this place.' She waggles her eyebrows at me.

It's not the place, it's the people. Person, I mean. If she'd experienced what I'd experienced this weekend, she'd understand implicitly.

'Who knew, indeed?' I run a finger over the platter of afternoon treats in front of us before selecting a small square of moist lemon drizzle cake. 'Will you cover for me again this weekend?'

'Again?'

'Yes, and every other weekend from now until I'm dragged back to my usual duties.'

'Is that a wise idea? Getting so attached?'

'I'm not getting attached. I'm getting an education.' Or maybe both.

I can't fall in love with him.

Can't, and won't.

Chapter Twenty-One

SEAN

I almost caved. Almost texted her for a midweek meet up. I had to give my phone to my PA, so I didn't do something stupid like call the princess. She lives in my head rent-free all day every day, and it's beyond distracting. I'm impatient to be alone with her, not because I want to have sex with her—I do, of course but the urge to spend time with her is consuming me.

I want to know how her week's going.

I want to know if the hours apart are dragging for her, like they are for me.

And I want to know if she's thought about me as much as I've thought about her.

Which is why I asked Larissa to bring her straight to the Throne Room tonight. It seemed fitting for the princess.

I survey the space stretching around me. Dimly lit, strategically placed amber lighting illuminates the throne dominating the far end of the room. Carved from midnight-black wood and upholstered in deep crimson leather. Floor-to-ceiling mirrors line one wall, angled to reflect every sordid angle. A bottle of Beckett's Black Label and two glasses sit on the small table beside it. I pace the room several times before dropping into the throne and pouring myself a generous measure while I wait.

I tap my foot impatiently to the low, hypnotic music pulsing through hidden speakers, something richer and more atmospheric than the club's usual electronic beats.

The minutes feel like hours.

Finally, a short, sharp rap on the door sets my pulse soaring.

The princess enters wearing a black silk bodysuit and those damn patent heels that I love. Her hair is tied back into a sleek low ponytail, which emphasises her long slender neck and exquisite bone structure. Our eyes lock as she struts towards me like she owns the place. If she was anyone else, she might well do—one day anyway. I've never contemplated marriage before, but looking at her right now, I'd lock her down as my wife in a heartbeat, if I thought I could get away with it.

Oh, fuck, that is one wayward, dangerous thought.

'Good evening, sir.' She struts across the room, slowly, seductively. I sink back into my seat again to stop myself from running to her.

'It is now you're here.'

She drops to her knees on the floor, but truthfully, she's bringing me to my knees.

'Did you miss me?' The words are out of my mouth before I can stop them. I cup her chin and tilt her eyes up to meet mine. That invisible chemistry short circuits between us again.

'Yes.' She pulls the silk strings at the back of her head and removes her mask. It feels like she's removing mine in the process. I've never told anyone about Hannah before. Never admitted I'd been foolish enough to fall for a woman who clearly didn't feel the same way about me. Never admitted out loud that despite the fun I have down here, a part of me feels broken. Not until her, anyway. She's a fucking princess. And she sees me, she knows what I am, what I'm into. And still, she keeps on coming back, night after night. 'Did *you* miss *me?*' she asks, almost coyly.

I stroke my thumb over her full lips. The urge to kiss them is all consuming, but I can't. I won't. Because this thing between us can't last. I'll never be enough for her outside of these walls. Despite what she said in the shower–I *am* broken. I don't trust easily. Yet there's an earnestness about her that makes me want to try. I'm torn between ending our arrangement and searching for a loophole to sign her up to a permanent contract.

If she feels the weight of the war raging inside of me, she doesn't show it.

'More than you can imagine,' I admit. Fucking whiskey has loosened my lips.

Dark eyes glint up at me as she inches closer, her gaze fixated on my lips. Her chin juts upwards until her mouth is millimetres from mine. She wants me to prove it. She wants me to kiss her.

I can't.

Because if I cross that line, I can never go back. And with her, there's no chance of moving forward. Which leaves me in limbo. She might be my sub in this club for the next few weeks, but she will never be *mine*.

I pull her up onto my lap, positioning her legs until she's straddling me.

'How was your week?' I brush my lips over the smooth line of her jaw, inhaling the scent of her skin into my lungs.

'Long and boring without you.' She tips her head back giving me access to her neck. I trail kisses along the column of her throat, it bobs as she swallows back a tiny moan.

'Ditto.' She rakes her hands through my hair and it feels

so good. Too good. We're playing with fire, dancing way too close to the flames, yet I can't bring myself to stop. This is so much more than what we signed up for. More—yet nowhere near enough.

'How's the painting going?' I've been wondering about her 'sensual pieces' all week.

'I'm producing quite the selection. What can I say? I've been feeling particularly inspired of late. Getting through my supplies quicker than I can restock them.'

'Inspired?' I pop open her bodysuit and pull it over her head.

'Yes.' Flames dance in her eyes. 'I blame you.'

'I've been blamed for worse, I suppose.' I run my tongue between her breasts. 'You are so fucking beautiful. What are you doing to me?' I groan.

'The same thing you're doing to me.'

'Which is?' I reach around to squeeze the firm globes of her ass cheeks.

'Hijacking my head, remember.' She hesitates for a split second. 'And my heart.' Her quiet admission kills me, as much as it turns me on.

'Princess.' I sigh. I'm in way over my head.

'Call me Layla.' She arches her back, pressing her breasts against my face. I kiss them until she's writhing needily on top of me.

'Layla.' The word drips from my tongue like honey.

'Kiss me,' she demands.

'I can't.'

'Can't or won't?' She arches a single eyebrow.

'Can't.' My mind wanders back to the last woman I kissed. To the pain that followed. 'You're already killing me. I'm already obsessed with you, woman.' I whisper, pulling her ankles up until they're either side of my thighs.

'The feeling is mutual.' She whispers and our eyes lock.

I reach across the arm of the throne to where a selection of restraints are attached to the side of the leather, patting around until my fingers tighten around cold hard metal.

Her eyes widen as I wave the handcuffs in front of her face. She wobbles, momentarily losing her balance as I clip her wrists, but I catch her, steadying her. 'I've got you.' Literally and figuratively.

But who's got me? I'm utterly fucking enamoured with her. I have been from the moment I met her, to the point I broke my own rules for her. Invited her into my home. Cooked for her. Washed her hair. Rode her bareback. Fuck.

The sex is the best of my entire fucking life. And it's not the usual Dom/Sub dynamics that's doing it for me. It's *her*. This is the worst thing that could possibly happen to me because even if I could get over what happened the last time I fell for a woman, even if I could learn to trust another implicitly with my heart as well as my body, the princess couldn't be more unavailable.

'Please, Sean.' She wets her lips again, and my eyes are drawn to her perfect Cupid's bow. I want to sink my teeth into her plump lower lip and then kiss it better. But I don't do this. I don't kiss women. It's been a hard limit since Hannah. But I'm finding it increasingly hard to deny this woman anything.

I place a steadying hand on her lower back, holding her in position as I use my free hand to yank open my suit trousers. Her eyes fall to my crotch. I place my hands on her backside and guide her until her entrance rests against the tip of my dick. It's weeping for her.

Her eyes bore into mine as she lowers herself onto my cock. I swear she can see my soul. 'Fuck it.' The last chord of my willpower snaps. My lips crash against hers, hot and hungry and claiming. I should stop this, but I can't. Hell, with her mouth melded to mine, I can barely remember why I'm meant to.

I rut into her again and again and again, swallowing every single one of her moans as I support her helplessly restrained body. She might be the one in shackles, but it's me who's been truly ensnared.

Fuck.

Her core tightens on me, and I know she's close. Thank fuck because I'm about five seconds from spilling myself inside of her. The thought of her dripping with my cum again is enough to catapult me over the edge. Thankfully, she's right there with me as animalistic pleasure courses through my body. She bites my lower lip, her core convulsing around my cock, milking me for everything I've got.

I'm so fucked.

When we finally still to catch our ragged breaths, I unfasten the cuffs from her wrists, peppering tiny kisses over her clavicle and her chest. She slumps onto my chest until we're heart to heart. We stay there, silent bar the deep bass and haunting melodies from the speakers. The music seeps beneath my skin, stirring something in my soul. Or maybe it's Layla's heart pressed against mine that's doing it.

I'm supposed to be teaching her about this life, but it's her who's teaching me— maybe, just maybe risking my heart is worth the heartache that will inevitably follow. Because even though I know this can't end well, holding myself back from her is hurting both of us almost as much as giving myself could.

I wish we could stay in this moment forever but we can't. Reluctantly, I rearrange her so she's sitting sideways in my lap. 'Drink?' I offer.

'Why not?' Her gaze shifts to the Beckett's Gold beside us. 'I tried it during the week. It's good.'

'I would say I'll pass the compliment on to my brother,

James, but naturally I can't.' I lean across her to reach the bottle and pour her an inch. 'I can get you some champagne if you prefer.'

'No, this is good, thanks.' She accepts the glass I hand her and clinks it against mine in a silent toast. 'What are they like, your brothers?' She lifts the glass to her lips and sniffs it appreciatively before sipping it.

'They're great. They'd kill for me. Die for me. Rian's a pain in the ass a lot of the time,' I admit, 'but I'm lucky to have them.'

'Why do you hide this place from them?' She sweeps an arm around the room.

I think long and hard before answering her. 'Because it's the one place that I have that's mine. That I can be myself in. I'm not just one of the "Becketts" here. I'm *the* Beckett. And I don't want to compromise that.'

She takes another sip, eyeing me over the rim of the glass.

'Do you have a place you can just be yourself? Or do you even have to keep the princess mask up behind closed doors of the palace?' Her words from the first night bomb back into my brain.

'Duties. Charity functions. Photoshoots. Every minute of my life is mapped out for me. I've been banished here to consider my options —the truth is, I don't have any. And I never will.'

We have more in common than anyone could guess.

She sighs, and the scent of whiskey carries on her breath. 'There's only one place I've ever felt... anonymous. St. James's Park, directly across from the palace. Sometimes I sneak out wearing a baseball cap and sunglasses, dodging security.' A wistful look etches into her glazed eyes. 'I sit on this one bench and watch real people living real lives—mothers with their children, couples arguing about nothing important, teenagers being reckless.' Her voice drops. 'For those stolen moments, I'm not a princess. I'm just... no one. And it's the most freedom I've ever tasted. Whenever I escape, that bench is always my first stop—the only place that's ever felt like mine.'

'I'll bear it in mind, just in case,' I joke, but the words drip from my tongue dark and serious.

'If only.' She gives a tiny shake of her head, and I glimpse how truly trapped she really is.

Chapter Twenty-Two

LAYLA

I stand before the floor-length mirror in my private chambers at Ardmore, barely recognising the woman staring back at me. A midnight blue silk gown flows like liquid sapphire against my skin. The bodice clings to my curves before flowing into a dramatic train that pools at my feet.

My hair cascades in loose Hollywood waves over one shoulder, leaving the other bare save for the glittering drop earrings that catch the light with every movement. The sapphire and diamond parure—necklace, earrings, and bracelet create a constellation of blue fire against my throat and wrists. The Queen is clearly keen for me to make a good impression on Lord Ashworth. But as I adjust the necklace one final time, it's not him at the forefront of my mind. It's Sean.

This feels so wrong.

Perverse, even, after the last few weeks, but it's just another one of my duties. If I don't at least make it look like I'm interested in Lord Ashworth, my parents will bring me home. Mad how only a few weeks ago I was desperate to get back to the bright lights of London, now I prefer the dark shadows of Dublin. Day and night, my thoughts are consumed entirely by a billionaire who knows my body more intimately than I do.

Each time we're together is more thrilling than the time before. I can't even try to deny it; I'm falling hard and fast for a man I can never have. A man without a title. A man whose family has been splashed across the papers for sex scandals, and that's not even including Sean's sex club.

We haven't been back to the main lounge for a couple of weeks. I get the impression he's reluctant to share me. We still haven't communicated outside of his exotic underground chambers. I've thought about texting him so many times but calls and texts can be tracked, and we're supposed to be strangers.

Would he care if he knew I was attending a ball with another man tonight?

Would jealousy flicker behind those controlled ebony eyes?

Or would he simply revert back to clause 6.2—that what happens outside Reveal's walls is none of his concern?

He has no claim on my time, my attention, or my body beyond our scheduled sessions—by his own stipulations. But after everything we've done in the sultry confines of his club, my treacherous mind keeps wondering if he'd want one.

I smooth down the silk of my gown and reach for my evening bag. My date is due to arrive any minute. I need to get a grip.

'He's downstairs, Your Highness,' Kat announces, poking her head round the door with barely concealed excitement. 'And the Queen wasn't lying— he's handsome!'

I tut and shake my head. It wouldn't matter if Chris Evans, Chris Hemsworth, or Henry Cavil was downstairs. There's only one man I want, but there's no way my parents would permit me to date him—even if he wanted to, which I can't even be sure of.

There's so much more to our arrangement than just the sex. It's the way he looks at me. The tender way he takes care of me afterwards. The way he's breaking his own rules for me. But he's been hurt, and I have no way to reassure him it won't happen again–because even though I'd never give myself to another man while we're together, I could be ripped away from him at any given moment, should my parents decide to bring me home.

'Princess,' Kat steps in and takes my hands. 'I know you and Mr Beckett have this insane chemistry, but no matter who you end up with, that won't last. That electricity fades for everyone.'

'Does it?'

I don't agree. It's been six weeks since I met Sean at Sub Night, but I can't imagine the chemistry ever fading. We have a connection that feels like a force more powerful than life itself, not that I'll admit that to Kat. If she had any idea how obsessed I am with the billionaire next door, she'd never agree to cover for me.

She shrugs. 'Grant and I are happy; we really are, but after six years together, our priorities have changed. It's the same for most people. That initial high wears off and you're left with someone who, at best, will be your best friend—if you're lucky. I'm all for you having a little fun, but you have to think of your future too.'

I inhale a breath. 'Most people.' I repeat. 'Not everyone. I refuse to settle for less than what I need in my life.' I blow out a sigh of frustration. 'Even if they do have the right breeding.'

Kat shoots me a pitying look. 'I hope you find what you're looking for. I really do. I'm just not sure it exists.'

Oh, it does. I know, because I already found it. Sean

Beckett may not have a title. His family may be shrouded in scandal, but he has confidence, charisma, and the way he looks at me when he's inside me makes me feel like he can see my soul.

I sigh, take one last look in the mirror, then follow Kat from my chambers. The corridor stretches before us, lined with those ever-present ancestral portraits. Tonight, they seem to nod approval as I pass. Huh.

Lord Ashworth stands at the foot of the stairs like something from a period drama—tall, broad-shouldered, and devastatingly handsome in perfectly tailored black tie and tails. His auburn hair glints beneath the light. Kat was right. He is handsome. He's no Sean Beckett, but his green eyes hold genuine warmth, and his smile is bright enough to light the city.

'Your Highness.' He executes a perfect bow as I reach the bottom step, then straightens with athletic grace. 'Lord Caspian Ashworth, Earl of Wicklow.' His voice carries that particular public-school polish that screams wealth and entitlement. I can see why my mother has high hopes for him.

'It's a pleasure, Lord Ashworth,' I lie, extending my hand in the precise manner that's been drummed into me since I was a tiny child.

He lifts my fingers to his lips, holding them to his mouth for several seconds longer than appropriate. 'Please call me Caspian,' he says breathily. Yuck. 'Your Highness, you look absolutely radiant this evening.' His eyes home in on my cleavage and I swear he's practically drooling. A shudder rolls over my spine.

'You're very kind,' I force myself to mutter, as I accept the wrap Kat settles around my shoulders, then pull it tightly around my chest.

I don't say, 'Call me Layla.' The way I did to Sean. It feels too informal. Formal is good. Formal keeps people at arm's length—or it's supposed to at least.

Kat winks at me as he offers his arm. It's a battle not to roll my eyes.

Caspian's Aston Martin waits in the circular drive, its British racing green paint gleaming under the castle's lanterns. Grant and Toby, another one of my security detail flank the front entrance. They'll follow us to the Shelbourne in their own vehicle, maintaining a discrete distance.

As Caspian helps me into the passenger seat, his fingers brush against mine, lingering too long the same way his lips did. I yank my hand away and settle into the leather, resigning myself to my fate for the evening.

I glance out at the countryside whizzing by as Caspian keeps up a steady stream of conversation, naturally all about himself. If he's trying to sell himself to me, he's doing a terrible job. As he navigates the winding country roads toward Dublin he drones on about his land, prospects, and his excellent golf skills. It's like groundhog day, every date is the same. Give me something real for Christ's sake! I have a sinking sensation Sean Beckett has ruined me for anyone else who comes after him. What a depressing prospect.

'I hope you don't mind the Hunt Ball,' Caspian says, downshifting smoothly as we approach the city outskirts. 'I know some find the whole tradition rather archaic, but there's something to be said for maintaining connections to the countryside.' He drops a presumptuous hand to my thigh.

I swat it away and glance at him pointedly. 'I rather like tradition—when it serves a purpose.' The irony isn't lost on me —here I am, defending tradition whilst secretly rebelling against everything it represents.

'Excellent. I'm rather excited to introduce you to my friends.'

I bet he is.

My stomach tightens. This is the crux of it. Every conversation will be analysed, every glance catalogued, every interaction dissected and reported upon—by the press—and to my mother. Which is why I should at least try to make it look like there's a chance of a future with Caspian. If someone had told me a month ago I'd be desperate to prolong my stay at Ardmore Castle, I'd have laughed in their face. Yet, there's nothing funny about the things Sean stirs in me.

Finally, we reach the Shelbourne Hotel. Elegant topiary flanks the entrance, their winter-bare branches wrapped in thousands of fairy lights that twinkle like stars. Despite the cold, small clusters of well-dressed guests gather on the pavement, their breath misting in the frigid air as they await their turn with the valet.

Caspian pulls up to the red-carpeted entrance, and the uniformed valets spring into action. One opens my door whilst another approaches the driver's side.

'Good evening, Your Highness, Lord Ashworth,' the valet says with a respectful nod. He's clearly been expecting us. 'We'll take care of your vehicle.'

The hotel's entrance blazes with light—crystal chandeliers visible through floor-to-ceiling windows, red carpet extending from the kerb to the revolving brass doors. Photographers wait behind velvet ropes, their cameras flashing as various notables arrive. My protection detail materialises from their vehicle, assuming casual proximity whilst maintaining professional distance.

Caspian offers his arm. I stare at it for a long beat before finally linking mine through it—purely for my mother's benefit. It feels so wrong.

Together, we step inside the Shelbourne's grand reception area. The marble-floored lobby soars overhead. 'I can't think of a better way to spend Wednesday evening.' Caspian murmurs into my ear as we join the stream of guests heading into the open ballroom doors.

I can.

He offers my arm a small squeeze and strokes and I cringe.

Every head turns as we enter. Their collective gaze feels like a physical weight. Conversations halt mid-sentence, champagne flutes freeze halfway to lips—the usual subtle shift in energy that occurs when I enter a room.

People rush to greet Caspian, but let's be honest, it's not him they're rushing to. That's not vanity, by the way, it's the harsh truth of being royalty. Everyone wants a slice. It's everything I haven't missed.

I attempt to wiggle my arm free from Caspian's, but he pins my elbow firmly against his side, staking a silent claim as we make small talk. I feel like a piece of meat. My mouth is dry. My head is pounding, and I'm silently praying someone, anyone, will get me a drink. God knows I could use one. Or five.

When we finally get a brief reprieve, instead of going to the bar, Caspian looks around, almost inviting the next round of guests to greet us. Not for the first time in my life, I feel like an endangered species—rare but not properly protected. I glance desperately around, searching for Grant and Toby. They're five feet behind us, relentlessly surveying our surroundings.

'Every eye in the room is on you.' Caspian murmurs, eyeing my cleavage again as he moves his hand to the small of my back. My spine stiffens. 'On us,' he gloats. I'm just a royal trophy to him. One that he wants to own—for all the wrong reasons.

My eyes sweep the crowd, silently screaming for someone to help me. To get me the hell out of here. I shouldn't have come.

You had no choice, a tiny voice in my head reminds me. It's no different to any other public appearance I've had to make.

Faces blur together—a sea of black dinner jackets and designer dresses. Caspian dips his lips to whisper in my ear in a gesture that's offensively intimate, but I don't hear a word because my gaze collides with a pair of burning black eyes across the ballroom.

The world stops.

Everything else fades.

Nothing exists except those big black familiar eyes.

Sean Beckett stands by the bar. A fitted dinner jacket sculpts his broad shoulders to perfection. His crisp white shirt clings to his body in a way that should be illegal. Full lips press together in a grimace.

My pulse hammers.

He looks magnificent, but there's no missing the jealousy blazing in his eyes. Jealousy and barely concealed fury. His jaw ticks as his gaze homes in on Caspian's arm around my back

We stare at each other across three hundred guests, me silently trying to explain to him that this isn't what it looks like. Him silently demanding answers that contractually, he doesn't deserve, yet I feel compelled to provide.

He claimed me in Reveal, mounting me in front of every man there, and the way he's looking at me now, I don't trust him not to do the exact same thing. And given the sensations that prospect is inciting over my skin, I don't trust myself not to let him.

He strides toward us without breaking eye contact.

The crowd seems to part instinctively for him; he commands as much attention as I do.

Imagine how much we would command together.

I squash that thought.

We can never be.

But tell that to the man stalking over here radiating a dark promise, and barely leashed fury.

Chapter Twenty-Three

SEAN

And this is exactly why I prefer to keep my underground life separate to the life I live above ground.

I opened up to Layla, revealed parts of myself I've never revealed to anyone, I kissed her mouth for fuck's sake, and here she is, hanging off another man's arm. A man, who I know for a fact, gets through more secretaries than cups of coffee. The man is a walking sleaze. But that's only part of the reason it's killing me seeing them together. The other part, well, that's the part of me that wants to beat his chest like a caveman and shout 'she's mine' at the top of my lungs. But she isn't mine. Not really. And she never will be.

To make matters worse, she looks positively fucking edible in a sapphire dress that showcases every single one of her curves. She looks every bit the princess that she is—utterly stunning—and utterly untouchable. But Caspian Ashworth didn't get that memo. He's parading her around like the latest car in his collection. Pawing at her like she's a prize pet, not a woman.

It's impossible to tear my eyes from her. The second I saw her, I spotted the rigidness to her posture, the tension lining her shoulders, and the way her lips are pursed into a tight line. Ashworth strokes the back of her hand and she flinches.

Either he's more stupid than he looks, or he's simply ignoring her body's cues. What the fuck is she doing here with him anyway? She's supposed to be on house arrest by all accounts.

I come to an abrupt stop in front of them. The princess's jaw drops. Her eyes are wild with panic, like I'm about to make a scene. I'm not. I just need to make sure she's okay, because every fibre in my body is screaming at me that she's anything but okay.

'Take your hands off her.' The words are out of my mouth before I can stop them.

'Excuse me?' Caspian's green eyes glare at me.

'I said take your hands off the princess.' My voice is low and controlled but inside I'm seething. 'Before I remove them—from your body as well as hers.'

'Sean.' Layla steps forward and rests her fingers on my chest, shrugging off Caspian in the process. The second she touches me, the relief is instant, for both of us, if the slackening in her shoulders is anything to go on.

'Princess?' Caspian's curious gaze flits between us.

'Mr Beckett is a friend of mine,' she offers her date a cool smile. There's a silent warning in her eyes.

'A very close friend.' I snap. A growl rumbles in the back of my throat. 'And you're parading her around like she's a prize possession. Where are your manners, Ashworth?'

His face falters for a split second, but he recovers quickly. 'It's Lord Ashworth actually, *Mr* Beckett.'

Subtext... I'm above you.

'It's not a dick measuring contest,' I hiss. My glare is sharp enough to make him take a step back. 'But if it was, trust me, I'd win.' I turn my attention to the princess.

The urge to claim her claws at me. I've had years of practice wearing this mask of politeness, but tonight is my biggest test yet. Everything about this situation feels wrong. Her being here with him. His hands on her. Us hiding the thing that's been growing between us for weeks. But it's what I signed up for. It's me who insists on restricting activities to Reveal.

Because blurring lines is how people get hurt, but here I am, blurring them anyway.

'Allow me to get you a drink seeing as your date clearly forgot you're a person, as well as a princess.'

'That would be lovely.' Her shoulders relax a fraction more.

'The usual?' I arch an eyebrow. Lord fucking Limp Dick's head whips up.

I never said I'd play fair.

'Yes, please.' A small smile touches her lips.

'I'm borrowing the princess.' It's not a request. 'She prefers my family's range to the shit they're serving here.' I motion to the bar at the far end of the ballroom. 'There's a crate of Beckett's Black Label in the back bar. It was donated for the toasts, but no one will mind if I open one early.'

Caspian Ashworth's jaw locks as he watches me guide her across the room. I give him a sarcastic wave over my shoulder then guide her toward the small private bar room, replacing his hand for mine on the small of her back. Even that minimal contact sends electricity through me.

Of all the women in the world, why am I obsessed with the one I can't have?

It's fucking cruel.

I usher her into the small bar area. Two of her security detail follow. Funny how they're paying attention tonight when they miss her sneaking out on a regular basis.

'It's fine, Grant.' She raises her hand, and they assume their positions outside the door.

I close it in their faces. The urge to touch her is overwhelming, but I don't. I'm vibrating with too many emotions
to depict. Emotions that are as unfamiliar to me as they are
unwelcome. 'Are you okay?' No matter how mad I am, how
upset, or disappointed, first and foremost I need to know
that she's okay.

'I am now.' She offers me a small smile. 'Thanks for the
reprieve.' She sighs. 'It doesn't get any easier.'

'What the fuck are you doing here with *him*?' I rake my
fingers through my hair and pace the small space.

Her eyes narrow. 'I'm not *with* him. I'd never be *with* him.
I'm *with* you. Even if it's limited to the confines of your club.'
Her voice shakes with the same despair that's bleeding into
my veins. She tilts her head up to meet mine. 'Do you think I
want to be here?' She demands incredulously. 'This is one of
those formal duties I told you about. My mother is basically a
pimp dressed in pearls. She won't be happy until she's secured
the highest price for me.'

I blow out a breath. 'Do you know how sick it makes me
feel, watching that fucker pawing at you?'

'I can imagine.' Her voice cracks with the same raw need
that vibrates inside me. 'I get that it's a shock running into
each other outside of the club, believe me, it's just as heart-
wrenching seeing you out tonight too, knowing I have no
right to touch you, to be with you. I bet women are throwing
themselves at you left, right and centre and I wouldn't blame
them.'

'This is all wrong.' The realisation hits me like a blow to
the chest. This is my doing—partly, anyway. Because I can't
risk a real relationship. Then again, the princess wouldn't
want one—not with me, anyway. Would she? She said the
Queen is determined to set her up with someone with a title.
I'm pretty sure "Ireland's most eligible billionaire" doesn't
count.

Her eyes rake over my shoulders before meeting my gaze again. 'It does feel wrong, but the contract stipulates I can't be with other Dominants, not out on staged duties with the opposite sex. Believe me when I say, this is all this is.'

'Ashworth couldn't dominate a donkey.' I spit. 'And I bet the ginger fucker has tried.' She reaches for me, but I sidestep.

'Please, don't.' My voice is wary. I move to the sidebar and open the champagne to avoid looking at her, because every time I do, I'm reminded what she is. What I'm not. That we can never be. Not out here in the real world. I shouldn't have broken my own hard limits. Shouldn't have kissed her. Shouldn't have let her into my club, or into my heart.

'I would never betray you, Sean. I'd never do what *she* did. This entire evening is to appease my mother.' Her tone is softer now. 'You have no reason to be hurt, and no right to be angry with me.'

My hands still on the bottle. I turn slowly, 'You're absolutely correct, Princess. I have no right to anything concerning you outside those club walls. We pretend I'm in charge, because it gets you off, but we both know the score in the real world.'

'Last time I checked, it got you off too—'

'Look, forget it.' I shake my head.

I can't tell her how I feel about her. Can't tell her that seeing her with another man is as painful as having a knife slice my chest open.

'It's all just a fleeting bit of fun for you. It's a lifestyle choice for me.' I pour two glasses of champagne, hand her one, and down the other.

'I told you already, Sean, I don't have any life choices.' She shakes her head, sadly. 'My parents are insisting I get engaged before my next birthday.'

'What?' The thought sends another irrational surge of

jealousy through my stomach. Her birthday is only seven months away. I know, because I Googled the ever living shit out of Princess Layla the night she stumbled into my club, and almost every night since.

'Of course they are. Marriage strengthens relations, raises public interest, and produces royal heirs.' She rolls her eyes. 'If I don't put on a convincing performance with someone "suitable" in Ireland, my parents will send the plane for me. Now Patricia is married off, and Sabrina is engaged, the heat is on me. I am the sole focus of my mother's unwanted attention.'

'Do you want to get married?' I reach for her hand now, unable to stop myself. Her proximity, her scent, her skin— everything about her draws me in. Instinctively my fingers trace circles on her skin. Her gaze drops, and we both watch as goosebumps ripple beneath my touch.

'Yes, but I want to marry for love. I refuse to settle for... less,' she admits.

So the princess is looking for a love match.

It's uncommon in families like hers. And utterly unlikely. An ache forms in my chest—for her, and for me. I don't even know if I could do the relationship thing, but something about her makes me want to try. But even if I could get over myself, I'd never be a good enough match for her family.

We stare at each other for a long beat, the weight of everything I can't say pressing down like a physical weight on my chest. The urge to kiss her is all-consuming, but every time I do, I fall a little deeper.

Fall?

Oh fuck.

This can't be happening.

I can't let it happen.

I drop her hand, inhale deeply, then take a long sip of champagne, using the moment to rebuild my composure.

'I better let you get back to your date, Your Highness.' I set down my glass and straighten my cufflinks. She flinches, the formal address lands like a slap. A sliver of guilt snakes into my stomach but I can't be here. I need to put some distance between us. I need to leave before I do something I can't take back.

She sets down her untouched champagne and moves toward the door, pausing with her hand on the handle. 'Sean?'

Our eyes lock. 'Yes?'

'Will I still see you on Friday?'

I should say no. End this before one of us—I—get hurt. But I can't. I'm not strong enough. 'Yes. It's a straightforward arrangement.' My voice doesn't waver despite the tumultuous emotions tormenting me inside. 'Assuming your social calendar permits, that is.'

She cocks her head to the side. 'Are you going to punish me for this?'

I don't respond. A part of me wants to punish her—well *him* actually— but I can't. The only person who crossed the line here is me. My contract. My rules. What goes on outside of Reveal is none of my business—a stipulation I demanded myself. The situation is so fucked up, it's not even funny.

'Watch him.' I nod towards the door where Ashworth is undoubtably waiting. 'He's not as gentlemanly as his title suggests.'

'I gathered as much, but don't worry, I'm leaving anyway.' She fires me one final look over her shoulder before leaving me alone with the crate of champagne and the knowledge that I just lied through my teeth. Because nothing about our arrangement is straightforward anymore.

Fuck the ball.

Fuck the fact I'm supposed to be networking.

And fuck the fact I'm falling in love with the one woman I can never have.

Chapter Twenty-Four

LAYLA

'Is everything quite okay, Your Highness?' Caspian's pacing outside the door with Toby and Grant. He reaches for my arm but I shrug him away. His jaw clenches. Sharp eyes narrow as they dart towards Sean who is making his way back towards the bar.

'I have an awful headache. I'm sorry, I need to go home.' Truthfully, it's not my head that hurts. It's my heart. It's stupidly aching for a man it can never have.

Caspian's face falls. He glances around the room at the throngs of people circling, waiting to greet us. 'Perhaps some water might help?'

I bite back my scoff. Whiskey is what I need, not water. And lots of it. I reach out to touch Grant's arm. 'Let's go.'

He offers a curt nod and motions for Toby to flank my side.

I turn to Caspian. 'Enjoy the rest of your evening.'

His gaze rakes over my cleavage again. I can't bear to have him look at me like I'm the last cake on the baker's shelf. He gathers himself quickly. 'I'll drive you, Your Highness. It would be my pleasure.'

But it wouldn't be mine. Sean was right. To him—I'm a princess, a possession, not a person. 'No need. Thank you for an enlightening evening.'

Worryingly, the most enlightening part about it was seeing Sean Beckett in the real world, away from the dark confines of his club. Because now I'm in no doubt; it's not the lifestyle that's doing it for me, it's him. The chemistry pulsing between us is the same, whether we're nearly naked in his sex club, or drinking amongst Dublin's elite. If he'd have kissed me out here in front of everyone, I'm not sure I'd have been able to stop him.

No matter how straightforward he insists our arrangement is, my feelings have become dangerously complex. Technically, I am well within my right to go out with whomever I choose, or in this case, whoever the Queen chooses. Yet it feels so wrong, and seeing Sean here tonight reinforced precisely why. Sean Beckett is a deeply private man outside of his club, yet he opened up to me about his previous hurt, and whether I'm within the realms of our contract or not, part of me feels like I let him down. Worse, I feel like I let myself down–because I've never had the courage to stand up to my mother. But then again, I've never had a reason to either.

'Perhaps we could...' Caspian's voice trails off as I march out of the ballroom with Toby and Grant.

———

The call comes at precisely nine o'clock the next morning, as I'm nursing my second cup of coffee, replaying the look of hurt and hopelessness etched into every line of Sean's face.

I stare at the screen for a long beat before swiping to accept. After last night's early exit, keeping the Queen of England waiting isn't advisable. Besides, she'll only call Kat.

'Your Majesty.' If she detects the sarcasm in my tone, she ignores it.

'Layla.' My mother's voice cuts through the phone with surgical precision. 'I understand you left Lord Ashworth's company early last evening. Another headache, I believe?'

My stomach clenches. 'Yes, Mother. It came on quite suddenly.'

'How convenient. And how did Lord Ashworth respond to your... sudden illness?'

I hesitate, remembering Caspian's suggestion of water whilst glancing around at all the people waiting to meet us. He cared more about being seen with me, than seeing that I'm okay. Asshole. 'He offered me water.'

'Water,' she repeats flatly.

'He was more interested in parading me around to greet the other guests—'

'Of course he was. Because Lord Ashworth understands duty and public responsibility. Unlike some people.'

Naturally, she's taking his side. Does anyone on this earth actually give a shit about me? About what I want?

I take a sip of coffee, buying myself time. 'Mother, I've been thinking—'

'Dangerous habit, darling,' she tuts.

I ignore her patronising remark and press on anyway, because if I don't voice the question that's been going round and round in my head, I'll always wonder. 'What if I were to find my own match? You know, in this day and age, it's not uncommon to marry commoners.'

The silence stretches so long I wonder if the connection has dropped.

'I beg your pardon?'

'I mean, what if I met someone who understood me? Someone I could genuinely care for? Build a life with—built around love and—'

'Layla Sinclair.' The use of my full name is never a good sign. 'You seem to have forgotten who you are and what you represent. You are not some celebrity blogger free to follow her heart wherever it fancies.'

'I understand that, but—'

'But nothing. You *will* marry someone appropriate. Someone with a title will strengthen our position and serve the Crown. This romantic nonsense is beneath you.'

Actually, it's not. I stand and begin pacing, my bare feet silent on the cold tiled floor. 'And if I refuse?'

'Refuse?' Mother's laugh is sharp enough to cut glass. 'My dear girl, you seem to have forgotten that your lifestyle, your security, your very existence depends entirely on the Crown's good graces. Should you choose to... step away from your duties, you would find yourself quite alone indeed.'

'You'd cut me off?'

'Without hesitation—emotionally and financially. And don't think the public would support such selfishness. The people despise nothing more than someone who turns their back on privilege and duty. You'd be reviled, darling. Completely and utterly reviled.'

My hand tightens on the phone. 'I see.'

'I sincerely hope you do. Lord Ashworth called this morning to express his continued interest despite your... episode.'

'Mother, please. He might be a match on paper, but he is not a match for me. He showed his true colours rather quickly, and a lifetime of looking at them would render me miserable.'

She sniffs disapprovingly. 'I suppose there's still Lord Montgomery. Though, unfortunately, he's been called away on business. If you'd have bothered to meet with him the first time he visited, we could have saved a lot of time.'

'Let's arrange something for his return. You sent me here

to consider my options. Please give me a few weeks' grace to do that.'

I really do need time to seriously consider my options—just not the ones she thinks.

Silence greets me while she contemplates.

'Please, Mother.' My voice cracks, not because I give a flying fuck about Ashworth or Montgomery, but because the one man I want to make happy is miserable with me, and it's all because of these archaic, patriotic duties.

She pauses for a long beat. 'You will entertain Lord Montgomery graciously upon his return, and you will conduct yourself as befits your station. And I want a full report. Is that understood?'

'Perfectly.'

The line goes dead, leaving me staring at the phone in my trembling hand.

Outside, the Irish rain continues to fall.

I've never felt more trapped or helpless in my life.

Chapter Twenty-Five

SEAN

The weights crash back onto the rack with more force than necessary, metal on metal echoing through the exclusive gym like a gunshot. It's been twenty-four hours since I left Layla with another man. And every single second of those hours, that knowledge has niggled me, eating at the lining of my stomach.

There's no denying it.

I'm in love with the princess.

I can't concentrate on anything longer than thirty seconds without my mind replaying last night's—along with fifty thousand other images of Princess Layla over the past few weeks.

'Easy, boss,' Ben says, adding another twenty kilos to the leg press without breaking stride. Ben and I have been working out together for the past five years. He's one of the few men mad enough to step into a boxing ring with me. Tonight, I opted for a weight session. Given my concentration levels this week, there's a good chance he could put me in a body bag.

I grab my water bottle and take a long pull, trying to wash away the taste of failure from this afternoon's meeting. The forestry deal I've been pursuing for six months just slipped through my fingers because I couldn't focus long enough to counter their final offer properly. Some twat of a Lord from the golf club I attend swooped in and stole it from right under my nose—not Ashworth, thank fuck. Another stuffy "suitable" bore though.

'Rough day?' Ben settles onto the bench press, his movements economical and precise. Twenty years in the military followed by a decade protecting wealthy arseholes like me has given him an uncanny ability to read situations.

'Rough twenty-four hours. Lost the Forestry deal.' I position myself as his spotter, hands ready above the loaded bar. 'Stupid fucking mistake.'

'That's not like you.' He begins his set, the 140 kilos moving smoothly despite his conversational tone. 'You'd normally close that in your sleep.'

That's the problem. I didn't sleep a wink last night.

'Just distracted,' I mutter, which is the understatement of the fucking century.

A brunette in expensive workout gear chooses the treadmill directly in my line of sight, her sports bra strategically chosen to showcase what are undoubtedly surgical enhancements. She catches my eye and offers a smile that's pure invitation, but I barely register she exists.

Ben racks the weights and sits up, following my gaze. 'That one's been circling since we got here. Along with the blonde by the free weights and the redhead pretending to stretch by the mirrors.'

I glance around and realise he's right. Half the women in this place are positioning themselves within my orbit, a ballet of casual proximity and meaningful looks that I'm usually much better at navigating. Dublin's social scene isn't exactly vast at our level—everyone knows everyone, and while I don't have a title, my Forbes bachelor status makes me something of a target.

'Fuck's sake,' I say, moving to the cable machine.

Ben follows, adjusting the weight stack with military efficiency. 'Maybe you should … relieve some tension. I could drive you to the club.'

'No point. Layla won't be there until tomorrow.'

'Just call her.'

'We have a contract,' I remind him.

'Rules are made to be broken.' Ben shrugs, like it's that simple. 'You've been checking your phone every five minutes like you're expecting a call from the Queen herself.'

The problem is, every time I break another, I give a little bit more of myself away to a woman who will never be mine. The phone check is unconscious, even though I know Layla won't contact me. If she was going to break that particular stipulation, she'd have done it before now. But after last night, a part of me keeps hoping for that breach in protocol —the sign that she's as affected by me as I am her.

'Don't even joke about the Queen.' I can't contemplate the magnitude of shit I'd be in if Layla's family got even a hint of what I've been doing to their darling daughter the past six weeks.

Ben settles into position for his next exercise. Silence falls between us. When I finish my set, I move to the rowing machine. The brunette from the treadmill approaches.

'Sean Beckett, isn't it?' She has that polished accent that comes from the right schools and the right connections. 'I'm Siobhan Fitzgerald. We met at the Hunt Ball last night?'

Did we? The minute I saw Layla, everyone else ceased to exist in that room. 'What can I do for you, Siobhan?' I can barely maintain the façade.

'I was just thinking we should grab coffee sometime.' Her smile suggests coffee isn't exactly what she has in mind.

She's attractive, confident, and if she was at the gala, then she's from a family with the right connections. Exactly the sort of woman my mother would approve of. Safe. Appropriate. Boring as fuck. Even if I hadn't been ruined by a certain royal brunette, I'd have no interest in this one.

'Perhaps another time. I'm really busy at the minute.' Busy dreaming up ways to simultaneously torture and tease my new submissive, though truthfully, she's the one torturing me.

'Of course,' she recovers quickly.

I shoot her a clipped smile, and she drifts away, though not nearly as fast as I'd like.

'Not posh enough for you?' Ben teases. 'Or not dirty enough?'

'I think a certain royal spoiled me for anyone else.' I shake my head.

Turns out, having a predictable submissive who follows the rules isn't nearly as satisfying as having a dangerous black-mailing one. In one calculated move, Princess Layla made it clear that everything I thought I should avoid in a woman, is everything I actually crave.

Ben snorts.

'Time to go,' I decide, towelling off. 'There's something I need to do.' Something hasn't been sitting right with me. Something I need to rectify.

'Other than the Princess?' Ben whispers and I thump his arm.

'Don't push it.'

As we head toward the exit, I catch sight of myself in the mirrored wall. Something's different. There's an edge I haven't seen before, a restlessness that has nothing to do with business and everything to do with a woman I can't have.

'I need to speak with Killian.' As we walk toward the Bentley, I pull out my phone. A shitload of emails. Four stupid memes from Rian. Nothing from Layla, of course. She's probably negotiating a marriage contract with Prince Fucking Charming whilst I'm losing million-pound forestry acquisitions because I can't stop wondering if there's a way we can be together—really be together—and if she'd actually want to.

One more day until I see her.

Twenty-four hours.

I can manage.

Probably.

I pull up Killian's contact details as I slide into the back of the Bentley. The Princess's security guards are ridiculously slack. If she can sneak out so easily, what's to stop someone sneaking in? I want eyes on her at all times—and eyes on her "suitable" fucking suitor should he make an appearance. I did some digging. Ashworth is as ruthless as he is resourceful. Layla needs real protection, not men who stand back and watch her being pawed at.

Killian answers immediately. 'Sean.'

'Where are you?' He could be in the Beckett Enterprise building, but more than likely, he's working from his home office. He's been doing that a lot since he hooked up with Avery.

For a man who seemed like he'd never settle down, he's done a full one eighty. He's even walking around with fucking hearts in his eyes. It's... confronting. Out of all of my brothers, I was certain Killian would keep me company in my eternal bachelor status. Given how much Rian puts himself about, it's only a matter of time before he knocks someone up and our parents force him into doing the right thing.

'At home, why?'

'Just checking you're not surrounded by our prying, pedantic brothers.' I pause for a second. 'I have a request.'

'Go on,' he drawls. Killian is not a man of many words. He

never has been, although he's opened up a good bit since he got with Avery.

'I need extra security detail. Maybe eight more men. And more cameras.' I stare out the window, watching the city lights whizz by, praying my brother hasn't developed the same meddlesome curiosity about my private life as Rian, Caelon and James.

'Is everything ok?' Killian's voice is sharp with concern.

'Everything's fine. It's...' There's no point lying to him. Killian has the means to find out pretty much anything he wants. The fact he doesn't pry into my private life is something I've always been grateful for. 'It's for a friend.'

'A friend,' he repeats, not entirely convinced. 'You would tell me if you were in trouble?'

'Of course.'

'I'll have them with you in the next hour.' He hangs up without asking any further questions.

I lied.

I am in trouble.

Just not the type he's referring to.

Chapter Twenty-Six

LAYLA

Friday takes forever to arrive. I check my phone obsessively, hoping Sean will text. He doesn't, despite the fact we've broken pretty much every other rule this month. But this time the silence between us feels different. I hurt him by going out with another man. It was unintentional, but undeniable. Yet despite that, his main concern was for me. If *I* was okay. My own mother didn't give a continental crap about how I felt, only how things looked. Sean is the only man I've ever met who treated me like a person and not a possession. His hurt, and the jealously I glimpsed in his eyes stemmed from something real, something raw—which thrills me, and terrifies me in equal measures.

By the time I sneak out of Ardmore, my nerves are shredded. I've replayed the events of the Hunt Ball a thousand times in my head. Is he going to punish me? There's a darkness in him that suggests he's capable of it, yet, here I am, about to willingly walk into the lion's den, because I'm utterly infatuated with him. I've never met anyone quite like him, nor am I likely to again.

I spent the last couple of days considering my options,

but I have no idea if those options include a real relationship with Sean Beckett. Every time I close my eyes, I see his face. His anger. His despair. His disappointment. And I want to fix it. I want to get back to us, because even though there technically isn't supposed to be an us—this is the most real relationship I've ever had. And if his reaction this week was anything to go by, he feels the same—whether he'll admit it or not is a different matter entirely.

Could we have a real relationship?

Would he want one?

Would the public really despise me?

I wouldn't be the first royal to step down.

I'm damn sure I won't be the last.

Obviously, there's the issue of financial security. I have a degree. I'm just not sure anyone would employ me. I have no real work experience. No references. No clue what kind of work I could even apply for.

Could I really do it? Step down and give myself a chance of finding real happiness?

And if I summon the strength to turn my back on duty, would Sean stand with me through the wreckage that would follow?

Each time we're together, he exposes me not just physically, but mentally too—drawing out dark desires I didn't even know I had until I stepped in here. He said it himself; he's done a lot more down here.

Would I be enough for him?

I negotiate the Range Rover into a parking spot just outside the club's discreet entrance with a heavy heart. The familiar black granite entrance looms ahead, but nothing about this feels familiar right now. I'm heading into totally uncharted territory—emotionally and physically.

My stomach churns with anxiety I haven't felt since that first evening. My mask is firmly in position; my diamond encrusted collar feels heavy at my throat. The short, sheer ebony dress feels like too much compared to the casual nearly nakedness of some of the women I've seen in here, but I teamed it with stockings and suspenders that I know Sean loves.

'Good evening, Princess.' Dominic's greeting is polite but lacks his usual mischief. He's guarded. Wary. Did Sean tell him about the other night?

If only I had someone to talk to about things.

Poor Kat doesn't know what to do with me brooding about the castle, which is why I locked myself up painting for the past two days. Painting and pondering my life as I know it.

'How is he?' I ask tentatively, slipping out of my coat.

Dominic sighs. 'As you might imagine.' He takes my coat and hands it to the receptionist. 'Sean is... complicated.'

'The entire situation is complicated.'

Dominic walks me through the darkly lit corridors. 'It doesn't have to be.' He keeps walking past the main lounge. 'I predicted this would happen, you know.'

'That a princess would stumble into the club?'

'That he would eventually find a sub he'd want more from.'

My stomach flips, hope spiking in my sternum.

'It's just unfortunate that you're not in a position to provide more. Or perhaps I should say, he's not in a position to ask you to.'

'My family has certain expectations for my future.' I slow my walk to draw this conversation out. I have no idea where Dominic is taking me, but it's not to the main lounge. My heels click against the polished floors. Members nod as I pass. I barely register them.

'But if the tabloids are anything to go on, you live to rebel against those expectations. What's another one?'

He's only voicing what I've spent the last few days thinking. His feet slow to a stop outside a room I've never been in before—the room with the Saint Andrew's Cross.

'He's waiting for you.' He motions for me to enter. 'I told you before, I think he's been waiting a long time for you.'

I pause, staring at Dominic for a beat. 'I was searching for him too. The trouble is, now I've found him, I'm not sure what I'm going to do about it.'

'You don't have to decide tonight, but unless you want lords to start turning up in body bags, I suggest you keep a low profile outside of here.'

His words should terrify me. They don't.

I push inside with my heart hammering in my chest.

Sean stands rigid backed beside the Saint Andrew's Cross. He's dressed entirely in black tonight; a black shirt sculpts his muscular torso. The dramatic lighting casts shadows across his shoulders, making him appear larger. More intimidating.

He doesn't turn when I enter. Doesn't acknowledge my presence at all.

The cross looms between us like a monument. My chest is tight with terror.

'Close the door, Your Highness.' So we're back to this again. Two can play this game.

'Yes, sir.' The soft click echoes in the vast chamber. He sucks in a ragged breath, but still, he doesn't turn.

'Strip.' The single word hits like a physical blow. No greeting. No champagne. No 'how's your week?' Just a command—probably like he gave to every other submissive he ever had. The thought makes my stomach sick.

Is that how he felt seeing me with Caspian the other night? Probably.

My hands shake as I reach for my zip. I'll do whatever he asks of me, because it's the only way I can show him I'm his.

The dress pools at my feet. I leave on the lingerie.

Goosebumps rise across my skin. Still, he doesn't look at me. I untie the silk strings and place the mask on top of my dress.

As I near the cross, Sean finally turns. The impact of his attention nearly brings me to my knees. His dark eyes rake over me, burning with something beyond possession. There's pain there. Raw and unfiltered. Mixed with hunger that takes my breath away.

This isn't just about the other night. This is about everything we can't say. Can't have. Everything that's been building between us since I first crawled across his floor.

He prowls towards me, rolling up the sleeves of his shirt like he means business. Veins pump furiously on his tanned forearms, the only indication his heart is working as hard as mine.

'Face the cross. Arms up.'

I press against the smooth ebony. The wood is cool against my heated skin. Sean's presence behind me overwhelms me. Heat radiates from his body. Subtle notes of cologne combined with his natural raw masculinity. When his hands touch my wrists, his fingers linger a moment longer than necessary. Electricity sparks between us. Every nerve ending in my body stands to attention.

Kat's wrong. She has to be. Because I can't imagine this intensity between us ever fading.

'You know why you're here.' His breath ghosts my ear.

'Because you want to punish me. You're disappointed in me.'

'No. I'm not disappointed in you. I'm disappointed in the situation.' His lips brush my shoulder. So light I might have imagined it. 'You're here because I need to claim you. I need to at least try to keep up the pretence that I'm in control here, because it's becoming painfully clear that whenever you're near me, I'm anything but.'

'Why is control so important to you?' What is it that makes this beautiful man so sure he's broken?

He's quiet for so long, that I'm not sure he's even going to answer, but then his voice comes, rougher than I've ever heard it. 'I told you about my original sub—the woman who introduced me to this life.'

'Yes.'

Tension radiates from his body. 'It wasn't just the fact she was unfaithful, it was the fact that I was naïve enough not to see it. My life was completely out of my own control, and I hated it. Hated how much she hurt me. How much I let her. In the confines of this club, bound by a contract, I know exactly where I stand. There are no games—well apart from the ones we opt to play together. There are no lies. No expectations from either party. And no surprises that can destroy me. Well...' he pauses for a long beat. 'Until you. You're the biggest surprise of my life.'

'I'm taking it as you don't like surprises?'

'Not when they're bound to end in pain.'

'I would never hurt you. I'm yours. In every way.' If only I could rip open my chest and show him—he has my heart. It beats for him—whether I want it to or not.

He fastens the cool chrome restraints around my wrists, and then my ankles with a definitive click. I'm trapped. Not just by the metal, but by the weight of everything we can't have. 'I need to explain. About the other night.' I twist my head to the point of pain to meet his eye. 'But I don't want to... terrify you.'

His shoulders tense as he folds his arms across his chest. 'You're the one shackled to the cross, and you're worried about terrifying me?' A disbelieving laugh rumbles from his throat. He stalks around the back of the cross to save my neck—I think.

'Yes,' I swallow thickly.

'Go on.' Curiosity blazes in his pupils.

'I went out with Ashworth in public in order to buy time with you in private. I... I want to be with you.' My eyes fall to the floor. Why is baring my heart to him so much harder than baring my body?

The answer slams into my stomach like a slap-because if he rejects me now, my heart would hurt so much more than any torture he could inflict on my flesh.

The truth of it hits me like a sledgehammer. I've fallen for him. Hard and fast.

The dim spotlight spills across his darkening expression. 'You want to be with me?' he repeats, the words rolling slowly off his tongue.

No point holding back now. 'Every minute of every damn day,' I whisper.

His eyebrows furrow.

'I know it's not what we signed up for. I didn't plan on developing feelings for you. But how could I not, when we have this? When you make me feel more alive than I ever have in my life.' I move my arms as much as the restraints will allow, which isn't a lot.

Understanding lights his ebony orbs.

'I'm not ready to go home. I'm not ready to go back to a life without this.' I meet his eyes again. 'A life without you. If I don't at least look like I'm making some progress on finding a marriage match, my parents will drag me home.'

His expression softens as he steps forward and brushes his fingers over my cheek in a rare show of tenderness. 'I don't like it. Not one fucking bit. Because I want to be with you too, princess. Every second of every damn day.' His nostrils flare. 'I can't bear to see you with another man, Layla. So help me God, I won't be able to stop myself next time. If someone so much as lays a hand on you, it sets me feral.' He steps back again.

'No one is going to touch me. No one but you. I'm yours. Every single inch of me.'

'Every single inch?' His eyes blaze with heat and hunger as he circles back around the cross, to place his hand on my ass cheek.

Understanding dawns. Lust pools in my stomach and lower. He wants to go where no man has gone before. And I'll let him, because I trust him with my body and oddly enough, with my heart. I'm utterly in love with the man, and he has no idea. 'Every. Single. Inch. Take me, I'm yours.'

Chapter Twenty-Seven

SEAN

The princess is a vision spread legged against the cross. I could stare at her all damn night. But it's not her body that's making me hard. It's her words. Trust hasn't come easy to me, not since Hannah, but there's something about Layla that makes me want to try. She's giving every inch of her body to me. I need to man up and do the same.

'Do you trust me, princess?'

'Yes. But more importantly, do you trust me?'

'I'm working on it.' I stride towards the glass cabinet at the far end of the room, my shoes thwack menacingly across the marble. I deliberately muted the music in here tonight so I could savour every single one of her moans.

Running my hands over the carefully curated selection of paddles and crops before settling on a silk flogger with chrome tipped falls that will sing against her skin. Her shaky breath fills the air as I stride back towards her.

'Do you remember your safeword?'

'Am I going to need it?' she pants as I trail the instrument over her spine, watching goosebumps rise in its wake. Her breath catches as I trace patterns across her skin. She arches into the touch instinctively seeking more.

'Not if you answer correctly.' I crack the silk across her backside, hard enough to sting but not actually hurt. 'Who gets to touch you?'

Her squeal pierces the air, followed by a moan of pleasure. 'You.'

'Who do you think about when you touch yourself?' I trail the flogger over her ass cheek where a red mark is already beginning to form, caressing it gently.

'You,' she pants, twisting her head round. Our eyes lock. Hers are glassy with need.

'Who does this pretty little cunt belong to?' I lower the flogger, trailing it between her legs, teasing her sex.

I need to be certain she's as invested in this—us—as much as I am.

She squirms against the flogger seeking friction. 'You.'

Satisfaction sweeps through every cell in my body, rapidly eradicating any last trace of lingering jealousy. 'Good girl.'

I toss the flogger to the floor and tear off the scrap of silk between her legs. It's soaked. I bring it to my face and inhale it before shoving it into my pocket.

My gaze roams over the silk suspender belt, the exposed flesh of the tops of her thighs above her stockings. They can stay on. I reach between her legs, swiping a finger through her slick folds, and she gasps.

'Sean,' it's a plea and a prayer. She twists to meet my eye again. I bring my finger to my mouth and lick her arousal off my finger. She wets her lips.

'You taste utterly delectable.' I'm on my knees for her in less than three seconds, lapping at her wet cunt, revelling in the taste of her and the needy little moans that spill from her mouth. When her thighs start to tense, I slow to a maddeningly slow pace, and she bucks against my face. I stop completely.

I rise, replacing my tongue with my fingers, thrusting them in and out of her tight channel. Just when she's ready to blow again, I stop.

'Sean,' her voice cracks with need.

'Trust me, you'll thank me for this when I'm fucking your ass.'

She gasps. 'Do it. I told you, I'm yours.'

Her words are a balm to my jealous soul. 'Patience, princess.' I swipe the slickness from her pussy and drag it higher until I find her tight little hole.

She shivers as I sink a finger in. Goosebumps rip over her skin. 'How does that feel?' I press tiny kisses over her shoulder blades and up over her neck.

'It feels,' I feel her throat bob as she swallows, 'so good.'

'My dirty girl,' I growl.

I tear open my suit pants and my cock springs free.

'Take everything off.' Layla twists to look at me again with a fresh set of need in her eyes. 'I want to feel your skin on my skin.'

I hold her gaze for a long beat.

She watches as I reach for my shirt buttons and unfasten them one by one. 'You're going to be the undoing of me.'

'I think it's you who's going to be the undoing of me,' she admits. Something flashes through her eyes. Something that mirrors every single one of my fragile feelings. I'm in way over my head. This thing between us is so much more than what we signed up for.

But this princess has no way of getting her traditional fairy tale ending. Not with me anyway. I'm no prince. I'm a predator. But at least we have this—for now.

I shrug out of my shirt and toss it to the side, then drag

my trousers down my thighs, kicking my shoes off in the process. Getting fully naked with a sub feels like relinquishing control. But this situation is already so far out of both of our control, we may as well embrace it together.

Pressing my body against hers, I nuzzle into her neck. She arches back into me, our bodies saying the things that our mouths can't.

This is so much more than anything before.

I nudge my cock into her slick slit. 'You feel so fucking good.' I inch myself into her, stretching her until she's full of me.

'So do you.' Her head rolls back against my chest. She tilts her chin up until our eyes meet. The last time a woman did that, I ended the arrangement immediately. This time, I want the woman before me to stare at me forever.

I thrust into her slowly, repeating the motion until my cock is coated in her arousal. 'This pussy is mine.' I drag myself out of her, repositioning my dick until it rests between her ass cheeks. 'This ass is mine.' I ease myself into her, slowly, gently, with a tenderness I've never used on anyone before.

'Ohh.' She hunches forward as she takes my cock, inch by magnificent inch.

'How does that feel, baby?' I steady her hips with one hand and reach around to play with her clit with the other. It's swollen, throbbing with need.

'Amazing.' Her head rolls back against my chest as I gently rock into her. She's so tight. So responsive. I don't stand a hope in hell of lasting like this.

'My dirty girl loves getting fucked in the ass.' I stroke from her clit to her slit then back again, driving my dick into her again and again.

'Only by you.'

I thrust into her, revelling in every little moan and mew.

'Sean,' she screams a split second before her body convulses with pure primal pleasure. I'm a second behind her, my own hedonistic high hijacking my entire body until I'm spilling myself in her, jerking through every wave of my hedonistic high.

'Fuck. I love you.' The words blurt out of my mouth before I can stop them.

Her body stills. She freezes, face forward, with my cock still in her ass.

Man, I'm such a twat.

Her words at my house float back through my mind: *'Don't worry, Mr Beckett, I can categorically assure you, I will not fall in love with you.'*

She's looking for a love match. Match being the key word in that sentence. I'm no match for her. Not in the real world.

Her silence speaks volumes. It's on the tip of my tongue to apologise, but I don't truly feel sorry. Stupid, yes, but not sorry. I'm glad she knows.

I drag myself out of her, peppering tiny kisses across her back as I do, then reach for the restraints. She says nothing as I uncuff her ankles first, then her wrists. Flexing them as she turns, her eyes finally meet mine. In just the stockings and suspender belt, dripping my cum, she looks absolutely ethereal.

Her eyes hold mine for a long beat before she speaks. 'I wanted to look into your eyes when I said it for the first time.' She swallows thickly, placing her hands on my bare chest. 'I love you, Sean Beckett. I have no idea what that means for us, but I do.'

My mouth crashes onto hers, claiming, cementing, celebrating that this thing between us is not in my head. That she's as mad about me as I am about her.

I have no idea if we have a future, but we have right now.

'You're coming home with me tonight. I want you in my bed.'

And in my arms.

I'm so fucked.

Chapter Twenty-Eight

LAYLA

He finally releases me from his crushing embrace. 'Let's go home.' He whips up my dress and pulls it over my head, dressing me like a child.

Home. If only. Imagine building a home with him. Having him hold me all night every night. I sigh. 'I need to be back at the castle before five am.'

'Or what? Your outfit will turn into rags?' he teases, touching his lips to mine.

'Or someone will notify my parents, and they'll tear me to rags.'

'I told you I'll take care of you. I'll sneak you back in personally.' He reaches for my mask and secures it over my face.

'I wish I didn't have to wear this. It weighs a tonne.'

'I know.' Sean's huge, deep dark eyes bore into mine. 'Believe me, I wear one all day every day. Unless I'm in here. Or with you. Tried my best to keep it in place at the ball. You saw how that ended up.'

'What are we going to do?' I whisper.

'Each other.' A smile curls his lips, but it doesn't meet his eyes. 'How does one acquire one of these titles your mother is so hell bent on?'

'With great difficulty.' I watch as he dresses, then heads for the restroom at the side of the room. He returns with a warm wet wash cloth and proceeds to clean me up. The expression on his face is one of utter tenderness.

'You're stunning, you know that?' He dips his face to brush his lips over mine.

'I feel like you're the first person to really see me.'

'I see you, Layla. I see you.' He pulls me into his chest, enveloping me in his huge embrace.

I wrap my arms around his broad shoulders, resting a hand on the nape of his neck. 'I want a tour of your house so I can dream of you sleeping there when I get back to the castle.'

'I won't be sleeping. I'll be lying awake thinking of how I can keep you here. Three months was never going to be enough.' He releases me from his arms, takes my small hand in his huge one and guides me out into the corridor.

'You'll need your sleep for tomorrow night.' I fire him a wink.

He winces. 'About tomorrow night.'

'Don't tell me *your* busy schedule doesn't permit our date?' I throw his own words back at him with a smile, but my heart is sinking inside of me. The idea of not seeing him tomorrow is already killing me. Especially after tonight's admissions.

'It's Caelon's stag night.' He sighs.

'Your brother?'

'Yep.'

'Where is it?'

'Rian's club.'

'Is it a club like this?' It's a battle to keep the jealousy from my voice.

'Not exactly.' A sheepish look creeps across his features. 'It's a gentlemen's club.'

'Strippers?'

'Dancers,' he corrects.

'Naked dancers?' I snap as we reach the end reception area. Dominic eyes us warily.

'Don't worry, Dom,' Sean flashes his friend a smirk as he reaches for my coat. 'We're just having our first domestic. The princess doesn't want me going to the Gentlemen's club.'

Dominic guffaws. 'I could entertain her here for you, if you're busy?' His eyes flash with mirth.

'Don't even think about it,' Sean snarls, all trace of a smirk evaporating from his face.

'You still owe me money for the bet.'

'What bet?' I narrow my eyes at Dominic.

Sean shrugs, placing his hand on the small of my back. 'He and Larissa bet I couldn't share you.'

'And we were right.' Dominic gloats, folding his arms across his broad chest. 'His obsession with you was crystal clear the second he laid eyes on you. It was written all over his face.'

'Thanks for that, mate.' Sean knocks his shoulder against Dominic's roughly before wrapping my coat around my shoulders. The elevator doors open and two members enter. I freeze for a second before remembering I have my mask on.

'I'll transfer the money later,' Sean shakes Dominic's hand good naturedly, nods at the members, then guides me into the lift. He slips his hand into mine. The gesture feels so intimate. I squeeze his fingers, and he squeezes mine back as we exit the building.

The February air is crisp and cold, but I feel a warmth inside that I didn't feel when I arrived tonight. Sean guides me towards a Santorini black Jaguar and opens the passenger door for me.

Moonlight spills across his darkening expression. 'If you have to attend any other public events to "buy time with me in private" he grimaces, 'can you please forewarn me so I don't have to sit through the show?'

'Absolutely.' I draw an X across my chest in promise. 'But you can trust me, Sean. I won't let you down.'

'Slowly, slowly, I'm starting to believe it.' He closes the passenger door, then strides around to the driver's side and drops into the seat beside me. 'Now, can we talk about something else?' He twists his head to meet my gaze across the console. 'Time is precious; I don't want to waste it imagining you dating another man.'

'What do you want to talk about?'

'You.' He takes my hand and presses it to his lips as he reverses the car out of the parking lot. 'I want to know everything about you.'

'You already know more than most.'

'What's your favourite food?'

'Pasta.' I shrug. 'Carbs have been my best friend since I got here. Carbs and Kat, my lady-in-waiting.'

'Favourite movie?'

'*Love Actually*. But it still bugs me that one couple didn't get their happy ever after.'

'And that Alan Rickman cheated on his wife!' He shakes his head in disgust.

'You saw it?' I squeal. It's hard to imagine a man like him watching a romance movie.

'I have a sister—and sisters-in-law.' He cocks a brow. 'Christmas isn't Christmas without that crap blaring, apparently. Every Christmas Eve, we have a family movie night. It's always the same two, *Love Actually* and *The Holiday*. The women always blub, and the men always slug. Thank God we own a distillery, given the amount of whiskey we get through at "the most wonderful time of the year".'

'It sounds idyllic. Our Christmases at the palace are a little different.' I pull a face. 'I'd love to have a family like yours,' I sigh wistfully.

'Maybe you will,' he inclines his head towards mine. 'Stranger things have happened.'

My stomach somersaults at the mere suggestion as we pull up outside Blackstone House. It feels like a lifetime ago that I was last here, that first night with the contract.

Sean carries me up the sweeping staircase, past the bathroom with the clawfoot tub, and into his bedroom. It's dark, masculine, and expensively finished, just like him. Floor to ceiling windows overlook the grounds below. I don't have time to appreciate the view because he lays me gently on his enormous bed. Onyx-like eyes hold mine through the moonlight.

'This is getting dangerous.' He whispers. 'Suddenly I don't want to tie you to a cross anymore. I want to tie you to my bed and never let you leave.'

'If I thought for a second we could get away with it...'

His lips find mine, parting them, tenderly sweeping his tongue through my mouth, savouring me like it's the first time. He unbuttons his shirt without breaking our kiss, then pulls my dress up over my head. When he's removed every single item of clothing from both of our bodies, he nudges my thighs open.

'I love you,' he says again, brushing my hair back from my face, kissing from my temple, to my jawline, then back to my lips. 'Sometimes I wonder if you're real. Sometimes I worry that one day, I'm going to wake up and you'll have vanished, never to be seen again.'

'It won't happen. I won't let it happen.'

He pins my arms above my head and guides himself into me, grinding slowly, like he's savouring every movement, every moment of this. His palms map out every inch of my body, like he's committing every millimetre to memory. It's unlike anything we've done in the sultry confines of Reveal. At Reveal, our bodies meet. Here, in the private confines of his bed, it feels more like two sacred souls meeting for the first time.

Afterwards, we lie entwined. He wraps his arms tightly around me like he really is afraid I might vanish. In the silence, something shifts between us—something deeper than desire, more profound than any contract. He strokes my hair with reverent fingers while I press closer, resting my cheek on his chest, listening to the steady thrum of his heartbeat. Sleep seems like a waste when these stolen hours feel more special than anything I've experienced in my entire life. I lie soaking in every second. A contentment that has no place there fills my heart.

He gently shifts beside me. 'We better get you home, princess.'

'I know. I hate leaving you. Especially when I'm not going to see you tomorrow.'

'I'll text you.'

'You will?'

'We're breaking all the rules now, anyway...' He brushes his lips over mine. 'This is no longer an arrangement. This, us'—he motions between us—'is everything to me now.'

Chapter Twenty-Nine

SEAN

Caelon's stag night is in full swing at the Luxor Lounge, the club Rian bought when its previous owner, Christopher Cole, mysteriously disappeared—coincidentally right after he came on to Scarlett when she worked here.

James and Killian are deeply engrossed in conversation at the bar. I'm nursing a Beckett's Gold in one of the circular booth seats beside the main stage, where three dancers glide around polished steel poles in various stages of undress. A deep bass thrums through the club. It's not open to members tonight. Every single man in the room is here for Caelon. Business contacts. Friends. Cousins. Caelon himself sits beside me with Dermot, Ivy's brother, beside him, then Rian on the other side, Rian's best friend Anthony on the end.

One of the young, lithe, barely dressed dancers approaches the booth. Her entire outfit comprises a cerise lace thong nestled between her legs. 'How about a dance?'

Dermot shoots Caelon a look that suggests if he even thinks about a private dance, he'll murder him. Guess he hasn't lost the older brother protective edge yet. At least Layla doesn't have one of those. Although having the King and Queen of England for parents will certainly bring its challenges.

'No thanks.' Caelon raises his hand at the dancer, keeping his eyes firmly trained on her face.

'It's on the house.' Rian offers. He is such a fucking stirrer. He can't seem to help himself.

'No, thank you.' Caelon's tone is sterner this time. He shoots Rian a look that would make other men flinch, but Rian merely laughs in his face.

'What about you?' The dancer turns her attention to me.

'Oh, don't waste your time there, love.' Rian snorts. 'You haven't got the equipment to satisfy Sean.' He slaps the table and roars with laughter. 'Come on, bro, when are you going to come out? It's okay.' Rian shrugs. 'No judgement here.'

I maintain my cool. Years of practice have served me well. 'You haven't got the equipment to satisfy anyone. Not long enough to keep them, anyway.' I raise my glass to my lips and take a deep drink. 'How many women have you fucked this year? Ten?'

'Twelve.' Rian gloats as Anthony beckons the dancer towards him

'And exactly how many of them have banged the door down for seconds?' I stare at him levelly over the rim of my glass as Caelon and Anthony dissolve into fits of laughter.

'Okay, smartass. How many women have you fucked this year?' Rian exudes a cockiness that stems from being the youngest and being handed everything in life. His idea of working is buying a strip bar and a string of nightclubs and alternating his time drinking in each of them.

I never reveal anything about myself, but tonight, it's too tempting not to. Plus, even talking about Layla in a round-about way brings a grin to my face. Inviting her into my bed last night was another surprising first for me, but it won't be the last. Watching her as she curled contentedly into my chest was every bit as satisfying as watching her come. I'm going to need more—of both. 'One.'

'What?' Caelon turns to me, eyes wide and incredulous. He's consumed enough Beckett's Gold to forget this entire night, let alone this conversation.

'Yeah, right.' Rian rolls his eyes. 'Who is this mystery woman? Why haven't we met her?'

'Because she's too good for any of us, and I refuse to have you pawing all over her like you do with our sisters-in-law.'

'Convenient.' Rian teases with a smirk. His attention shifts from me to his friend Anthony, who's guiding the dancer onto his lap. His hands snake from her waist up over her breasts in front of everyone.

Rian's entire demeanour flicks like a switch. All trace of teasing evaporates as he eyes Anthony tweaking nipples and kissing the back of the dancer's long slim neck. 'I'll take a dance.'

We all know it's not a dance she's offering.

She slides off his lap and places her hand in his. His navy suit pants are tented with his excitement. Rian narrows his eyes. 'Thought you were married, man.' He shakes his head.

'What's it to you?' Anthony shrugs, then follows the dancer through the club, no doubt to one of the private rooms.

'Asshole.' Rian snatches up the whiskey in front of him. 'His wife is way too good for him.' He slides out of the booth. 'I'll order us another bottle.' He nods towards the almost empty bottle of Beckett's Gold in the centre of the table.

'Not for me,' Caelon slurs. 'I'm going home.'

Dermot nods his approval. 'I'll give you a ride. My driver's outside.'

'Thanks, bro.' Caelon slaps Dermot's back as he helps him up. He definitely won't remember the earlier conversation. 'See you, Sean. Thanks for coming, man.' He slaps my back.

'As if I'd miss your stag night.' I'm just grateful he had it in Dublin. Given it's not his first, he opted to keep it low key.

'I love you, man.' He bumps his fist against my bicep.

'Yeah, yeah, I love you too, bro.' I pat his back as he staggers away with an amused looking Dermot.

There's no need for me to stay now Caelon's gone. Ben is outside in the Bentley waiting for me. I glance at the chunky silver on my wrist.

The need to see Layla claws at my insides. I was going to call her anyway, but perhaps it's not too late to make a house call. I pull out my phone and fire off a quick text.

> You awake?

The three answering dots that appear serve as my answer. I don't wait for her reply, the same way I don't hang around to say goodbye to my other brothers.

Thirty minutes later, I'm climbing up the drainpipe of the castle, doing a very clumsy impression of a prince trying to rescue a princess from her tower. The truth is, it's her who's rescuing me—from a life of black and white lines. Who knew grey could look so good?

'You okay, boss?' Ben calls through the darkness.

'Fine.' Thank fuck for all the gym work. There's no way I could pull this off if it weren't for four days a week with Ben busting my bollocks in the gym. 'Go back to Blackstone. I'll call you in the morning.'

'It is the morning,' he chuckles.

'Barely.'

The old sash window screeches as it opens, and Layla's head pops out. Her long dark hair is loose, and it blows over her face in the winter wind. 'I can't believe you scaled the drainpipe. You're certifiably mad.' Her tinkling laughter floats through the air as I hoist myself up and swing onto the balcony outside her room.

I am mad—mad about her. 'Open the door; it's fucking freezing out here.'

Ben's laughter rings from below. The car door closes with a gentle click, and then he speeds away. The door slides open, and Layla stands like a vision in a white nightdress that stops just above her knees. It's far more conservative than the outfits I'm used to seeing her in, but it still renders my dick solid in seconds.

'Have you got any lingerie on under that thing?' I close the distance between us, finding her lips with mine. The relief is acute.

She breaks our kiss and drags me in through the doors, sliding them closed behind us. 'Come in and find out.' Her eyes flash with heat.

'I intend to.' My gaze travels around the room, cataloguing the princess's chambers. They're not what I expected. They're... cold, miserable, dark and utterly unfit for her. She did say she'd been sent here as punishment. She wasn't joking. If she was sent here to freeze and die of boredom for tipping a drink over someone's head, what punishment would she suffer if her family were to find out about me?

Layla slips her hands inside my suit jacket, mapping out each muscle beneath my shirt. 'I can't believe you're here.' It's barely more than a whisper. 'From the night I crawled across the stage, I wanted you in my bed, and now you're finally here.'

'Why didn't you say so?' I pull her against me, pressing a kiss to her lips. She tastes like toothpaste and temptation.

'Would you have come?' her eyes glitter.

'There's not a thing on this earth I wouldn't do if you asked me to,' I admit.

'Well, in that case, Mr Beckett, you can start by doing me.' Her hands reach around to squeeze my backside. 'Unless you're too tired, that is?'

I run my palms over her breasts. 'We can sleep when we're dead.'

'Which might be sooner rather than later if we aren't careful.' Her eyes bore into mine. 'The guards.'

'Fuck them. I need you every night. Every day. Every goddamn fucking hour.'

'Are you drunk, Mr Beckett?'

'Possibly. But that doesn't change how I feel about you.' I scoop her up into my arms, pressing my lips to hers again, swallowing her squeal of surprise as I carry her towards her bed. She wraps her arms around my neck and her legs around my waist, locking me in position. As if I'd leave. Not willingly anyway. The floodgates to my heart have been well and truly opened and there's not a thing I can do about it.

I lower her onto the bed without breaking our kiss. Her hungry mouth devours mine, fingers rushing to clumsily unbutton my shirt, like we're going to run out of time any second. I still her hands and place them above her head.

'Patience, princess.' I strip for her slowly, watching as her pupils dilate and her tongue darts out to wet her lower lips.

'I need you,' she whispers.

'You have me.' Whether I wanted to give myself to her or not, she has every fucking part of me. She's seen the kinks, the darkness, the jealous beast that hides behind the polished façade, and she still wants me here. When the last piece of clothing is discarded on the floor, I pull her nightdress up over her head. The moonlight pours through the balcony doors, illuminating every inch of her flesh. She's the most beautiful woman I've ever laid eyes on, and she's mine.

'Please, Sean.' Her voice cracks with need.

I crawl up the hard mattress to position myself between her legs. Her pussy glistens with arousal. It's too enticing not to taste her. I glide my tongue along her slit, and she drags her fingers through my hair. She writhes against my face. 'I need you inside me. Right now.'

I smile against her sex. 'And I thought I was in control.'

'Neither of us is in control when we're together.'

Isn't that the truth?

Her fingers dig into my shoulder blades as she tries to drag me up the bed. I don't need dragging when it comes to sliding my cock in her. I push against her dripping entrance and slide into her, kissing up her neck, along her jawline until I find her mouth. Her hands settle on my ass cheeks, fingers biting into the skin, thrusting me deeper into her. She's so goddamn responsive. So fucking perfect. She's everything I never knew I needed.

I feel the tiny pulses of her pussy fluttering on my cock, dragging me over the edge with her. She shatters, and I swallow her moans. They mingle with my own as white-hot pleasure tears through me. Pleasure and a sublime sense of something else.

Contentment.

As she lies on my chest, I stroke my fingers through her hair as she sleeps. It occurs to me this is the first time in years I've had vanilla sex. But with Layla, there's nothing vanilla about it.

Chapter Thirty

LAYLA

Sean has snuck into my bedroom every night for the past three weeks. The sex has been epic, but the most epic thing ever is having his body curl protectively around mine, feeling his warm skin against mine, hearing the soft soothing sounds of his breath as he sleeps. I never fully appreciated how alone I felt until suddenly I wasn't.

Twice, Kat almost caught us. Thankfully, I managed to stall her while Sean slipped out the window. Friend or not, this new development will alarm her. It's one thing to have a bit of fun with the billionaire next door, and another entirely to fall in love with him. I'm alarmed about it myself—by the intensity of my feelings for him.

The nights have shown a tenderness, a deeper level of intimacy to the raw, animalistic sex we've had at Reveal. The second he leaves, my body aches for him. I need his touch, his kiss, and his undivided attention. And I need it like a heart needs a beat. I don't care if it's kinky sex, crazy sex, or sleepy sex, I'll take it. But after a week of vanilla-ish sex, I can't wait to see what he's going to unleash on me tonight at Reveal.

Unfortunately, I have to get through an afternoon with

Lord Finegan Montgomery first. He's finally back from his business trip, and the pressure is on. My mother sprung this surprise on me at nine o'clock this morning. Sean had already left. I didn't have the heart to call him and break his. It's just tea. It means nothing. It's another duty—one he'll at least be spared from witnessing. That's what he asked for, wasn't it?

Like my mother did before me, I'll sit here and think of England. The only difference is, my legs will remain firmly closed—until tonight, at least.

I'm doing this for him. For us. To buy us more time. Because unfortunately, we're running out by the hour. Sabrina's wedding is rapidly approaching. My mother will want me home for the preparations any day now, unless I can prove to her that there's something worth staying here for.

There is, of course. Just not what she's hoping for.

I would stay here, given half the chance.

Mid-afternoon, Kat knocks on my studio door. 'Lord Finegan is in the drawing room.'

'Fantastic.' My sarcasm isn't lost on her.

'Do you want your parents to send the jet for you, or not?' Her fair eyebrows wing upwards.

'Fine. I'm coming.' I slide off my painting overalls and go upstairs to change. The scent of Sean's cologne lingers in my bedroom. Or maybe it's in my nostrils because Kat hasn't mentioned it.

For today's dull date, Kat laid out a midi-length dove grey dress. It's fitted and elegant without trying too hard, which is precisely the point. She's teamed it with my grandmother's pearl strand and matching studs, probably at my mother's request. I'm a twenty-five-year-old woman, and my mother still picks out my outfits for me. Well, some of them at least. I pull my hair back into a sleek sort of chignon. I barely recognise this version of myself anymore.

I make my guest wait a further ten minutes before

descending the wide sweeping staircase to greet him. The
drawing room door creaks as it swings open. Lord Montgomery pounces from the vintage sofa to his feet, raking his
hand through his blond, short, wavy hair. Piercing blue eyes
land on mine.

'Princess,' he bows his head.

'Lord Montgomery,' I stride across the room and extend a
hand to shake his. He glances up as he brings it to his lips and
brushes a kiss on the back of it. At six foot two, with an
athletic frame, Lord Montgomery is infinitely more attractive
than I remembered. Or maybe he's simply grown into the
man that he was always meant to be. Still, he has nothing on
the man living in my head each day, and my bed each night.

'Please, call me Finegan.' His voice is deep and polished in
that clipped, expensively educated way of our world.

'Very well, Finegan. It's a pleasure to see you again.' I'm
lying obviously, although it's not as painful as I'd imagined...
so far.

'Likewise, Princess.' His startling eyes rake over my frame,
and then he takes a step back, like he caught himself looking
at something he's not sure he can afford.

'Please, have a seat. The staff will bring through tea shortly.' I sweep a hand towards the couch, and he lowers himself
to a sitting position again. I take the large chair beside it.

'How are you enjoying Ireland?' He begins. 'I trust you've
recovered from your migraine?'

'I'd enjoy it infinitely more if the Queen allowed me to
leave this estate.' I shrug. 'And yes, thank you, I'm feeling
much better.'

His lips quirk upwards, revealing years of what has to be
impeccable orthodontic treatment, another positive change
since the last time we were acquainted.

'I heard a rumour you were grounded of sorts.' He cocks
his head to the side, arching his brows in question.

'Unfortunately, it's true. Sometimes I wish I'd been born with a penis. Then at least I might have some say in my own life.' I shrug.

I can only blame Sean Beckett's filthy mouth for my vulgarity. I open my lips, and everything tumbles out. My tolerance levels for anything less than real are through the floor. I'm tired of being a show pony for my family. Especially now I know what it feels like to have someone love me— really love me, for who I am, not for my status.

He splutters, coughing through his shock, but his eyes gleam with intrigue. 'Quite,' he finally agrees.

Mrs Medway enters carrying a tray full of delicacies and steaming hot tea. She flashes a smile and bows her head respectfully, but I'm under no illusion—she's spying for my mother again. I'd love to give her something really shocking to report, but instead I sit forward, straighten my spine and stare at Finegan like he's the most interesting creature to grace this earth. Perhaps that will buy me more time. I'm acutely aware that one way or another, I'm running out of it.

Finegan graciously accepts a cup of Earl Grey, stealing curious glances my way until we're finally alone again. I take a sip of my own and leave the ball in his court.

My mind wanders back to Sean, wondering where he is, what he's doing. If he's in his Grafton Street office, or out for lunch with his brothers. But mostly, I'm wondering if he's missing me as much as I'm missing him.

Finegan stares at me intently, his eyes ablaze with curiosity. 'I must say, I'm rather glad you weren't.'

'Weren't what, sorry?' I force myself to pay attention to the man occupying my time instead of the one occupying my brain.

'Born with a penis.' A smile touches his lips. 'I think you're rather perfect the way you are.'

My phone vibrates in the discreet pocket of my dress.

Probably my mother, reminding me to behave. I ignore it. 'Thank you, Finegan. Sorry if my manner is somewhat crude. It's rather frustrating being the third daughter sometimes. First world problems, I know.'

He arches forward, closing the space between us. 'I can relate, believe me.' He tugs at the material of his cream suit pants, adjusting the material over the thighs bulging beneath. 'While I may have been born with a penis...' his eyes flare with mirth '...there are still certain restrictions enforced in families like ours.'

'Yours can't be as restrictive as mine. But still, we didn't meet to form a pity party. Tell me, what have you been up to these past few years?'

My phone vibrates again. I ignore it, listening as Finegan regales his recent antics travelling in Asia. Thankfully there's no mention of gardens or sheep. In fact, this Finegan is actually rather entertaining compared to the one I last met.

'How is the gardening coming along? And the sheep farming?' I lift my teacup to my lips, wishing it had a drop from Kat's flask in.

'Oh.' He shakes his head; a small smile twitches at his lips. 'Honestly, I hate both, but last time we met, my mother insisted it was an appropriate topic to discuss with a lady such as yourself.'

'So what does interest you, Finegan, if it's not sheep and gardening?'

'Property acquisition. Golf. But mostly... you, princess.' His piercing eyes bore into mine. 'You interest me a great deal.'

Before I can answer, a knock sounds on the door. Kat's head pops around before I can say 'come in'. Her face is pale and tight. Panic lights her eyes.

'Whatever is the matter, Kat?' I frown.

'You have another visitor, Your Highness. And he's very insistent.'

'Who?' No one knows I'm here except…

'Mr Beckett is adamant he joins you.' Her eyebrows shoot skyward.

My lips twitch. Is it wrong that I love that my boyfriend is crazily possessive? I turn to Finegan and shrug. 'Send him in.'

Chapter Thirty-One

SEAN

Unfuckingbelievable. Who the fuck does Finegan fucking Montgomery think he is? Bad enough he snatched forestry from under my nose a few weeks ago, but there's no way he's taking my woman as well.

You can imagine my surprise when I got a phone call from Ben informing me my girlfriend had a visitor. Okay, we haven't put a label on what she is to me, on what I am to her, but given I spend every night in her bed, and we've said those three little words every day for the past few weeks, I kind of assumed.

Killian's security detail have been keeping Ben updated with progress reports from Ardmore. They surround the property from a respectable distance at all times, accompany her when she goes riding. They're discreet but deadly. I take comfort in knowing that *someone* is guarding her properly.

I know she's under pressure from her family to settle down, but she promised to warn me about things like this. What is she doing entertaining that blond pretentious prick in her home? Him *and* his fucking title. The public date with

Ashworth was bad enough, but Lord Finegan Montgomery's arrival at the castle is an abomination.

I stride into the drawing room, forcing a neutral expression onto my face. Thank god it's my superpower. No one has any idea of the jealous beast I am beneath the polite, polished façade. No one but her. And yet somehow–she still loves me.

'Good afternoon, Your Highness.' I bow my head at Layla, and she quirks an eyebrow at the formal address.

In a fitted grey dress, she looks conservative, yet utterly stunning. From the minute I left her this morning, I've been counting down the seconds until I can hold her again. These past few weeks have been the best of my life. There's no way I'm letting this pretentious prick take her from me. Him or anyone else.

'Mr Beckett.' She raises a dainty, manicured hand, pressing it at the base of her throat. 'What a surprise.'

Finegan Fuck Face rises from his position on the couch. He glowers at my interruption. 'Beckett, I wasn't expecting to meet you here.'

'I could say the same about you.' I manage to keep my voice level, despite my disdain for him.

'I'm here by invitation,' he says smugly, adjusting his baby pink tie. I'm tempted to string him up by the fucking thing.

'Really?' I turn my attention back to the princess. She shrugs and raises her eyebrows and I gather it wasn't her who invited him, but her meddling mother.

'Our families go way back.' Finegan may as well have taken his entitled cock out of his suit pants and slapped it down on the thick plush carpets. If he wants to get into a dick measuring competition, there's only one of us who's had our dick inside the princess.

Isn't there?

A sliver of doubt curls in my core.

No. Layla isn't Hannah. She wouldn't do that to me. Layla

lives to rebel, to test boundaries. The only boundaries this cunt would test is her patience. 'How charming,' I snort. Translation: How boringly aristocratic.

I stride across the room to Layla, and drop a kiss on her cheek, letting my lips linger a little longer than appropriate. Her familiar perfume engulfs me along with a flashback of her curled across my chest in bed this morning.

I step back, and our eyes lock. That familiar intensity pulses between us.

'Mind if I join your little tea party? I'm between meetings. Thought I'd drop by and check my neighbour is okay.' I shoot Layla a wink as I drop into the chair opposite her. 'I've been keeping her company while she's on house arrest.'

'How very neighbourly of you.' Finegan's jaw ticks as he reaches for the teacup on the table in front of him. 'I didn't realise you two were acquainted.'

'We are *very* well acquainted.' I hold his gaze unwaveringly.

The nosy old bat of a housekeeper chooses this precise moment to bustle in with a fresh tray of tea. She places it down on the table in front of us. 'I don't suppose you've got anything stronger?' I have a feeling I'm going to need it.

'Yes, certainly, Mr Beckett. Wine? Brandy? Whiskey?'

'Whiskey, please.'

'I'll have the same.' Layla's eyes twinkle, which makes me think she's grateful for the interruption. Coming here was reckless, but that's the effect she has on me. 'Would you like one, Finegan?'

'I'm driving, unfortunately.' His eyes dart between the princess and me like he's trying to work out exactly how well acquainted we are while the housekeeper shuffles over to the drinks cabinet at the far side of the room.

I thrum my fingers over the arm of the antique chair. It wouldn't look out of place in my grandmother's house. In fact, the whole room looks like it hasn't been updated since the eighteen hundreds. Like her bedroom, it's fucking freezing—despite the roaring open fire. There are creepy portraits staring down from every wall in the house. I don't know where Layla got her looks from, but it certainly wasn't these miserable, judgy bastards. If I thought for a second, I could get away with it, I'd move her into Blackstone House this second. Now there's an idea.

Imagine not having to sneak out every single morning. Imagine having a leisurely breakfast together, then crawling back to bed again. Date nights. Sunday lunches with my family. A normal life never looked so appealing.

I force that thought away because it's futile.

Isn't it?

Every night we talk until one of us inevitably falls asleep, but this is the one subject we've both avoided. The clock is ticking, and I'm still nowhere near ready to give her up. Quite the opposite, in fact. I'm prepared to fight for her—dirty—if I have to.

'Carry on,' I sweep a hand languidly in front of my face. 'I'd hate to interrupt what must be a riveting conversation,' I accept the heavy crystal tumbler from the housekeeper and swirl the amber liquid in the glass before bringing it to my lips.

'Finegan was just telling me about his interests.' Layla takes a small sip of her own whiskey.

'Captivating, I'm sure.' I take a large mouthful of mine. Beckett's Gold. Thankfully the Royals have better taste in alcohol than they do in interior décor.

'Property acquisition specifically.' Is the princess trying to find common ground or antagonise me? 'Isn't that your department?'

'That's just work.' I scoff, shooting a look Finegan's way.

The smarmy fucker is positively preening about the forestry. 'There's nothing interesting about it.'

'Do share your interests, Sean, please.' Finegan blurts, puffing out his chest like a fucking pigeon. Oh he has no idea what he's asking.

I take another sip of whiskey, eyeing the princess over my glass. She squirms in her seat, like she's reliving my 'interests' in her head. The air short circuits between us.

'Testing limits.' I don't break our stare. 'Mine, and other people's.'

Layla's tongue darts out to wet her lips.

'Pleasure, Finegan.' I snap my eyes to his. 'I'm interested in pleasure. Spending time with the people I love.'

She takes a huge gulp of whiskey and then coughs.

Finegan continues to stare quizzically between the princess and me like he *still* hasn't got the missing piece of the puzzle, i.e. that she's my absolute world. Before he can work it out, his phone chimes from his cream suit pants.

What kind of a fucking chump wears cream suit pants?

I shake my head, glancing back down at my own black custom-made suit.

Finegan winces apologetically as he pulls his phone from his pocket.

'Please, take it,' Layla sweeps a hand in front of her face.

'Sorry, but I've been waiting for this call all day.' He stands, excuses himself, and takes his call out to the hallway, leaving the princess and me alone together.

I down the remainder of my drink and place my glass on the table. He's barely closed the door before I pounce on her, wrapping my hands around her waist, tugging her up until her body is flush with mine. Heat radiates from her, despite the cool room temperature.

'I thought we clarified that I don't want to see you with another man?'

'You wouldn't have, had you not barged into my home...' She smirks, quirking an eyebrow, defiant as ever. I should put her over my knee this second.

'As I recall, you don't normally mind me barging into your bedroom.'

'It's my favourite time of day,' she admits, biting her lower lip. 'But you shouldn't be here.'

'Do you want me to go?' The prospect makes my heart sink to my stomach but if she wants me to, I will. My presence here is putting everything in jeopardy, but a part of me deep down knows that it's deliberate.

I almost want someone to find out about us.

Want our relationship brought out in the open—one way or another because we can't go on sneaking around like this indefinitely.

'You know I don't. You know I have no interest in Finegan.' She looks up at me from beneath those huge dark eyelashes and winks. 'Although he is slightly more interesting than I remember.'

My nostrils flare. 'Careful, Princess, or I'll tie you to the table with my tie right now and we'll see how interesting Finegan is then.'

'Maybe that's what I'm hoping for,' She smirks, 'Sir. Out of curiosity, how did you get by the castle's security detail during the day? Did you come in the balcony again?'

I laugh and lean closer until our lips are mere millimetres apart. 'There isn't a thing on this planet I can't get if I want it, sweetheart.'

Well, except maybe her.

Isn't that the fucking painful truth?

She raises her hands, resting her palms on my chest. The contact feels good. Too good. 'I've a good mind to bend you over this couch right now and show Finegan fucking Montgomery who you belong too.' I slide a hand over her breast, then her hip, and over her dress until I find the hem. My hand is beneath it before I can stop myself. She's wearing stockings and suspenders. A growl sounds from the back of my throat.

'Are you wet for me, Princess?' I stroke up the inside of her thigh while she stares over my shoulder at the door. Like I said, part of me is almost hoping we get caught.

'Always,' she pants.

'Always, sir.' I remind her.

The door opens, and I yank my hand back and turn my back to the princess and pretend to be admiring the artwork.

'I didn't know you were an art fan,' Finegan drawls deeply.

'I have an extensive collection. The princess will tell you; she was rather taken with it when she visited.' My mouth is running away with me, but I can't help it. I glance at Layla to see if I've said too much, but she doesn't seem concerned. Is it possible she's as sick of sneaking around as I am?

Finegan scowls. 'I'm terribly sorry, Princess, but I need to go.'

Well, I, for one, am not sorry. Not one fucking bit.

'I trust everything is okay?' Layla says, glancing at the phone in his hand.

'Bit of a family emergency.'

Yeah, his mother probably needs fucking.

It's actually hilarious that my brothers regard me as the polite one. If they had any idea what went through my head, they'd realise I'm just as dark as the rest of them. Maybe even darker. I simply hide it better. Except from her. She sees my broken and she still calls it beautiful.

'Perhaps we can continue this another time?' He stares intently at the princess like a fucking puppy.

No, you cannot continue this another time you desperate prick.

Layla flashes Finegan an award-winning smile. 'That would be nice.'

Nice. Pah. Who wants nice when you can have naughty, dirty, depraved and primal?

Finegan's focus shifts to me, his eyes narrowing. 'Beckett.' He nods a wary goodbye as he strides towards the door, like he resents the fact he has to leave me alone with her. Good. I can't go on like this.

Maybe Finegan's visit isn't an entire disaster.

It's forcing forward the one conversation we've been avoiding—the future—and if we have one.

Chapter Thirty-Two

LAYLA

Finegan's barely closed the door when Sean reaches for my hands. His cologne wafts through the air, rich and darkly enticing, just like him.

'I hate you spending time with other men,' he admits, dragging his fingers over his scalp.

'I know, believe me, I know, but the Queen is threatening to bring me home with immediate effect unless there's something worth staying here for.'

'Does my cock not count?' He teases, but there's a hint of helplessness in his tone.

'Did your cock gain a title since the last time I saw it?' I press my palms over his chest, feeling the solid slabs of muscle beneath. We can joke about it all we want, but the truth is far from funny.

'Yes. Lord I'm Going To Fuck You So Hard You Won't Be Able To Walk For A Week.' He presses a tender kiss to my lips.

'I'm not sure the Queen will approve of that one.' I take a step back to put some distance between us before I do something stupid like throw myself at him, right here, right now.

'Don't give me those come to bed eyes right now. Anyone could walk in.'

'Maybe we should let them.' He murmurs, closing the distance between us again. Black eyes blaze with a heat that mirrors my own. 'Maybe it's time we tell the whole world we're a couple.'

I suck in a breath. This conversation was inevitable, yet I'm not sure I'm ready for it. I'm not sure I'll ever be ready for it. 'What about the consequences?'

'We'll deal with them together.' Sincerity rings in his tone.

'Really?' I swallow thickly. 'You'd stand with me, through all the backlash and uproar? It'll be ugly. Really ugly.'

'Of course.' A puzzled look forms on his face. 'I can't lose you, Layla.'

'I don't know if you know what you're signing up for.' I sigh.

'A bit like you didn't know what you were signing up for when you agreed to be my submissive—and look how that turned out. It was the best thing that ever happened—to me at least.' A hint of uncertainty creeps into his tone. 'I'll never force your hand, but at some point we're going to have to make a decision.'

I blow out a breath. 'Not for the first time in my life, I don't actually have a choice.'

'You do Layla.' His face falls. 'God, I'm so sorry, I'm pushing you into this. I assumed...'

'You assumed correctly. The reason I don't have a choice is because I love you. There's no way I can give you up, but if we go public, it'll put a target on both our backs. Your family might be billionaires, but your brothers have dominated the tabloids for all the wrong reasons for years. The King and Queen will never accept our relationship. My entire family will disown me. The public will hate me—us. Your name will be dragged through the press. Your family. Everything.'

'From what you've told me about the dynamics, being disowned would be like being released from prison.' He tilts my chin up until our eyes lock. 'I'm your family now.' His eyes bore into mine, and I swear he can see my soul. 'Let's do this. Let's build a life together. Step down. We'll deal with the consequences together. You know my family is no stranger to scandal. I love you. I want you. All of you. Not just the stolen moments. The seconds feel like hours when we're apart. I want to be with you properly, all day every day preferably.'

'You do?' A shiver rips over my spine. Excitement. Anticipation. Sheer terror. 'Are we really going to do this?'

'I'm ready if you are.' He nods. 'Because now I've found you, a life without you isn't a life at all. I want to be the man you have tea with.' He scowls at the door Finegan just left through. 'I want to be the man you wake up with. Go to bed with. Eat dinner with. The man you discuss the trivial details of every day with.'

My heart melts. It's official—I'm going to have to step down from my role.

I open my mouth to speak, but the buzzing of his phone cuts me off before I can utter a word. He winces, plucking the phone from his pocket. 'I'm late for a meeting with my brothers. They're all looking for me.'

'It's okay.' I reach for the lapels of his jacket and tug him down for a quick kiss.

'It's not okay,' he pulls back and glances towards the window then back to meet my eyes. 'We need to talk about this.'

'We'll talk more tonight, okay.' There's a lot to consider.

Sean presses another kiss to my lips just as a knock sounds from the other side of the door. We jump apart just before the handle jerks down. Mrs Medway bustles in, her beady eyes taking in the room. In her eagerness to snoop, she slams directly into Sean's solid frame and bounces back like a ball.

'Oh, my goodness, I'm so sorry, Mr Beckett. I wasn't expecting you there.' She takes another step back, gawking at the god-like creature in front of her. She might be a nosy old bat, but even she admitted how attractive our neighbour is. I swallow back my giggle.

'I wasn't expecting him either.' Literally and figuratively. 'Mr Beckett was just on his way out.' Unfortunately.

'And where is Lord Montgomery?' Her hawk eyes roam around the room.

Sean arches a single eyebrow, then stares at her pointedly—expectantly—as if to say, 'who actually works for who around here?' I stifle a laugh as he silently defends my entitlement to privacy, without even opening his mouth. I was in love with him before, but now... No one has ever stood up for me. Ever.

The silence echoes painfully around the room.

Mrs Medway's mouth opens and closes like a trout, until finally she gets a hold of herself. 'Sorry, I don't mean to pry.'

Of course you didn't.

'I only ask because chef is preparing dinner, and we wondered if Lord Montgomery might stay.' She smooths her hands over her apron, and I'd bet my life they're clammy. Sean Beckett has the ability to do that to any woman on the planet. I know from experience.

'He's gone. Family emergency.' Sean answers for me, and I don't mind one bit.

It's on the tip of my tongue to beg him to stay, but even if he didn't have a meeting with his brothers, Lord I'm Going To Fuck You So Hard You Won't Be Able To Walk For A Week definitely isn't on my parents' list of approved matches and Mrs Medway is bound to report back.

Besides, I should take some time before we talk again to figure out a way to support myself.

Figure out where I'm going to live.

And what exactly I'm going to do with my life—other than spend it loving Sean Beckett.

'That's a pity; we'd prepared for a visitor.' Mrs Medway gazes at Sean in open awe. She bristles, opens her mouth, then closes it again. Finally she says, 'I don't suppose you'd like to stay for dinner, Mr Beckett?'

My breath hitches.

My heart leaps ridiculously in my chest.

He's going to say no, of course he is. There's no way he's going to sit here under the prying eyes of my mother's staff. It's one thing creeping into my bedroom, but staying for dinner will bring a lot of heat on us. And no matter what he says, I'm still not entirely sure he's ready for it.

He turns to look at me, pausing thoughtfully, then rubs a contemplative thumb over his jawline.

Stay. Stay. Stay. I will him silently.

He whips out his phone. 'Do you know what?' He flashes Mrs Medway a killer smile. 'I'd love to stay for dinner. Thank you so very much. I just need to rearrange a meeting.'

Right there in that moment, I realise he *is* ready.

The question is, am I?

Chapter Thirty-Three

SEAN

I never want to leave her. Doing something as normal as eating together is something we've been denied for too long, along with so many other small milestones, like first dates, and dances, and introducing her to my family.

'Wonderful,' the housekeeper says, backing out of the room.

I don't miss the smile that Layla bites back. 'She will report your presence to my mother. Thankfully, I think she's rather taken with you.'

'If that's her idea of being taken, I'd hate to meet her if she wasn't.' I brush a hand over Layla's cheek. I can't stop touching her. My gaze strays to her lips. The urge to take her in my arms and steal her away from this glorified prison is overwhelming. If this is what love does to a person, I can see why people try to avoid it. It's all-consuming. Makes me irrational. Whatever terrible consequences we have to face, it'll be worth it if it means I get to do life with her.

'Another drink perhaps?' Layla nods towards the drink's cabinet.

We might need it. Now I've broached the subject, it's imperative we continue our conversation now—not later. 'Yes, please.' I drop my hand abruptly and fetch my glass for a refill. 'Does the housekeeper always hover over you like that? It's very intrusive.'

'Unfortunately, yes.' Layla puts her hand out to take the glass from me, and as our fingers brush, every hair on my forearm stands on end.

'It must be suffocating.' I watch her ass sway as she struts towards the drinks cabinet, snatching up her own glass in the process. It's on the tip of my tongue to tell her to move in with me. To beg her if needs be. I could protect her, provide for her.

'You get used to it.' She shrugs. 'Thank goodness I'm a spare and not the heir.' She pours two generous measures of whiskey and hands one to me.

'I should be waiting on you.' I bet she's never poured anyone a drink in her life. It occurs to me that my royal etiquette is shocking. 'You know, I have no idea of how to act appropriately around you. What the proper etiquette is when it comes to the Royal Family.'

She laughs then, low and sweet. The sound makes my stomach flip. 'I love that you don't *act* any way around me. You are what you are, and I respect you for that.'

We cross the room together, side by side, hovering in front of the fireplace. Flames lick over the logs, crackling and spitting, piercing the silence that's fallen between us. It's not an uncomfortable silence. Far from it, actually.

I glance around at the panelled walls and antiques, drinking in the princess's privileged prison. The portraits on the wall stare accusingly back at us. 'I take it these aren't your pieces.'

'No,' she scoffs. 'Mine are much more colourful.'

'Tell me more.' I've been wondering about her work for weeks. Wondering about the paintings that pour from her soul.

She spins on her heels to face me, swirling the whiskey in her glass contemplatively 'My recent pieces are,' she pauses, 'darker, yet somehow more vibrant than anything I've ever produced before—thanks to you.' She stares at me from under those thick dark eyelashes.

'Show me.'

Her eyes meet mine. 'They're quite personal ... It would be like laying my soul bare for speculation.'

'It's the laying yourself bare that draws people in. That's true intimacy.' I reach out to cup her face, brushing a thumb over her lower lip. 'I want to see them. I want to know every piece of your soul. Lay it bare for me, the way I've laid mine bare to you. I already know they're going to be exquisite. They come from you; they could never be anything else.'

'Very well.' She knocks back her drink. I do the same. 'I hope you're not underwhelmed after all of this. My parents think I should spend my time pursuing other interests. But art is the only way I know how to express myself.' She shrugs.

'Which is exactly why I need to see it.' If I can see how she views the world, perhaps then I can work out a way to give her everything her heart desires. If she's really stepping down to live an ordinary life with me—I need to ensure it's extraordinary. I want to give her all the happiness she's been denied.

'I should warn you, I'm no Van Gough.'

'Van Gough was crazy.' I follow her across the room, placing my empty glass on the table as I pass it.

'Aren't we all?' She glances over her shoulder at me.

'Maybe.' I shrug. 'Though, I keep my crazy well under control.'

'Like this afternoon?' She teases.

She has a point. I'm not sure what was crazier, barging in on her afternoon tea with Finegan, touching her in her own drawing room where any of the staff could have walked in, or agreeing to stay for dinner when clearly it will get back to her family. Yep, I'm definitely losing it.

I follow her through the huge wide corridors, taking in the majestic décor; gilded portraits, crystal chandeliers, and enough candles to stock a factory. We pass by several members of staff, all who bow or curtsey for the princess. It's a stark reminder of who she is. Who her family are. The power that they wield. They're not going to let her go easily, but I'll fight for her, harder than I've ever fought for anything. Because I love her, more than I've ever loved anything or anyone.

We reach the far end of the building, and she pauses outside a doorway. 'Promise you won't laugh, okay?'

'As if I'd laugh at you.'

Vulnerability flashes through her chocolate eyes for a split second. I place my hand on the base of her spine. 'Don't you think I felt vulnerable sharing my space at Reveal? It is the essence of who I am beneath the mask. The things I orchestrate down there are the way I express myself. It's different, but it's also the same.'

Understanding flashes through her eyes. She touches my forearm, conveying something words can't, then pushes the door open.

I follow her into a bright airy room with floor to ceiling windows overlooking the grounds. Several canvases dot the edge of the room, some finished, some unfinished. Discarded overalls hang on the back of a chair to the left of the room, alongside a selection of brushes and paints. What really draws my attention is a giant canvas punctuating the centre of the room on an easel.

It beckons me over, demanding my attention. Swirls of crimson bleed into black, creating a shadow unfolding like a secret. It's dark and discreet, and if I hadn't been part of the scene itself, I'd never see the truth to the sweeping curves that subtly portray arched backs, and bodies that are entwined and writhing. Sensuality screams from every stroke. It's by far the most erotic art I've ever seen. I need it for my bedroom.

A low whistle escapes from my mouth. 'Wow. This is exquisite.' I trace a finger tentatively over the spot where the two dark forms are joined.

The princess stands beside me; her arm brushes against mine. 'Do you see it?'

'I see it. I see us. And I see you.' Not just in the painting, but in her portrayal of the scene. The boldness of the colours. The bleeding of one form into the other. The unapologetic desire pulsing from the picture. I swallow, drinking it all in. 'And I feel it.' I grab her hand and place it over my heart.

She stares up at me from under thick dark lashes. They sweep across her cheekbones as she exhales a sigh of yearning. The painting reflects every part of her personality—her depth, her sensuality, and exactly how suppressed she is by this life that she's living. I need to get her out of here. Not just for my sake, but for hers.

'I want to buy it.'

'It's not for sale.'

'Everything's for sale for the right price.'

'Even my freedom?' She cocks her head to the side.

'Even your freedom—though the currency is rather different.'

'How are we going to make this work?' She exhales heavily. 'I'll have to find a job. A home.'

'Move in with me. We'll deal with everything together.'

She sighs. 'As much as I love the idea of living with you, I point blank refuse to go from being dependent on the crown, to being dependent on you.'

'Stubborn woman.' I brush a thumb over her lips. 'Don't you realise I'm equally as dependent on you—just in a different way. I want to be with you all day, every day. I want to take you out, show you the world, spoil you the way you deserve. I'm going to marry you, Layla—public revolt or not. Fuck them. Everything I have will be yours then anyway.'

Her eyes well with tears. 'I'll step down. As soon as Sabrina's wedding is over. But we have to find a way for me to work. I have a degree in arts, but who will hire me when I'm the star of yet another scandal?'

'We'll make this work, baby, I promise.'

'I love you,' she whispers.

'I love you too.'

The clicking sound of footsteps approaching sends us darting apart. A knock sounds on the door. This time, the person behind it waits before barging in.

'Yes.' Irritation clips my tone.

The door opens and Mrs Medway enters, her beady eyes raking over the scene in front of her. At least she knocked this time. Maybe she got my less than subtle message earlier.

'Dinner is almost ready. Please be seated in the dining room.'

'Thank you,' Layla smooths a hand over her dress.

'We'll continue this later,' I whisper. As we walk towards the doorway, my eyes do a final scan of her art collection. 'You know these pieces are exceptional.'

'You're just biased.' She shoots me a small smile.

'I'm not, I swear. You're exceptionally talented. They're better than anything I've seen in my life. They'd sell for tens of thousands each. Maybe more.'

The realisation hits me like lightning.

This is it.

Her independence hangs on these walls, waiting to be discovered.

She's been sitting on her own escape route without even knowing it. Not through marriage. Not through me. Through her own talent. I know just the man to showcase it.

Chapter Thirty-Four

SEAN

In addition to creeping into Layla's bed each night, I've called to the castle for tea twice this week under ruse of discussing fencing between the estate boundaries. Maybe Layla is right; maybe the nosy housekeeper genuinely has a thing for me because it would seem Mrs Medway hasn't passed the information on. Or if she has, it hasn't flagged as a red warning to the Queen. But it's only a matter of time now before she finds out either way.

I called Jaxon the second I left Ardmore and told him that I'd stumbled across some paintings of interest. He agreed to review them. All I have to do is persuade Layla to let him.

She's agreed to step down, so I need to step up—be everything she needs and more. I want to give her the world. I want to be everything she's never had, and to shower her with the love and attention she's never experienced. Romance isn't my forte, but I'm trying. Which is why I sent her a thousand red roses this morning, and enough art supplies to keep her going for a year.

'Earth to Sean?' Caelon clicks his fingers in front of my

face. I must have been staring into space again. It's been happening a lot lately, which isn't ideal—especially while I'm out with my brothers.

I asked Caelon and James to help me scope out a potential purchase: an old manor house with a thousand acres of land in the Kildare countryside. Though I'm the only one scoping out anything. They might be dressed for business in sharp three piece suits, not entirely dissimilar to my own, but the only business they're interested in is discussing their sex lives, which for some reason, is bugging the hell out of me today. Probably because I'm dying to tell them about mine. To scream from the rooftops that I'm head over heels in love. But as usual, I keep my mouth shut.

'Is Ivy pregnant yet?' James says to Caelon, as Ben negotiates the Bentley around the perimeter of the land.

'I'm working on it,' Caelon shoots James a shit-eating grin. 'Morning, noon and night.'

'I bet you are.' James's eyes gleam as he elbows Caelon.

'She's insatiable,' Caelon says with a hint of pride. 'I'm not complaining. I never thought I'd have this again.'

'Wait until she is pregnant, and the hormones kick in. After the first twelve weeks, Scarlett is feral.' James lets out a long low whistle.

'I remember it well.' A wistful look mists Caelon's huge eyes. 'The hormones tend to bring tears too, though. Don't forget all the hearts and flowers stuff. Women like spontaneous presents. It lets them know we're thinking about them.'

'You don't need to give me marriage advice.' James scoffs. 'My wife got a nice little present this morning.'

Caelon smirks, eyes James's crotch, then raises his baby finger. 'You said it.'

'I said *little,* dickhead.' James shakes his head in disgust. 'Six carat diamond earrings, if you must know.' Now it's

James's turn to smirk. 'I did give her something big too, though.' He winks lasciviously and the two of them guffaw like fucking schoolboys.

I think I preferred it when my brothers were lonely, miserable fuckboy players. A hollow pang thrums my sternum. I rub it with my knuckles. I need to lock things down with Layla, because a life without her is unimaginable now.

'Am I the only one of us paying any attention to a property we're contemplating spending twelve million euro on?' I glance between my brothers pointedly, deliberately keeping my voice neutral, despite my irritation.

'Correction, *you're* spending twelve million euro on,' Caelon says. 'We might all operate under the Beckett Enterprise, but property and land is your department. I still can't believe you let that forestry slip through your fingers, though.'

I bite back the profanity on the tip of my tongue. 'I was distracted.'

I'm still fucking distracted.

'Distracted?' James's laser eyes home in on me like a torpedo.

Oh fuck. I'm even distracted enough to let the fact I'm distracted even slip out. Distracted enough that I felt the need to bring these two clowns along with me today to check this place out. I don't trust my judgement. I'm not on my A game and I don't like it. Not one fucking bit.

Caelon straightens up, staring at me like I've grown another head. 'Who is... *she*?' He says the last word tentatively. I know what's coming next. 'Or *he*?' He lowers his voice, even though it's only the three of us in the back here. Clearly he's forgotten his stag night. Rian hasn't though. He's asked me a hundred times since who my lady friend is. To which I reminded him gentlemen don't kiss and tell—which is why we can name every single one of his conquests.

'Who said it was a person?' I shrug. 'Can't I just have stuff on my mind?'

My brothers exchange a look that conveys an entire conversation.

Tread gently.

Don't joke.

Maybe today's the day he'll open up.

I can read them like a book.

'You know you can talk to us.' James brushes his thumb over his chin thoughtfully. 'About anything.'

'For all our teasing and joking—'Caelon rests his hand on his heart like he's swearing an oath'—we have your back. We won't judge.'

'Can I have that in writing?' I attempt to joke, but it comes out more serious than I intended.

'Seriously, Sean, if there's ever anything you need help with, we're here for you,' James says earnestly. 'Or if you just want to talk.'

I believe them. My brothers are my best friends. I know they have my back. But that doesn't mean I'm ready to reveal my secrets to them.

I stare out the window at the lush expanse of land stretching before us. The crumbling mansion comes into view as Ben turns the corner. 'Thanks, guys, but it's nothing.'

My phone vibrates in my pocket. I pull it out faster than a fifty at a strip bar, silently willing it to be Layla. Did she like the flowers? Were they too cheesy? Too much? Not enough?

I squint at the screen, but before I can open the message, I'm rugby tackled from two sides. 'It *IS* a person!' Caelon yells, snatching the phone from my hands. I scramble to snatch it back. 'Who the fuck is P?' He shrieks gleefully. 'Paul? Peter? Parker? The Pied fucking Piper?'

'Thank fuck,' James grins. 'I thought you were hiding some rare illness or something!' James clutches his chest. 'To clarify—I wasn't worried about you, I was just praying it wasn't contagious.'

'Passcode,' Caelon demands, with a devious glint in his eyes. 'Let's see what P has to say.'

'In your fucking dreams.' I bite, attempting, and failing, to grab my phone back again.

James's eyebrows shoot up. I never lose my composure. Correction—I never *normally* lose my composure.

Caelon is loving every second of this new development. 'Don't make us pin you down and face ID this thing.'

The only saving grace is Rian isn't here.

'You know we can have Killian hack your phone and trace P down in a heartbeat?' James teases.

'Killian, unlike you two baboons, respects my privacy.' I hold my hand out. 'Hand it back, or you'll see a side of me you've never seen before.'

'Maybe we want to see that side of you.' Caelon's tone is goading.

'Trust me, you don't.' I finally prise the phone free and grip it like it's a lifeline.

'Ohhh.' My brothers tease in unison. Caelon makes jazz hands. I've never wanted to punch my brother as much as I do today, but of course, I won't. I've already let enough slip for one day.

I hold my mobile up to my face, swatting away the arms that are swinging at me. The Bentley is spacious, but nowhere near spacious enough to avoid these two brutes. If I had any sense, I'd put the phone in my pocket and read the message privately later, but the need to know how my gift was received is eating me alive. I click into the message, holding the phone as high above my head as I can, keeping it moving.

> You spoil me. Thank you. Are you calling for tea today? X

. . .

One tiny X makes my stomach swoop. I'm worse than a teenager.

'Tea?' Caelon yells. 'How fucking boring can one person be?'

'Mind your own business.' If only he knew. I shove the phone back into my pocket, biting back the grin that's threatening my lips.

But there's no way I'm sitting through another pot of Earl fucking Grey.

I'm breaking the princess out for the night. And I have the perfect place to take her to give her a taste of our future.

Chapter Thirty-Five

LAYLA

'He must really like you.' Kat is scooping up bouquets of roses and rearranging them around my private sleeping quarters. As far as the rest of the staff are concerned—especially Mrs Medway—the flowers and the art supplies were from Finegan. For everyone's sake—especially my mother's—it's better that way.

'I like him.' I bite my lower lip. 'A lot.' Understatement of the century. We're in way over our heads. I twist to face her. 'I'm thinking about stepping down from royal duties.'

'Oh, Princess.' Kat's voice is low and gentle. She halts her floral arranging and strides across the room to where I'm sitting at the vanity station. 'Is it worth throwing everything away for? You know the Queen will never accept him. Your sisters will be caught between a rock and a hard place. And with Princess Sabrina's wedding only a couple of months away, imagine the uproar. Is it worth it? Is he worth it? You need to be certain before you do something you can't undo.'

Our eyes meet in the gilded mirror. She takes a brush and runs it through my hair like she has done a million times before.

'The thing is Kat, he is.'

Her hand slows to a stop on my scalp. 'Don't do anything rash. Promise me.'

'I promise.' But I've already done something rash. I've fallen head over heels in love with a man who not only lacks a title but owns a BDSM club.

'Is he stopping by today? He seems obsessed with your paintings.'

He's obsessed with what they represent. He's the only one who sees the truth in them. He's the only one who sees me. And he seems certain they're my way out of this life.

'I'm not sure.' I check my phone again, but he hasn't replied to my thank you message yet. If I don't see him today, I'll see him tonight. Not that I'll admit that to Kat. It's for her own sake. Plausible deniability if the Queen discovers our dalliances.

My phone vibrates on the vanity station in front of me, and I snatch it up eagerly.

Not today, Princess.

My heart sinks. I guess I can wait a few more hours.

I'm breaking you out. We're going on a date.

A date? Butterflies swirl and soar in my stomach. This is a new unexpected development. Unless he means a mid-week date at the club?

My fingers fly over the keys.

> To the club?

No, somewhere else.

You know I can't be seen anywhere. They'll drag me home before we have time to figure out our future.

I'm going to give you a glimpse of the future. The only eyes on you will be mine.

A shiver of apprehension skates over my spine, and my stomach flips. 'Kat,' I swivel on my stool to face my friend and confidant. 'Will you cover for me tonight?'

She stares at me for a long beat, concern etches into her huge blue eyes. 'I will, you know I will, but for the love of God, be careful.'

'It's not like I'm going out with some gangster.'

'You may as well be as far as your parents are concerned, Princess,' she reminds me slightly more firmly this time. 'You know, there are rumours circulating that Princess Sabrina has been sneaking out too.'

My eyebrows skyrocket. 'Sneaking where and with whom?' Is it possible she too is choosing for herself?

'I have no idea, but Judy said the Queen is fraught with worry that the wedding won't go ahead. And apparently relations are tense between your family and Prince Harold's family already.'

'If it doesn't, it might be the best thing that ever happened to Sabrina. I am surprised though. She seemed rather taken with Prince Harold. Maybe the two of us could join forces and form a united rebellion.'

'Don't joke, princess. I'm already worried sick about you. Not just about you getting caught with Mr Beckett. Anything could happen to you while you're out without security. Will you at least take Grant with you?' Kat gnaws on her lower lip. 'If something happened to you, I'd never forgive myself.'

'I'm not taking anyone. Sean has his own security. Nothing is going to happen, don't worry.' I pat her arm.

Nothing except a glimpse of the future... whatever that means. I can't wait.

I make a mental note to call Sabrina tomorrow as I wait by the stables for Sean. The stable boys have retired for the night, so I pop in to see Temptation. He stamps his hooves when he sees me, readying himself to break free. 'Not tonight, boy.' I rub my hand over his face, and he nuzzles into me. I've been neglecting him lately with Sean taking up so much of my time.

The low purr of an engine cruising towards us sets my heart racing. 'We'll go out tomorrow. I promise.' I stroke his cheek before darting out into the cold, crisp night. The moon hangs low, illuminating the pathway to where Sean's Bentley is parked outside the stable. I glance up at the main house before making a dash for the car. A man I don't recognise waits with the door open. 'Princess.' He bows his head and motions for me to get in.

Sean is in the backseat already, looking especially delicious in his trademark black suit, although instead of the black shirt he usually wears in the club, tonight he's wearing a crisp white shirt and a bronze tie that matches the flames dancing in his huge dark irises.

'Good evening, Princess.' He pats the seat next to him, and I slide in.

'Good evening, sir.' Our eyes lock through the moonlight, and that ever present energy thrums between us.

The door closes behind me, and I jump, breaking the moment. 'Who is your friend?' I nod towards the driver.

'That's Ben. He's my driver, and my security.' Sean's eyes don't leave mine. 'Don't worry, I trust him with my life. And yours.' He presses a button, and the screen between the front and back of the car slides down. 'Ben, may I introduce Princess Layla.'

'Evening Princess.' His tone is full of mirth. 'I've heard a lot about you. Sean hasn't shut up about you. It's a pleasure to finally meet you.'

'Thanks for that,' Sean says with a little shake of his head. 'Let's see if you're as cocky in the ring tomorrow.'

'I bet I'll have more energy than you, *sir*.' Ben quips.

Sean presses the button, and the screen slides closed again. He reaches for my hand as the car starts to move, stroking a thumb over the back of my hand. 'Ben has been with me for a long time. He's like another brother, to be honest. One who doesn't constantly ask if I'm gay.'

'I suppose you don't help yourself.' I rest my head on his shoulder and gaze up at him through the moonlight.

'What's that supposed to mean?'

'You've never been photographed with a woman.'

'Have you been stalking me again?'

'Says the man who hired extra security to surround my family's castle and climbs a drainpipe to let himself into my bedroom every night.' I squeeze his hand.

'I don't hear you complaining.'

'That's because my mouth is usually full of your body parts.' I lean into his neck, breathing in his intoxicating scent. 'Where are we going?' I hope it's not too far because with his aftershave wafting through the air and the way he's stroking my hand, I'm about to combust with lust.

'It's a surprise.' His pupils gleam through the darkness.

'I hate surprises.' I pout, though that's not entirely true.

'I thought you'd like them, given the way your life is so regimentally planned out for you.' He quirks a brow and squeezes my hand. 'Right down to your suitors.'

I shake my head. There's no point in denying it. Sean knows me better than any other person in the world. In fact, he treats me like I am his world.

'Is it far?' I glance out across the spiralling countryside.

'Twenty minutes.' His gaze falls to my lap. 'So spread your legs and let me play with your pretty pussy until we get there.'

Heat suffuses my skin. I crave his touch like a drug. I glance towards the front of the car.

'He can't see anything.' Sean is a mind reader. 'And even if he could, he wouldn't open his mouth. Trust me.'

I do trust him.

'Do I have to make a detour by the club for that spreader bar I know you love?' His voice is low, rough and commanding and it reminds me exactly who is in charge here. 'Open your legs, Princess.'

'Yes, sir.' I undo the belt of my cashmere coat, revealing the little black Stella McCartney I picked out for tonight. Its scoop neck reveals enough cleavage to make his eyes flare. My legs fall open for him, and he wastes no time slipping his hand beneath my dress. His palm glides over my silk stocking until it meets the straps of my suspender belt. He hisses out his appreciation, and I smile. Wait until he feels what's between my legs—nothing. And as usual, I'm already soaked for him.

His fingers glide higher until they find my wet flesh. His moan reverberates around the car. 'You are officially the worst submissive I've ever had.' His voice is gritty with need.

'How so?' I part my legs further to accommodate the fingers that are circling my entrance, sweeping through my slickness.

'Because I am supposed to remain in control at all times.' He crooks a finger an inch inside my core, which is already pulsing with the need to come. 'And when it comes to you, I have zero control. You're in my head all damn day every day. I've missed out on several lucrative business opportunities because I've been thinking with the wrong head.' He pushes deeper into my core, and I whimper. 'I've drunk approximately seventeen pints of perfumed tea just to watch you paint, and now I'm sending you roses. I've never sent anyone roses before. So yeah, tell me who's really in control here.' His eyes bore into mine as his thumb skirts over my clit.

'Well, it's clearly not me,' I pant, glancing down at where his hand disappears under my dress.

He adds another finger, stretching me and filling me.

'Good. Now be a good girl and come on my hand, we're nearly there,' he demands, but I'm one step ahead of him; the first shockwave of my orgasm is already pulsing through me.

For a woman who has spent her entire life rebelling, surprisingly, I have no problem taking orders from Sean Beckett. Especially when they result in orgasms.

Chapter Thirty-Six

LAYLA

If Ben has any idea of what just occurred in the back of the Bentley, he is exceptionally discreet about it when he opens the back door.

'Where are we?' I take the hand he offers and step out into the narrow street. Lantern lights on high poles line both sides of the quiet, cobbled lane tucked away between Dublin's main thoroughfares where tourists never venture. March frost makes the old stones slick beneath my heels, and I glance around, checking no one is ready to pap me out of habit, but the coast is clear. The street is eerily deserted, our car the only sign of life apart from a tabby cat picking its way delicately across the wet cobbles.

Most of the buildings look residential—tall, narrow Georgian facades with peeling paint and darkened windows suggesting flats converted years ago for students or young professionals. But halfway down the street, one building stands apart.

Sean's hand rests on the base of my spine, sending tingles shooting in every direction. 'Patience, my love. You're about to find out.' He guides me towards a converted Victorian warehouse with industrial brick and oversized windows that have been painted black from the inside. No signage, no hint of what lies beyond those imposing doors—just sleek steel numbers mounted beside the entrance and a single spotlight illuminating the threshold. The entrance looks deliberately anonymous, expensive in that understated way that whispers rather than shouts about exclusivity— expensive mystery wrapped in Victorian brick and modern steel.

I have absolutely no idea what I'm walking into.

'Trust me.' Sean arches an eyebrow my way as he punches digits into the keypad next to the entrance. The heavy door clicks open. Ben takes position beside the entrance as we step inside. My breath catches in my throat as I take in the soaring space above us—a cathedral of art.

Exposed brick walls and steel beams disappear into shadows twenty feet overhead. Spotlights create intimate pools of illumination around each painting, turning the gallery into a constellation of colour and emotion. Contemporary works line the walls—bold abstracts that pulse with life, haunting portraits that seem to follow our movement, sculptures that twist and flow like frozen music.

'Sean, this is incredible.' I drift toward a massive canvas dominated by violent reds and deep purples, the paint so thick I can see every brushstroke. Sean takes my hand, his fingers intertwining with me as we take it in together. 'Is this your friend's place?'

His thumb brushes the back of my hand. 'Yes. This is Jaxon's gallery. He specialises in emerging artists, alongside established names.' His voice is weighted with meaning, and I realise he's watching my reaction more than the art. 'I know you said your paintings aren't for sale, but trust me, this is the best way for you to keep your independence. I've already spoken to Jaxon. He'd love to see your work.'

'Did you tell him who I was?'

'Of course not.'

My heart thumps double time in my chest. Sean's offering me something I've never had before—true freedom. A way to support myself—away from the rest of my family—other than starring in a questionable Netflix series that would surely give my parents a heart attack.

But would people really buy my work?

'Please, Princess.' Sean pulls me against him, supporting my weight, like he senses the weakness in my knees. 'I want to build a life with you. I know what I'm asking you to give up for me, but I will spend the rest of my life making it worth your while.'

'Oh, Sean.' I melt into his embrace. He has no idea what he's asking. 'You're asking me to give up nothing compared to what I'd gain from being with you, but what about you? I know how much you value your privacy. When the tabloids get wind of our relationship, every paper in the world will want to dig up dirt on you. It's only a matter of time before Reveal is exposed.'

'I'll deal with it. My family has powerful connections. And yours won't want that splashed all over the headlines. I love you; I want to be with you, whatever the consequences. Let Jaxon see your work, please.'

'What if he hates it?'

'He won't.'

'But what if he does?'

'Then you'll just have to pad around my kitchen barefoot and pregnant, waiting for me to come home from work.'

I suck in a breath. 'Sean!'

Being married and pregnant used to feel like a fate worse than death, but that was when I thought I was going to be forced into an arranged married. Given half the chance, I'd arrange this one myself—for tomorrow morning. I can't imagine a life without Sean, and I don't want to have to.

'Do you want kids?' I ask.

'I didn't.' His eyes hold mine. 'Until I met you. I love my nieces and nephews like they're my own. I'd kill and die for those little terrorists. I can only imagine how I'll feel about our child.'

My ovaries combust. 'Okay.'

'Okay, as in you'll let Jaxon see your work? Or okay, you'll tell the world that you're mine and I'm yours and pad around my kitchen barefoot and pregnant?'

'All of the above,' I nod, feeling more certain with every passing second. 'It's frankly terrifying. All of it. And it's probably going to cause a war. But if it means I get to be with you, it's worth the casualties.'

'We'll fight it together.' He crushes me against his chest, and I've never felt more loved, more secure, more sure that I'm doing the right thing.

We hold each other for a long time until finally, Sean releases me. 'Come on, let's explore. See where your pieces could be displayed.'

He takes my hand, and we wander through the building, examining each piece with wonder. It's an evocative collection. Each piece demands attention, conversation, thought. Even I have to admit, the red and black pieces I painted the past few weeks would fit alongside these perfectly.

'I still want to buy that painting, the first one you showed me,' Sean brushes a kiss over my temple.

'You may have to speak to Jaxon about that.'

His throaty laugh is music to my ears.

Finally, we reach the back of the building. Candlelight flickers between the shadows. A single table, elegantly set for two, sits before floor-to-ceiling windows overlooking the city lights in the distance. White linens, crystal glasses, silver that catches the light. A single red rose sits in a slim glass vase. A bottle of wine is uncorked on the table.

'You arranged this?' The logistics must have been extraordinary.

'Jaxon owed me a favour. He's going to owe me another one when he sees your work.' He pulls out my chair and gestures for me to sit. 'There's food keeping warm in the back kitchen. Pasta.'

'My favourite!' I shrug off my jacket, hang it on the back of the chair and sit, overwhelmed by the attention to detail. 'This is the most thoughtful thing anyone's ever done for me.' I'm not talking about the food and the wine; I'm referring to the way he's fighting for us, for a way for us to be together, when in all honesty I was certain there wasn't one.

'Even more thoughtful than tying you to my kitchen table and eating you like dessert?' His eyes glitter with mischief.

'Now you mention it, it's a close one.' I smirk. 'Both experiences left quite an impression.'

'Good, because when you move in with me, it's going to be a regular occurrence.'

'Promises, promises.' My stomach flips. I gesture around the gallery. 'Kudos. Credit where it's due, Mr Beckett. Not exactly a typical first date venue.'

'You're not exactly a typical woman.' His gaze holds mine steadily.

I agree, reaching for the wine. 'I've always found typical to be rather overrated.'

'And how do you feel about getting bent over the table and fucked into next week?' His black eyes blaze with a hunger that no food can satiate.

'It's decidedly underrated.'

'That's settled then.' He winks.

Chapter Thirty-Seven

LAYLA

Sean doesn't hang around. A mere twelve hours after I agreed to showcase my art for Jaxon, he arrives at the Ardmore, with my beautiful, burly boyfriend. I'm sitting at the breakfast table pouring over the morning papers when Kat enters to inform me of their arrival. 'If Mr Beckett keeps turning up like this, it will get back to the Queen.' Worry washes over her features.

'She's going to find out sooner rather than later.' I shrug, speaking with more bravery than I feel. Stepping down is the right thing for me. But I'm under no illusion—it's not going to be easy.

'Oh, Princess.' Kat rounds the table to stand beside me, touching my shoulder and squeezing. 'Are you absolutely certain about this??'

'I've never been more certain of anything in my life.' I close the paper and stand. Sean said he'd bring Jaxon, but he didn't mention it would be first thing, which is why I'm dressed in my riding gear. 'Show them in, please. I'll receive them in the drawing room.'

The two men rise as I enter. Sean looks devastatingly

handsome in a black impeccably cut suit and white shirt. His eyes sparkle when they meet mine. 'Princess.' He crosses the room with four long strides and presses a chaste kiss to my cheek. 'Thought you'd have had enough riding this morning,' he whispers with a snigger before turning to introduce his friend.

'This is Jaxon Clayton. Jaxon, may I introduce Princess Layla Sinclair.'

'Your Highness, it's an honour.' Jaxon steps forward and offers his hand. In navy chinos and a suit jacket, he's far more casually dressed than my boyfriend—but he still radiates a certain air of authority.

'The pleasure is mine.'

'Sean told me you'd come across some paintings in the studio here. He seems very taken with them. I'd love to take a look.'

I bite my lip. Vulnerability rises in my chest again. Silence stretches between us as I try to regulate my erratic heartbeat. There's so much riding on this. Sean might be comfortable with me being pregnant and waiting for him to come home, but I need my independence. If Jaxon likes my work, this could be the perfection solution.

'Layla?' Sean's tone is filled with concern. He dips his head towards me. 'Are you feeling okay?'

I can't answer him. I can only nod as every one of my mother's clipped remarks about my artwork attacks my ears.

'Would you like to sit down? I can escort Jaxon to see the paintings, if you prefer?'

I swallow down my nerves and suck in a deep breath. 'No. It's fine. Sorry. I was just a bit light-headed there. This way.' I pivot on my heel and stalk out of the room. The quicker we get this over with, the better. At least then I'll know where I stand.

The sound of Sean and Jaxon's footsteps bouncing off the

tiles assures me they're right on my tail. The short walk to my studio feels like walking the green mile. I feel physically sick. Jaxon must think I'm a complete weirdo.

My hand hovers on the door handle for a beat. I glance up at Sean. He offers one encouraging nod and mouths, 'You've got this.'

Whether I do or I don't—I have him. And that means more than anything.

I take one more deep breath and fling the door open. Brilliant morning sunlight floods in through the huge floor to ceiling windows, illuminating the canvases, which I arranged in a perfect semicircle at the far end of the studio.

There are twelve finished pieces in total, each one a piece of my soul laid bare. They pulse with the dark sensuality that's consumed me these past months—vibrant crimsons bleeding into deep purples and charcoal blacks. Abstract impressions of everything I've experienced at Reveal, translated into paint and passion.

Sean's eyes find mine immediately, that familiar intensity making my pulse quicken further. Jaxon moves first, drawn like a magnet toward the largest canvas—the one that dominates the centre of the display. The piece Sean had mentioned wanting to buy. He stops directly in front of it, clasping his hands behind his back as he studies it without uttering a word. Seconds feel like hours as he says absolutely nothing. The silence stretches. One minute. Two. The only sound is the distant ticking of the grandfather clock in the hallway.

I turn to Sean. He fires me a reassuring wink. I wish I had his confidence. He drifts towards me, and I slip my clammy hand in his.

Finally, Jaxon releases a long, low whistle that seems to echo in the high-ceilinged room. He turns slowly to meet my eye. 'These are,' he breathes, 'Absolutely magnificent. I would love to feature these in my next exhibition.' His gaze darts between Sean and me, falling to our entwined fingers, then back up again.

'Thank you.' I exhale the breath I'd been holding. The relief is palpable.

Jaxon's brows furrow. 'Did you ...? Are they...?' He sweeps a hand towards the paintings. 'He told me you'd "come across some art."' He frowns at Sean. 'He didn't tell me it was yours, Your Highness.'

'I asked him not to. I didn't want to influence your decision because of who I am.'

'These would sell for six figures without your name attached to them. With your signature?' Jaxon pauses, calculating. 'We're talking serious money. Museum-quality money.'

'That would mean going public with them.' I swallow.

'We're going public anyway, baby.' Sean wraps his arm around my shoulders and pulls me into him.

Jaxon shakes his head; a huge grin parts his lips. 'Looks like your identity isn't the only thing he's been keeping a secret from me.'

'It's essential that our relationship, and any deal we reach with the paintings is kept under wraps until the princess has officially stepped down from her royal duties.'

'You have my word.' Jaxon pretends to zip his mouth shut. 'When are you thinking of stepping down? I don't mean to pry, but I'm keen to get these pieces on display. Genuinely, they're unique.'

'After my sister's wedding.'

Kat's words from last night float back through my mind. It doesn't make sense. Sabrina was so excited about the wedding. Excited about Prince Harald, as much as the big white dress and televised production.

'When is that?' Jaxon enquires politely.

'Six weeks away. My stepping down will cause outrage. It's only fair I wait until after she's had her big day. She's dreamed of this big white wedding since we were children. I refuse to taint it for her... It's only a few weeks.'

Sean kisses my head. 'I can't wait until you step down.'

'Neither can I.' Jaxon smiles. 'Obviously for very different reasons. Will you be attending the royal wedding?' He arches his eyebrows at Sean.

'I wish,' I sigh, at the same time as Sean says, 'Not a hope. Even if I did make the guestlist, which I didn't, I've had my fill of pompous lords for one lifetime.'

So have I, but there's no way I'd miss my sister's wedding. Even if the thought of being apart from Sean is killing me already.

Jaxon turns to the pieces again. 'Where did you get the inspiration for these?'

'Probably better if you don't ask.' Sean grins. 'Now, let's talk about commission.' He winks and nudges his friend.

'I'll discuss the finer details with the artist herself.'

'Sean can negotiate. Call him my agent.' He's not just my agent. He's my absolute everything. If it weren't for our time together at Reveal, I could never have produced anything remotely like these pieces. Submitting to him secured my freedom. Oh, the irony.

'I'll meet you back in the drawing room. I'll ask Mrs Medway to organise some tea for us.'

'Never mind tea.' Sean pulls me against him, despite being in company. 'I have some Beckett's Black Label in the car. This calls for champagne.'

I nuzzle into his chest. I spent years wishing for an ordinary life. Wishing I was free to choose my own life, to choose who I wanted to love, where I wanted to live.

Turns out, there's nothing ordinary about any of it.

Life with Sean Beckett is miraculous.

Chapter Thirty-Eight

SEAN

Life has never felt this good.

I lean back in my chair at the head of James's dining table, watching my family argue over everything from football to politics with the kind of contentment I've never experienced. One day soon, Layla will be here with us. My family will love her—once they get over the shock that is.

Avery is obsessed with the Royal family. She basically stalks them on Instagram. She'll probably keel over when she finds out. My future sister-in-law is obsessed with my girlfriend, and she has no idea she's about to get a front-row seat to the biggest royal scandal in decades. It's hilarious—as well as exhilarating.

Layla is going to love Avery. And Scarlett, Ivy and Zara. From what she told me about her upbringing at the palace, she's closer to Sabrina than Patricia. Her parents didn't exactly shower any of them with love. My family will make up for that. I won't even have to ask them to—they just will. The prospect makes my heart swell. I'm as sickeningly obsessed with her as my brothers are with their women. James was right; it will be me next. The Queen wanted Layla to be engaged by her next birthday. If I get my way, she will be.

Jaxon assured Layla she'll get seven-figures for each piece —especially the centrepiece that's been haunting my thoughts since I first saw it. I've already instructed him that whatever anyone offers for that particular piece, I'll double it. I always get what I want and this won't be the exception. It's going on my—I mean *our*—bedroom wall.

The thought sends satisfaction coursing through me.

'More wine, Sean?' Scarlett asks, already reaching for the bottle of our family reserve.

'Why not.' It's too early to sneak up to Layla's room. I won't miss that fucking drainpipe when we go public, that's for sure. I hold out my glass, smiling at nothing in particular.

'Fuck. Me,' Rian says from my right. 'Who put that shit-eating grin on your face?'

'One day soon, I might actually tell you.' My lips stretch wider until I'm actually beaming.

'Oh, tell us!' Scarlett pours the wine. My focus falls to her slightly swollen stomach. Will that be Layla one day? I hope so. Though I'm nowhere near ready to share her yet. I'm going to have to install a creche at Reveal so someone can mind our kids while I have some kinky fun with their mother. Laughter bursts from my lips.

'Oh, my God!' Scarlett squeals, staring at me like I've got two heads. 'You're in love!' She points an accusatory finger in my face. 'Who is she?'

'He—you mean.' Rian scoffs.

Suddenly I have the attention of my entire family. Every eye in the room is on me. Even Zara's abandoned her perpetual scrolling on TikTok to stare at me.

'Come on, man. Spill.' Caelon calls from the other side of the table.

I lift my glass to my lips and drink. I'd love to tell them.

But it's too soon. Apart from the risk that Rian might open his mouth and tell that gobshite friend of his, Anthony, or worse again, one of his fleeting conquests, Layla and I need to come up with a suitable backstory for how we met, because there's no fucking way I can admit she snuck into my sex club and auditioned to be my submissive.

'There is someone.'

'Ahhh!' Avery, Ivy, and Scarlett squeal in unison.

'What's with the secrecy? Why can't you just tell us who she—'James glances at Killian'—or he is?'

'*She* has to sort some things out before we can be together.'

Rian's eyes narrow. 'Is *she* married? You dirty dog! Even I haven't crossed that line...yet.'

'She's not married. It's just... complicated.'

'Do we know her?' Scarlett demands, returning to sit on James's knee at the other end of the table. She curls an arm around his neck, and he wraps his arms around her waist, his hand settling on her bump.

'Not exactly.' I shake my head, biting back another laugh. 'Look, guys, I'm not playing twenty questions. I can't tell you yet, but as soon as I can, I will. I can't wait to introduce you.' Every time I think about how their jaws will hit the floor, I snigger.

'I still think it's an elaborate cover-up story.' Rian muses, eyeing me suspiciously. 'You're suddenly in love with a "woman",' he emphasises the word making quotation marks with his fingers, while simultaneously rolling his eyes, 'Yet no one's ever seen you with one. Where is she? Tied up in some sort of sex dungeon at your place?'

I almost choke on my wine. If only he knew how close to the truth he is.

'Don't be so crude, Rian,' Zara scolds. 'Unlike you, Sean is a gentleman.'

'Thanks, sis.' I flash Zara a guilty smile.

'Respect his privacy,' Killian says quietly. 'Sean will reveal all in his own time.'

'Here here,' Avery says, reaching for Killian's hand. Her phone buzzes on the table beside her. Her eyes flick to the screen. 'OMG guys!'

'What?' Ivy demands.

Avery snatches up the phone and peers at it intently. All eyes are thankfully on her now, instead of me. Thank God for small mercies. Her eyes are bright with excitement as she clutches her chest. 'You'll never believe it!'

Killian eyes his girlfriend lovingly. 'Did you get the bridal contract?'

Avery is a model. Former model. Whatever.

'No! It's even better! The Queen just made a statement.' She speaks about her like they're on first-name terms. 'Apparently they're pulling forward Princess Sabrina's wedding—to this weekend!' she squeals excitedly. 'It's never been done before in the history of the Royals. They're even moving the public holiday. Do you know how much work that entails? This is wild! I would kill to know why. There has to be something scandalous going on!' She clamps a hand over her mouth.

My stomach plummets. That can't be right. Why would they do that? From what Layla has told me about her mother, everything is executed to perfection. The Royals don't do rash. I'm only half listening to the conversation around me as I slide my phone out of my pocket. I glance down at the screen. There's nothing from Layla. Surely she must have heard the news. Maybe she's waiting to tell me in person. Naturally she'll have to go back to London. While I don't relish being apart, the quicker this wedding is over, the quicker she can step down, or step up, I should say—step into the life that she chooses for herself. Every night when I sneak into her room, I thank whoever is up there that life includes me.

'Fuck's sake, woman.' Killian rolls his eyes good naturedly. 'I thought it was something important.'

'It is important. It's the wedding of the year. It's going to be televised. I need to buy a hat!' Avery's waving her arms around dramatically. She and Killian could not be more different if they tried. He's calm, and she's chaos.

'Did you get an invitation?' Ivy shrieks.

'Not exactly, but I always have my own Royal wedding party. You know, watch it stream live on TV, dress in something fancy, and drink champagne for breakfast.'

'Sounds like every other morning, minus the TV,' Killian drawls, a slow smile spreading across his face.

'Has anyone else noticed that Princess Layla has been completely MIA since Christmas?'

It's a battle to keep my mouth shut.

'Maybe she's just taking a break from royal duties,' James suggests diplomatically.

'Princesses don't just vanish,' Avery insists. 'Sure, she tipped that drink over some posh guy's head, but it's like she's been grounded or something.' Avery pretty much has it sussed. 'She's completely disappeared.'

Her last sentence slices through my chest. It's my biggest fear—Layla just disappearing. Which is half the reason I have the castle surrounded by Killian's men.

'Scarlett, James, thank you so much for a lovely evening.' I push my chair back and stand. 'I'm going to head off. I've got a few things I need to do before bed.'

Rian snorts. 'Like what? This mystery woman.'

'Actually—yes.' I need to make the most of her before her family sends the jet for her.

'Have him followed,' Rian says to Killian with a wicked gleam in his eye.

'I'll do no such thing.' Killian scowls at Rian. 'Maybe I should have you followed, then we'll find out where you go every Wednesday night at six pm.'

Rian's jaw almost hits the table. 'What do you know about that?' he snaps.

'Not a lot. Because I respect people's privacy.' He draws the sentence out slowly to emphasise his point.

Wherever Rian goes every Wednesday, he doesn't want anyone knowing. Interesting. Maybe he's the one seeing a married woman. Right now, I don't have time to ponder it.

'I would normally say don't rush off.' Scarlett rises from James's lap. I don't dare look down in case he's sporting a boner, 'but none of us would begrudge you the chance to see your lady friend. We do want a full report—soon though.' Scarlett rounds the table and presses a kiss to my cheek. Ivy, Avery, and Zara follow suit. My brothers shake my hand as they say goodbye. Rian walks me to the front door, then punches my arm. 'Serious, bro, I know I'm always pulling the piss, but if you've found someone, I'm happy for you.'

'Thanks, that means a lot.' Perhaps my little brother isn't such a douche after all.

'Can't wait to meet HIM.'

Dickhead.

I sigh, shaking my head as Ben pulls up in the Bentley. 'Thanks, Ben.'

'How was your night?' He asks conversationally, as he negotiates James's large sweeping driveway.

'Weird.' I pull out my phone again. Still nothing. I dial Layla. It goes straight to voicemail. Uneasiness snakes into my stomach, curling round my intestines. 'Did you hear about Princess Sabrina's wedding being moved forward?' I type it into my search engine and, sure enough, every tabloid has an article on it already. None specify why the wedding's been pulled forward. I try Layla again. Voicemail—again. I don't like it. Not one fucking bit.

'Yeah, every news station on the radio is gushing about it.' Ben shakes his head. Clearly he doesn't feel as passionately about the Royal Family as Avery does.

'Straight to Ardmore Castle, Ben. Step on it.'

'Keen tonight, aren't you?' Ben teases, glancing back at me in the rear-view mirror. His smile freezes on his face when he spots my expression 'What is it?'

'I don't know. I just have a really bad feeling.' I try Layla again. 'I thought Layla would have told me about the wedding. It's a big deal for her family—and for us.' Ben's the only other person apart from Jaxon who knows she's planning on stepping down. 'But her phone's off.'

Ben's phone rings through the Bentley's hands-free system. It's Anderson. He's one of the men Killian sent me to help at Ardmore. Ben hits the button to accept the call. 'Four of Princess Layla's guards just bundled her into the back of the Range Rover. She didn't look happy. Do you want us to follow, or stay and guard the castle?'

'Follow,' I snap, answering for him. 'For fuck's sake. Don't let them take her from me. Fuck.' I slap my hand across the leather interior as Ben disconnects the call. Every fibre in my body screams at me that it's too late. They already have.

Chapter Thirty-Nine

LAYLA

I've never felt more like a prisoner than I do sitting in the back of the Rolls-Royce, watching London blur past the tinted windows. Grant and Toby hadn't given me a choice this evening—"orders" was the only explanation I got before they threw my phone out of the Range Rover's tinted windows, then bundled me onto the royal jet with only an overnight bag and a growing sense of dread. They were apologetic but immovable as granite.

'Your Highness,' Grant's voice carries from the front seat, formal and careful. 'We'll be arriving at Wyndham Palace shortly.'

Wyndham Palace, the family home, but there's never been anything remotely homely about it. I glance at the Cartier watch on my wrist. It's almost eleven pm, which means the Queen will be in her private chambers, leaving me to stew overnight.

Nausea rises in my stomach.

Did she find out my intention of stepping down?

Or about Reveal?

About Sean?

Sean. A sickness seeps into my soul. What must he think? As far as he's concerned, I've literally disappeared into thin air. I can't even text him.

'Grant, can I please borrow your phone for two minutes?'

'Absolutely not, Princess. It would cost me my job, and the ability to work ever again.' He shakes his head. 'I'm already hanging on to both by a thread.'

I open my mouth to speak, but words won't form. There simply aren't any. I knew this day was coming. Knew the Queen would send for me. But I didn't know it would be kidnapping style. Still, perhaps it's better to get this over with sooner rather than later, but it's not going to be pretty. Apprehension weighs on my chest like a concrete boulder.

My body aches for Sean. For his reassuring arms, for his strength, and quiet certainty. If only I could talk to him. Explain. He'd know what to do.

A wayward tear slips from my eye and streaks my cheek as the car sweeps through the palace gates, past tourists and photographers who snap pictures of the distinctive royal vehicles.

Toby opens my door, his expression carefully neutral. But I catch a flicker of sympathy in his eyes.

The palace looms before me in all its Georgian grandeur, a symbol of centuries of tradition. I can't believe I ever felt trapped at Ardmore. I might have been lonely there before I met Sean, but here I feel like I'm drowning and I haven't even stepped through the door.

I turn to Grant. 'Is Kat coming?'

'She's been dismissed.' His face is grim.

Fuck.

Toby and Grant escort me in through the front door, where Edmund, the butler who has worked here since child-hood, meets us. 'Princess Layla, welcome.' He greets me with his usual fondness, but I can't even pretend to be happy to be here.

Edmund takes my overnight bag and leads me through the familiar marble corridors. Grant and Toby follow, their footsteps echoing off the vaulted ceilings.

Edmund makes up for my lack of small talk by compensating with his own. 'It's wonderful to have you back at the palace, princess. I highly recommend you take a stroll around the walled garden in the morning. The daffodils are in full bloom—an endless sea of yellow even on the dreariest of days. Mind you, it's wonderful to see the mornings getting lighter and the evenings getting longer.'

Does he have any idea that I don't want to be here?

Does he even care?

Does anyone?

'The Rose Suite has been prepared for you, Your Highness,' Edmund stops before gilded double doors. Grant and Toby take position either side as I walk wearily inside. I feel like a naughty schoolgirl being sent to her room after misbehaving. The Rose Suite is as opulent as I remember. Silk wallpaper in pale pink, antique furniture, and a huge four-poster bed laden with plump, plush looking pillows.

'Would you care for some tea, Your Highness?' Edmund hovers at the door.

'No, thank you.'

He nods his goodbye and closes the door with a soft click. I don't bother changing out of my clothes. What little energy I have left, I'm saving for my mother tomorrow. No doubt I'm going to need it. I kick off my shoes and collapse onto the silk bedspread.

Every night for weeks, I've fallen asleep in Sean's arms, his steady heartbeat beneath my ear, his fingers tangled in my hair. Tonight, the massive bed feels like an ocean of emptiness.

I pull a pillow against my chest, trying to recreate the feeling of being held, but it's useless. Nothing can replace the warmth of his body, the safety of his presence, the certainty that I belong somewhere.

I've never felt more alone in my life.

———

After a night tossing and turning—staring at the intricate patterns on the ceiling, I take a long hot shower, then unzip the overnight bag I hastily packed yesterday. It feels like a lifetime ago. I reach for the grey formal dress and jacket set, folded neatly beside a set of equally conservative lingerie, and roll my eyes. Something sparkling catches my eye from the bottom of the bag. My collar. I have no idea what possessed me to grab it, but something did. I snatch it up, fingering the diamonds. It's cold and heavy, but the weight of it in my hands is familiar. Simply holding it makes me feel closer to Sean. I allow myself the luxury of a little wallowing before stashing it back at the bottom of the bag for safe keeping, then get dressed and apply a little make-up. No amount of concealer could hide the bags under my eyes this morning, but I apply some anyway.

Two unfamiliar security staff are outside my bedroom door when I open it. It's like being in prison.

'Your Highness.' They greet me with a curt nod.

'Am I allowed to go for breakfast or am I restricted to my room by order of the crown?' My sarcasm is lost on them. They fall into step behind me as I stride down the wide, bright corridors to the main dining area.

My mother is already at the table, immaculate in a cream silk blouse and navy blazer, her signature pearls catching the morning light. Her silver hair is swept into a perfect chignon, not a strand out of place. She doesn't even glance up as I enter.

'Leave us,' she says to the housemaid pouring her tea. The girl scurries away. My security detail step outside too, closing the door behind them. It's hilarious really, she's probably the one person I need protecting from the most. When she finally meets my eye, the look she gives me is positively lethal.

'Sit.' It's not a request.

I take the seat to her right. 'Mother.' I greet her with as much warmth as I can muster, which isn't a lot given she had me kidnapped.

'Welcome back.' Sarcasm drips from her tongue.

'It was rather a rushed departure. May I ask what the urgency is about?' I reach for the teapot and pour into the fine china cup set in front of me.

'Your sister is pregnant.'

'Congratulations. I'm sure Patricia will make an excellent mother.' She will do—if she parents completely the opposite way to how we were parented.

'Not Patricia.' Her tone radiates disapproval. 'Sabrina.'

'I see.' My shoulders relax a fraction. Is it possible the Queen has no idea about Sean? About Reveal? About my intention to step down. 'Who is the father?'

'Prince Harald, of course. She's been stupid, but she's not *that* stupid.' She gives me a pointed stare.

Good for Sabrina. At least if she's pregnant, that means she's willingly having sex with her suitor. I hope he's better in bed than Patricia's husband. Either way, he clearly gets the job done. Imagine, sneaking around with her own husband to be is a scandal. Seriously—this monarchy is so outdated.

My mother sets down her teacup with deliberate care. 'We've decided to bring the wedding forward.'

'Why?' Moving the wedding is a huge ordeal. Caterers,

florists, even the dress. Sabrina couldn't have a bump already, could she?

'Because relations are already tense with the Norwegians. If they decide to break off the engagement in the next six weeks, your sister will be ruined. Not to mention it won't take a genius to work out that when the baby is born, Sabrina will only have been married for six months. I refuse to have *another* daughter shrouded in scandal.' She looks at me pointedly, tapping her fingers on the white starched tablecloth.

'You look tired, Layla.' Her tone is ice cold. 'Sneaking a man into your room every night is clearly exhausting.' Her narrow eyes exude disgust.

I wince internally, but outwardly hold my composure. A hard hit of adrenaline courses through my bloodstream.

She picks up her tea without taking her eyes from me. 'And tell me, what exactly is that establishment beneath the ground on the edge of Mr Beckett's estate?'

Fuck. Fuck. Fuck. Fuck.

'Mother, I...' I'd rehearsed this speech in my head a hundred times.

'Don't say another word.' Her stare could level Westminster Abbey. 'It's finished. Over. To say I'm disgusted with you is an understatement. You've disgraced yourself, and this family. Yet I've managed to salvage your situation. You can thank me later.'

I open my mouth, but she raises her hand to silence me.

'You will marry Lord Ashworth in September. Your engagement will be announced next week, along with a picture of you together at the Hunt Ball.'

My stomach bottoms out. She can't be serious. 'And if I refuse?'

'Refuse, and you will have nothing. Be nothing.'

Chapter Forty

SEAN

Forty-eight hours. That's how long it's been since I watched the royal jet disappear into the Dublin night sky, taking Layla with it. Forty-eight hours of pacing the penthouse of Beckett's Bliss in Westminster like a caged animal. Forty-eight hours of making calls that go nowhere. Forty-eight hours of feeling more powerless than I've ever felt in my entire life.

I've never felt as sick as I did standing behind that chain-link perimeter fence at Dublin's private airfield, watching her vanish into the night.

Ben pulled every string he could—called in favours at air traffic control, customs, even tried to get Anderson and his team closer to the hangar. But the airspace had been locked down without warning. Armed guards turned us back before we even got within a quarter mile.

I flew to London immediately, Ben and Anderson insisted on travelling with me. I lied to my brothers. Told them I'm here looking at property—but the only property I'm actually looking at is Westminster Abbey. The whole of London is mad with excitement about the upcoming wedding of

Princess Sabrina this weekend. I'll be excited when it's over. Maybe then Layla will find a way to contact me.

We set up camp in the penthouse overlooking where the wedding will take place. In twenty-four hours, Layla will be inside that building. And I will be as close to it as life physically permits.

I'm at my wit's end, pacing the penthouse like a caged animal. Every fibre in my body is begging me to storm the gates of Wyndham Palace, but I'm not that stupid. We'd be gunned down without hesitation; the whole thing spun as a break-in or 'security incident.'

Ben hunches over his laptop, pulling up architectural blueprints of Wyndham Palace. Anderson spreads security schematics across the dining table. We've been looking for any way to get a message to her, any possible sighting, any proof she's even still in there.

'Anything?' I ask, though I already know the answer from their expressions.

'Palace security's been doubled,' Anderson reports grimly. 'No one in, no one out. Even the usual staff rotations have been suspended. No one's seen her since she arrived two days ago.'

'So we don't even know if she's definitely there?' I rake my fingers over my scalp. I'm physically and mentally exhausted trying to figure out a way to get her back in my arms. And when I do, I'm never letting her out of my sight again.

'She's there,' Ben glances up from his laptop. 'My contact saw the car arrive, but that's it. No movement since. No appearances at windows, no garden walks, nothing.'

'And legally? How are they doing this? It has to be unlawful imprisonment.' I turn to Anderson.

'My best guess?' Anderson's voice is bitter. 'They're probably invoking some sort of protective custody provisions. I've been reading up on royal protocols—there are archaic laws that theoretically allow the Crown to restrict movement of any family member if there's a perceived threat to their safety or the monarchy's reputation.'

'The perceived threat being me.' I have no idea how much Layla's family know about our relationship, but given the way her phone has been disconnected, there's no way she's just been whisked away for her sister's wedding.

'Exactly. And if that's what they're doing, it's totally immoral—but completely legal. They could hold her indefinitely until the threat is eliminated.'

I scrub my hands over the stubble lining my jaw. In my world, problems have solutions. Money opens doors. Power creates opportunities. But the monarchy operates by different rules—rules that have been refined over centuries to protect itself from people exactly like me.

I stare out at the Gothic spires in the distance, watching the morning sun catch the ancient stonework of Westminster Abbey. The Thames flows past like liquid silver, and London sprawls endlessly in all directions—millions of people getting on with their lives, boarding red buses, hurrying to work, completely oblivious to the fact that my world has collapsed. Street vendors are already setting up along the barriers for tomorrow's crowds, anticipating the celebration. Everyone else is excited about a royal wedding while I'm dying inside. 'Tomorrow is my only chance to see her.'

Anderson frowns. 'Sean, what's the plan here exactly?'

'There is no plan.' The admission tastes like ash in my mouth. 'I just need to be where she is, see she's okay with my own eyes, even if I can't reach her.'

'The security will be massive,' Ben warns. 'Armed police, military presence, counter-surveillance teams.'

'I know.' I press my palms against the cold glass of the window. 'But it's the only place I know she'll be.'

Anderson looks up from his schematics. 'The public

viewing areas will be cordoned off. You'll be hundreds of yards away behind barriers.'

Ben exchanges a look with Anderson. 'The crowds will be massive. Tourists, royal watchers, media. It'll be chaos.'

'Good. We'll blend in as we position ourselves as close as we can get to the entrance.'

'And then what?' Ben asks in a slightly gentler tone. 'After the ceremony, they'll whisk her back to the palace. You'll still be on the outside looking in.'

'Then I'll wait.' I turn back to the window, watching the morning traffic crawl past Westminster Abbey. 'She won't do anything rash during the wedding. She won't risk ruining Sabrina's day. But after ...'

My mind wanders back to that park she told me about. St James's Park. It's not much to go on, but I have fuck all else.

'I can only hope.' And it feels utterly fucking pathetic. I've spent my entire adult life being in control. In the club, in business, in every relationship I've ever had. I dominate situations, bend them to my will, make things happen through sheer force of determination and resources.

This is teaching me what true powerlessness feels like. I've never been less in control in my life. I hate it.

It's killing me but I can't save her. No matter how much I want to. I have to accept facts.

This is one battle Layla has to fight alone.

Chapter Forty-One

LAYLA

I stare at my reflection in the Rose Suite's ornate mirror. Today is the day. Sabrina's wedding day—and my last official appearance as a member of this family—a fact that they're not yet in possession of.

Tonight, after the last guest stumbles out of the reception, I'm telling my mother exactly where she can shove her marriage plans.

I'm done being the dutiful daughter.

Done being manipulated.

And I'm definitely done being treated like a broodmare for the monarchy's breeding programme.

The baby pink bridesmaid dress hangs from my frame. The weight has fallen off me this week. Being away from Sean is taking its toll, but thank God I have a small part of him here with me. My fingers drift over the collar automatically. The diamonds are cold against my throat, but the weight is familiar. Comforting. I might not have a phone or internet access, but I have other ways of communicating with him. When he sees today's television coverage, he'll know. I'm still his. No matter what.

I close my eyes and picture him somewhere out there. He'll be out of his mind with worry. The thought makes my chest tight, but it also makes me stronger.

Tonight, I'm going to take the first step back to him. And God fucking help anyone who stands in my way.

A knock interrupts my plotting. 'Come in.'

Sabrina floats into the room, and Christ, she looks stunning. Her wedding dress is straight out of the fairy tale she's been dreaming up since we were children—ivory silk that moves like water, lace sleeves that probably took some poor seamstress months to create, and a train that goes on for miles. The tiara holding her veil makes her look like an actual princess instead of the reluctant one I am.

'Well?' She spins, beaming. 'What do you think?'

'You look like you stepped out of a Disney film. The good kind.'

She laughs, tears threatening her perfectly applied makeup. 'I feel like I might throw up.'

'Nerves or morning sickness?'

'Both.' She blows out a breath. My sister is the only person in this entire palace who's excited I'm home. My father hasn't come near me, which means my mother has told him everything. Good. It'll save me a job.

I place my hand on Sabrina's still flat stomach and pray to fuck she makes a better job of parenting than our own parents did. 'I can't believe you're going to be a mother.'

'I know.'

She studies my face with that annoying sister intuition. 'Are you all right? You seem ... different since you got back from Ireland.'

'I'm fine.' She knows I'm in the bad books. Let's face it, I usually am. But she has no idea how bad those books actually are.

'Layla?'

'I'm fine,' I repeat, more firmly. 'Now, let's get you married.' I link my arm through hers, drawing strength from her joy. If Sabrina can find love within the royal circus, maybe there's hope for the rest of us.

My hope just happens to involve burning the whole thing down.

The ride to Westminster Abbey is surreal. London has transformed overnight into a patriotic fever dream—Union Jack bunting on every surface, crowds packed ten deep behind barriers, the air thick with excitement and exhaust fumes. People wave and scream as our convoy crawls past, their faces bright with the kind of joy reserved for people they'll never actually meet.

I watch them through the bulletproof glass as we approach Westminster Abbey. The crowds thicken and the noise becomes deafening. The ancient Gothic spires rise against a grey spring sky. Those stained-glass windows that have seen a shitload of royal drama.

The car slows to a stop. Photographers aim cameras like weapons. The red carpet stretches towards the abbey doors. One of the armed guards opens the door. The sound of the crowd crashes over me like a breaking wave, along with the flash of a thousand cameras. I step out into the crisp morning air, spine straight, chin up.

My heart races in my chest, the pounding of my pulse every bit as loud as the crowd.

Suddenly it hits me.

He's here.

Sean is somewhere in the crowd.

I don't know how I know, but I do.

The knowledge chases away the numbness of the past few days. I scan the sea of smiling faces, but there are too many. It's impossible. I raise my hand to my neck, fingers tracing the diamonds deliberately. I look pointedly at the closest camera and blow a tiny kiss.

I'm coming home.

———

The ceremony passes in a blur of Latin and organ music. I stand where I'm supposed to stand, smile when I'm supposed to smile, and I watch my sister marry the man she loves. Tiny tears threaten my eyes. Tears for my sister. Tears for me. I blink them back, and focus on getting through the day.

The reception is back at the palace. It's the usual royal circus—more flowers than the Chelsea Flower Show, and enough champagne to float a yacht. I play my part perfectly. The dutiful daughter. The supporting sister. The princess who knows her place. I make small talk with relations I haven't seen in years, and probably will never see again after tonight. I clap at Prince Harald's carefully rehearsed but heartfelt speech, and I eat my dinner like a lady, biding my time.

Only another couple of hours.

The society band launches into timeless classics—Etta James, Sinatra, the works. Some of the guests are dancing on the dance floor; others are making shapes to leave already. I'm reaching for a glass of champagne from a passing waiter when a familiar voice makes my skin crawl.

'Princess.'

I turn to find Lord Ashworth circling like a shark. His auburn hair glints under the chandeliers as he closes the distance between us. A smug smile stretches across his face. The two security guards assigned to me step forward. 'It's okay,' I motion for them to step back. This is one of three conversations I'm determined to have tonight.

'Lord Ashworth.' My voice could freeze hell, though it's not his fault my mother is a meddling witch.

'I've been trying to steal a moment with you all evening.' He moves closer, and I catch a whiff of his cologne. Expensive. Cloying.

'Why?' I deadpan.

A flicker of confusion flashes over his features. 'Well, to tell you how delighted I am about our ... arrangement.'

I blink slowly. 'What arrangement?'

His face is comical. I wish Sean were here to see it. I wish Sean were here full stop.

His smile falters slightly. 'Our engagement, of course. Your mother assured me you were thrilled about. I'm living for the moment we can announce it.'

'I'll die before that ever happens.' I take a sip of champagne, studying his face over the rim of my glass as it sinks in. I'm not going to be his trophy piece; I'm not going to be anything to him. Just as my mother threatened, I'm going to be nobody—to any of them— and that—as well as the knowledge my boyfriend is somewhere near—is what's driving me on tonight.

His smile falters. 'Princess?'

My fingers tighten around the stem of the champagne flute. 'Let me make something crystal clear, Lord Ashworth. There is no arrangement. There is no engagement. And there never will be.'

His face pales, then turns a similar shade to his hair. 'But your mother said—'

'My mother says a lot of things. Most of them are nonsense.'

The words come out sharper than I intended and carry further than I intended. Conversations around us falter. Heads turn. I feel the weight of a dozen stares, the sudden hush that falls over our section of the ballroom.

Lord Ashworth looks like he's been slapped. 'Your Highness.' His voice drops to an urgent whisper. 'People are watching. Perhaps we should discuss this privately—'

So he can put his hands on me again?

I don't think so.

'There's nothing to discuss.' I smile at him, but it feels more like a grimace. 'Enjoy the rest of the reception, Lord Ashworth. I certainly will.'

I turn on my heel and walk away, leaving him standing there like the fool he is. The conversations around us resume. Across the ballroom, my mother's eyes find mine. Even from here, I can see the fury radiating from her. She knows exactly what just happened. She knows I've just declared war. She can sense the shift in the air, the way all predators always can.

I drift towards the French doors leading to the gardens with my security close at my back. The lights of St. James's Park twinkle in the distance, and it hits me like a bolt of electricity that if Sean is anywhere near here, that's where he'll be. I don't know how I know, but I know it better than I know my own name.

The urge to run to him eats me alive, but I bide my time. I've come this far. Finally, Sabrina and Harald make their excuses and retire for the night. My sister's big day is officially over. My mother doesn't hesitate. It's time for the second difficult conversation of the night. She stalks towards me with her royal purple ensemble sashaying behind her. Her pearls gleam like armour as she approaches me. Her razor-sharp smile might fool our guests, but never me.

'Enjoying yourself, darling?' Her voice drips with disdain.

'Immensely, Mother.' The air between us crackles with the kind of heavy atmosphere that lingers before a violent thunderstorm.

'That was quite a performance with Lord Ashworth,' she says quietly, as the music plays on around us. Her eyes narrow.

'If you refuse him, if you embarrass this family in any way whatsoever, I will cut you off quicker than a Royal Decree.'

I meet her gaze steadily, feeling something cold and dangerous settle in my chest. 'Do it.'

'You will have nothing more than the clothes on your back.' Colour flushes her neck as she battles to keep her composure. 'Nowhere to live. Not a penny to your name.'

That's where she's wrong. I'll have more than I've ever had in my life. And I'm not talking about the paintings or the money they'll provide.

I'm talking about freedom. About happiness. About love.

'You think that Beckett boy will want you when you have nothing? When you are nothing? Pah.' She swats a hand in front of her face.

'I know he will.' I drain the rest of my champagne and place it on the table beside us. 'I'm leaving. Right now. And if you try and stop me, I will make a scene in front of every single one of your precious guests. I will shout it from the goddam rooftop that you are trying to keep me a prisoner here.'

'Fool.' She shakes her head. Disgust radiates from her every pore, but she doesn't stop me when I step out into the palace gardens, and into the cool starlit night.

Chapter Forty-Two

SEAN

I've been wandering around these grounds for hours, like a man possessed. St. James's Park, the place Layla used to escape to, should be peaceful at this hour of the night with its manicured lawns and ornamental lake, but it's hollow and empty, just like me. Anyone with half a brain has gone to bed. Probably because they've got someone to go to bed with.

I can't sit still, can't think straight, can't do anything but pace between the trees and stare at the palace gates across the road.

She's in there, somewhere, behind those imposing walls and endless windows, and I'm out here going slowly insane. But she's still mine. Hope sparks in my chest every time I remember the princess's televised arrival at Westminster. The kiss she blew.

It's just a matter of time.

I need to be patient.

I need to trust she's got this. I need to trust her. Trust what we have.

It's just so fucking hard having absolutely zero control of any of it.

Ben and Anderson are sitting on a bench near the Duck Island bridge; they gave up trying to convince me to go back to the hotel hours ago. Pretty sure they think I've lost my mind. Maybe I have.

My phone rings in my pocket. Hope jolts through me like an electric shock. I pull it out of my suit trousers with shaky fingers and squint at the screen.

Fucking Rian.

I cancel the call, and it rings again immediately. This time it's Killian.

I sigh, then swipe to answer. Out of all of my brothers, I trust him the most. 'Killian.'

'Is there a reason you were outside Westminster today?' He asks dryly. 'Or were you just watching history be made?'

'Did you put a tracker on me?' I snap.

'No. My girlfriend is a royal fanatic. The coverage was on the TV all damn day. Imagine my surprise when I caught sight of my younger, anguished looking brother in the sea of faces.'

'Don't tell the others.'

'As if I would,' he scoffs. 'Are you okay? I don't want to pry...' he trails off.

'Then don't.' I round past the memorial statue and glance up at the dark midnight sky. Any second now, it's going to piss down. I can feel it in the air. 'Just do me a favour.'

'Anything.'

'Double up everyone's security for the next couple of months. Don't ask me why. Just do it.'

'Are you in trouble?' It's not the first time he's asked, and it won't be the last.

'No. But I'm hoping to be.' While I don't think the Royal family would physically hurt any of us, when my relationship with Layla eventually does become public knowledge, we're going to be mobbed.

'This woman...' he trails off.

'I told you, it's complicated. Please, Killian, I'll explain everything when I can.'

The line goes silent. He doesn't like being kept in the dark, but he gets it.

'Do you need anything else?'

'No.' Even my resourceful big brother can't get me into Wyndham Palace. 'Actually, have Jenkins come to my place next week.' Surely by next week this princess will have managed to extract herself from the clutches of her controlling mother?

'Jenkins? Now you're worrying me, Sean.'

Jenkins is our family lawyer. He's the best in the world. It could take months to sort through the legalities of her officially stepping down from duties. Not to mention the media shitshow that will inevitably follow.

'Trust me. I'm okay.' I will be anyway, just as soon as I get the princess back where she belongs. With me.

'Consider it done.' Killian says curtly. 'Call if I can help you.' I swear he thinks I'm shacking up with a mafia princess. He'll find out the truth soon enough. They all will.

'I will, thanks, man.'

I shove the phone back into my pocket as the sky opens. The first drops of rain smash into my face like cold bullets, and within seconds it's a torrential downpour. Water streams down my face, soaking through my suit jacket, turning the manicured park paths into rivers of mud and fallen petals.

I should find shelter. Join Ben and Anderson under the bridge where they're no doubt cursing my stubbornness.

But I can't move. From this spot, I can see the palace gates through the sheets of rain. To my left, the lake churns with the impact of thousands of raindrops. To my right, the streetlights blur into halos of yellow light through the downpour.

My hair plasters to my skull. My shirt clings to my chest, but I don't give a fuck. Let it rain. Let it pour. I'm not going anywhere.

Not tonight. Not ever. Not until I see her.

Somewhere deep down, I'm still wondering if I'm enough for her. Still can't believe that she's real. That she's mine.

Where are you, Layla?

The wind picks up, driving the rain sideways, and I turn my collar up against the storm. Through the chaos of wind and water, I keep my eyes fixed on those palace gates, praying to a god I don't believe in for a fucking miracle.

Then—movement catches my eye.

A figure emerges at the edge of the palace gardens, distant at first through the curtain of rain. My heart stops. Even from here, even through the storm, I'd recognise that silhouette. I know the way her body moves.

She's running across the grass, her dress a pale blur against the dark parkland. Her hair streams behind her, soaked and wild. The ballgown clings to her legs as she runs, the fabric heavy with rain, but she doesn't slow down. She's a far cry from the picture perfect princess in the wedding coverage, but she's utterly fucking perfect to me.

Our eyes lock across the distance, and my heart swells.

She grins—actually grins—despite being drenched, despite everything. The layers of her dress billow and flow around her like liquid silk, and she's barefoot, her shoes abandoned somewhere in her escape.

She's all I can see.

I step forward, then break into a run as she reaches the edge of the palace gardens. She doesn't hesitate at the high stone wall that separates the royal grounds from the park. She hikes up her sodden dress and climbs, hauling herself up and over like a ninja. She stumbles slightly as the heavy fabric tangles around her legs, then breaks into a sprint. A black cab blares its horn as she darts across the street, but it doesn't stop her. She keeps on running, bare feet splashing through puddles, her dress streaming behind her like a pale banner in the storm.

I sprint toward her, my shoes sliding on the wet ground, and we meet halfway across the park. She launches herself the final few feet, then slams into me like it's been years instead of days.

I catch her.

Hold her.

Bury my face in her hair. She smells like champagne and freedom.

'Have you been out here all day?' She laughs, grabbing the collar of my jacket and yanking my face down to meet hers.

'Yes.' My shoulders sag with relief at being reunited.

'You're crazy.' Wild eyes dart excitedly over every inch of me, like she can't quite believe I'm here.

'Crazy about you.' I pull the princess tight against my chest, nuzzling into her, wrapping my arms around her, securing her against me. I inhale her neck, breathing in her familiar scent. 'I missed you so fucking much. No one is ever going to take you from me again.'

'Damn right they're not.'

'Not your mother. Not your family. Not the entire fucking army.'

She stares up at me as the layers of her dress blow around us like a blanket. 'I love you so much.'

'I love you.'

The Queen's fucked up.

They all have.

Because I've got her now.

And I'm never letting her go.

Chapter Forty-Three

LAYLA

I wake to the sound of rain against the huge windows. Sean's arms are wrapped around my waist. For a moment, I just lie there, breathing in the scent of his skin and listening to his steady heartbeat beneath my ear.

This is what happiness feels like.

A month ago, I was trapped in the palace, being told who to marry and how to live. Now I'm in Sean's bed, in his house, in his arms, and I've never felt more free in my entire life.

Blackstone House has become my sanctuary. The sprawling Georgian mansion sits on hundreds of acres of Irish countryside, neighbouring the very estate where my parents banished me before New Year. The irony isn't lost on me.

Ireland was supposed to be my punishment.

It transpired to be my salvation—not because of the place, but because of the man sleeping beside me. Before I stumbled into Reveal, I was so desperate to get back to the chaos of London—the traffic, the crowds, the constant noise.

I thought I needed all that stimulation to feel alive. Now in the quiet solitude, I can appreciate the truth. I was just using the buzz to fill a void. The quietness here doesn't feel empty anymore. It feels... complete. The weather still leaves a lot to be desired, but grey skies and constant drizzle are a small price to pay for this kind of freedom.

Outside the window, Temptation is secure in the stable below, waiting for his morning ride. Sean somehow managed to get him from Ardmore. When I asked how, he just smiled and said, 'The luck of the Irish.'

I don't believe in luck. I believe in love, hard work and fighting for what you want in this life, because no one else will fight for it for you.

'Morning, Princess.' Sean's voice is rough with sleep. He rolls his huge, muscular body to face mine and presses a kiss to the top of my head. His dark stubble is deliciously rough against my jawline.

'Morning.' I stretch against him, every muscle in my body deliciously relaxed. 'What time is it?'

'It's Saturday, so it doesn't matter.'

He's right. It doesn't. I don't have a schedule dictated by royal protocol. No morning briefings, no charity appearances, no photoshoots, no one telling me what to wear or who to smile at. Or who to date.

Just Sean and me and all the time in the world.

'True. Though, it will matter this time next week.' Sean's brother is getting married and his entire family are flying out to Portugal for the occasion.

'I wish I could bring you to Caelon's wedding,' he says, his fingers tracing lazy patterns on my bare shoulder.

'It would cause a media shitshow,' I remind him for the hundredth time.

Sean can't wait to introduce me to his family. And I can't wait to be introduced to them, because one day—soon I hope —they're going to be my family too.

The press is still hunting for me—'Missing Princess' headlines appear daily—but they have no idea I'm here. No one does—well, except my sisters, and the queen, but they're not going to be giving up my location anytime soon. My mother would rather the speculation than the world know the truth —that I chose love over loneliness. Desire over duty.

It's not like we can go anywhere, not yet, but these few quiet weeks together have felt like a gift rather than a curse. We've spent entire days playing in Reveal. Other days watching movies in bed together, just because we can. We've sat by the fire and talked for hours. Sean's trying—and failing—to teach me how to cook. I'm trying—and failing—to teach him how to paint. There's no one to answer to except ourselves.

Sabrina was shocked when I told her I was stepping down. Patricia merely put out—probably that she didn't have the courage to stand up to our mother, but she might find it yet.

'How does it feel to be officially free from duties?' His hand glides lower to cup my bum.

'I'm not free of all my duties.' I turn in his arms to face him, taking in the sight of his dark hair messy from sleep, his dark eyes gleam with devilment. 'Being a girlfriend comes with certain expectations.'

'It certainly does. I can't wait to get you to Reveal later.' His fingers pinch my ass cheek hard enough to make me squeal. 'I'm going to fasten you to the Saint Andrew's cross and fuck you into next week.' He rolls on top of me now, pinning my wrists to the bed and nudging his way between my thighs.

'Promises, promises.'

The scent of bacon drifts in the air, and he pauses kissing my neck and exhales a long, low groan. 'You need to tell Kat the only thing we want for breakfast is each other.'

When Mrs Walsh opted for an early retirement, Sean offered my former lady-in-waiting the position as our house-keeper. I nearly cried with relief. It's not just the guilt of getting her into trouble either. Having her here makes this place feel like home. She's still my closest confidant, and the best friend I have—other than him, that is.

Grant's here too, working as Sean's estate manager. He's brilliant with the grounds and the staff, and more importantly, he and Kat are finally free to be together without worrying about royal protocol. Funnily enough, Sean didn't offer him a security position. Maybe he's worried about me sneaking out? Ha! As if.

'The bacon can wait.' I'm nowhere near ready to leave the warmth of his arms. I don't think I ever will be. I melt into him, my body responding to his touch like it always does. This is what I was missing in my old life. This connection. This passion. This feeling of being completely and utterly wanted for who I am, not what I represent.

'I love you.' I murmur into his mouth.

'Marry me.'

'What?'

'You heard me, marry me.' He nuzzles into my neck.

'You're just trying to lock me down before Jaxon sells my paintings and I become a billionaire like you.' All joking aside, my heart is hammering in my chest.

His deep laughter brushes over my skin, sending goosebumps rippling in every direction.

'Answer the question.'

'You didn't ask one. It was more of a demand.' As ever, my dom likes to boss me around, and I am here for it.

He pulls his head from my neck to look at me. Our eyes lock, and that ever present chemistry pulses between us. 'Layla Sinclair, you might be my submissive in the bedroom, but in life, you're my partner, my equal, and my absolute fucking everything. Will you do me the greatest honour of becoming my wife?'

'Yes.' It's barely more than a whisper, but it's filled with certainty.

The rain continues to patter against the windows as Sean sinks himself inside me. Nothing else matters but him. He is my life now.

And it's everything I ever dreamed it could be.

EPILOGUE

Sean

June.

Tonight is the night. Where better to introduce my fiancé to my family than the grand opening of Caelon's new flagship hotel, Beckett Bliss Dublin.

'How do I look?' Layla asks, adjusting the diamond collar at her throat. The ring on her finger tells the world she's mine, but she still insists on wearing the first diamonds I gave her. And I love that.

In a black silk dress that hugs every single one of her sexy curves, she looks like a goddess, but more importantly, she looks happy. Free.

'You look like you're about to give my brothers heart attacks,' I tell her, straightening my bow tie in the mirror.

'Good.' That defiance flashes in her eyes—the one that first caught my attention in the club. 'I've been looking forward to this for months.'

The press had a field day with Layla's official announcement, but we weathered the storm safely tucked away at Blackstone House. The public were shocked, distraught even, but I'm confident they'll come round. She's agreed to feature in Okay magazine next month, and she's going to reveal all—well, all except Reveal, the BDSM club she now co-runs with me.

Tonight is our first public appearance as a couple. The hotel opening is perfect—high profile enough to make a statement, but controlled enough that we won't be mobbed.

'Are you nervous?' she asks, slipping her arms around my waist.

'Excited.' I admit, staring into her huge chocolate eyes. 'My family are going to lose their shit when they realize who you are.'

'Who I was,' she corrects, a wry smile touching her lips.

'You'll always be a princess to me.'

She laughs, the sound filling our bedroom with warmth. 'Flatterer.'

'Realist.'

'Come on, we've waited long enough. Let's do this.' She slips her hand in mine as we make our way downstairs. Ben is waiting outside the front entrance with the Bentley. Anderson and his team are in a Range Rover behind, ready to follow us.

'Good evening, lovebirds.' Ben opens the car door, and we slide in over the leather seats.

'Evening, Ben.'

He shakes his head and laughs as I hit the button to close the screen separating the back from the front. My hand gravitates to Layla's thigh, but she swats it away.

'Don't even think about it. I'm about to meet your mother, for goodness sake!' She fires me a warning look and crosses her legs. 'Besides, you'll ruin my make-up.'

'I wasn't aware you wore any down there.' I smirk.

'Whatever happened to delayed gratification?' she fires back.

'It's overrated, spoilsport.' I take her hand in mine as Ben drives us to Dublin. The plan is to arrive fashionably late, after the initial press frenzy has died down. My family are expecting me—I told my parents I was bringing someone special—but they have no idea who.

'What do you think they'll say?' Layla leans her head against my shoulder as the countryside rolls past.

'Rian will probably come in his pants. Avery will scream. Killian will pretend he knew all along.'

'And your parents?'

'They're going to love you. How could they not?' I squeeze her hand reassuringly.

'Where will we tell them we met?'

'We'll tell them you auditioned to be my submissive, then blackmailed your way into my life.' I snort.

'They'll never believe it.'

'Exactly.'

When Ben pulls up outside the hotel, it's easy to see this is Caelon's most impressive yet. The sun glints off the gleaming glass wall where Becketts Bliss is scrawled in italic font. Photographers line the entrance, but they're focused on the other guests arriving. They don't recognise Layla yet, not in this context.

Our security detail—Anderson's team—forms a subtle but protective circle around us as we slip through the crowd. They're good at what they do, blending into the background while keeping us safe. After the media circus following Layla stepping down, we can't be too careful.

My hand stays on the small of her back as we approach the entrance. Through the glass doors, I can see the glittering crowd inside, and somewhere up on the mezzanine level over-looking the entrance, I spot familiar figures—Killian, Avery, and Rian positioned at the balcony railing, drinks in hand, clearly watching for my arrival.

'Ready?' I ask.

'Ready,' she says, but I hear the slight tremor in her voice.

'I've got you.' I press a kiss to her temple.

We step inside—the effect is immediate and electric. Conversations around us stop mid-sentence. Heads turn. The murmur of recognition starts low and builds like a wave.

From the mezzanine above, I hear Avery's voice carry over the crowd: 'Oh my GOD!'

All eyes turn to us, and I watch as recognition dawns on face after face.

Avery is the first to reach us. She's fanning herself like she's about to combust. 'Oh my God,' she whispers, then louder, 'Oh my GOD!'

Killian is hot on her heels as usual.

Rian strides over, grinning like a lunatic. 'So you're not gay.'

I snigger. Before I can answer him, Layla jumps in. 'I can confirm he's definitely not.' She shoots me a look that translates to, *even if you do like anal.*

I pull her closer against me, and she snuggles in.

James stalks over, with Scarlett hanging off his arm. 'Sean, what the fuck—'

'Language,' I interrupt, grinning. 'May I introduce you to my fiancée, Layla Sinclair?'

The silence that follows is deafening. Then chaos erupts.

'Fiancée!' Scarlett's bawling—must be those pregnancy hormones they were harping on about. Ivy's fanning her face like she's about to start too. Zara's jaw is on the floor as her eyes quick fire between Layla and me. Killian is as cool as a cucumber—like he expected this all along. My mother's mouth is opening and closing like a fucking goldfish. For the first time in her entire life—she's short of words.

Suddenly everyone is talking at once, asking questions, demanding details, welcoming her to the family with the warmth that's always defined the Becketts.

'My dear girl, welcome to the family,' my mother gushes, squashing us both with a bear-like hug. 'You must come to dinner on Sunday. I need to hear all about this whirlwind romance. And mark off the last Friday of every month to come to the spa with us.' She glances around at Scarlett, Zara, Ivy and Avery. 'We go to Eden for a girls day.' She winks at Layla knowingly.

Layla beams. She wanted a family. She's getting more than she bargained for with the Becketts. I watch as she handles their questions with grace, laughs at their jokes, and wins them over within minutes. Though truthfully, it's me who is the real winner.

I'm the luckiest bastard alive.

She's mine.

And now, the entire world knows it.

I learnt the hard way in London, some things can't be controlled. My devotion to her is one of those things. I can't wait to spend the rest of my life showing her that.

THE END

If you want more of Sean and Layla's sexy romance, click here for a free bonus epilogue....

BONUS EPILOGUE

Click here to check out Dominic Kincaid's story. He was too dark and delicious not to get his own book! MINE- A Scorching Hot Irish Mafia Romance

Click here for Rian's story, the next book in the Beckett Brothers Series... RELEASE ME-book

. . .

RIAN:

What's worse than falling for my best friend's sister?

Falling for his wife...

One deep, stolen conversation at their engagement party, and my heart was ripped from my chest.

Years of craving. Aching. Burning.

I've lost myself in hundreds of women trying to forget her, but every time I close my eyes, it's her face that haunts my darkest fantasies.

Now she's in my club every weekend, her husband's latest betrayal written all over her face.

Watching my best friend destroy the only woman I've ever loved is a special kind of torture.

I'm running out of reasons to keep my distance.

Taking what I want will end in war—but some betrayals are worth the bloodshed—and she's worth everything.

REBEKKA:

I married the devil's prodigy to save my family's business —but my husband's true talents lie in sabotaging everything he touches—including me.

When he flaunts his latest conquest through his best friend's club, it's the final straw.

I'm done playing the perfect corporate wife.

Done playing by the rules.

Done fighting the heat in Rian Beckett's eyes each time they devour me.

My body aches for his touch, and there's only so much pain I can take.

It was supposed to be a fling.

But somehow, Rian became my everything.

Which is terrifying because no matter what I do, or where I go... my husband will never release me...

. . .

🤍Best friend's wife

   🤍Forbidden romance

   🤍Billionaire playboy

   🤍Reverse age gap

   🤍Pining

   🤍Forced proximity

   🤍Who did this to you?

   🤍Touch her and d*e vibes

   🤍Blush-inducing steam

ALSO BY L A GALLAGHER

INTRODUCING A BRAND NEW SERIES....

THE KINCAID SYNDICATE

Click here to learn more...

MINE

Dominic:

Aoife O'Shea ran from one dangerous monster...

straight into the arms of another—me.

And now she owes me a debt written in blood.

She asked for one month to repay it. But from the moment she stepped into my world, I knew I'd never let her walk away.

She's in my home.

In my bed.

Under my skin.

She thinks I rescued her.

The truth? I'm keeping her.

Because in my world, debts aren't cleared.

They're claimed.

And Aoife O'Shea just became mine.

WRECK ME

SCARLETT:

Pole dancing at the most exclusive 'Gentlemen's Club' in the country is lucrative, though the men are anything but gentle. They're all desperate to take the only significant possession I have—my virginity.

I've spent five years hiding in plain sight, burying my head in my books, courtesy of a scholarship at Dublin's most prestigious college. But now, for the first time in my life, I feel seen. Wanted. Desired. And I've awakened a need I never knew I had.

Enter James Beckett, a billionaire bachelor with a reputation as famous as his family's whiskey empire, and he wants *me* to be his fake girlfriend until he conquers the next part of his empire.

He'll even tutor me through my final exams... and anything else I require tuition in...

Our arrangement will either secure my future, or shatter my world...

JAMES:

Yet another sex scandal means I'm heartbeat away from being fired as CEO from my own family's whiskey distillery, unless I can prove to my father and The Board that I've shed my playboy reputation.

The last thing I want is a showpiece society wife.

Especially when I'm obsessed with The Luxor Lounge's newest pole dancer.

At only twenty-three, Scarlett radiates an innocence that drives me wild. Turns out, my little dancer is a virgin.

Fooling around with my fake girlfriend was *always* part of my plan.

Falling for her *wasn't*.

She's everything I crave, but everything my father forbids.

Even if I can convince him that Scarlett is the one for me, she's been keeping a secret.

One that could wreck me...

Get WRECK ME here...

REDEEM ME

IVY:

I'm the queen of handling tiny tyrants—I've been nannying since the era of bedtime bribery. But there's no guidebook for living with Dublin's most notorious grump and widower—my brother's brooding best friend.

Mr. Tall, Dark, and Tortured isn't just a challenge; he's a full-blown occupational hazard.

Under his icy shell, a fierce fire burns. Every fleeting touch ignites an attraction so intense it's impossible to fight.

He's broken.

And I'm compelled to fix him.

But who will fix me afterward?

Because if my brother discovers our forbidden fling, it won't just be fireworks—it'll be an inferno the size of hell.

And that's before Caelon's shadowy past comes bulldozing back into our lives...

CAELON:

I live for two things: my kids and a relentless pursuit of revenge for the love of my life.

Tragically, I'm failing at both.

Then Ivy Winters, my best friend's sassy little sister, blazes into my world in search of a job and a fresh start. And while she's babysitting my children, I'm stuck with a promise to her brother to keep an eye on her.

But Ivy defies my rules.

Challenges me at every turn.

And somehow, she manages to ignite a spark that threatens to melt the ice surrounding my heart.

But just as I start to see the possibility of a life beyond my pain, the past comes knocking, demanding its due.

Now, I'm faced with the ultimate choice: revenge or redemption...

💚 Brother's best friend

💚 Single dad trope

💚 Forbidden romance

💚 She's the nanny

💚 Grumpy/sunshine

💚 Forced proximity

💚 Billionaire possessive hero

💚 Dating the boss

💚 Opposites attract

💚 Touch her and d*e vibes

💚 Blush-inducing steam

💚 10 year age gap

💚 Set in Dublin

Get it here... REDEEM ME

RUIN ME

AVERY:

I'm a psych graduate turned glamour model, but it's not as glamorous as it sounds when I've got a stalker leaving black calla lilies in my dressing room with little love notes that say, "I'm coming for you."

Cue my worst nightmare: needing a bodyguard. But not just any bodyguard—Killian Beckett, the infuriating CEO of a global security empire, former soldier, and certified grouch.

Killian's all hard muscle, military precision, and absolutely zero charm. He insists on hovering around like I'm some kind of fragile damsel in distress.

Newsflash: I'm not. And his 'no-nonsense' attitude drives me straight up the wall. The guy radiates disapproval—of my job, my dates, my wardrobe. You name it, he's judging it.

Unfortunately, Mr Control Freak also looks like he was sculpted by the gods, and smells like temptation itself.

The more time we spend sparring, the more I realise there's something buried under all that brooding. Something damaged. Something that just might ruin us both if I get too close.

Sleeping with my bodyguard?

Bad idea.

Falling for him?

Absolutely fatal.

KILLIAN:

Babysitting a spoiled celebrity wasn't how I planned on spending my days, but when Avery's name lands on my desk, I can't say no, even if she's trouble wrapped in taffeta.

Avery is everything I can't stand: reckless, loud, and she lives for attention. Day and night, her smart mouth tests my patience, and her curves increasingly test my control.

I don't even like the woman, but my God, do I want her. But I can't cross that line. Instead, I watch, I wait, and I fight—both the outside threats and the escalating pull between us.

But the battlefield I learned to survive on is nothing compared to the war Avery stirs up inside me.

Getting involved with a client is the ultimate risk in my world, but when it comes to her, I'll risk it all.

Even if it ruins me...

Click here to learn more about RUIN ME.

🩶Bodyguard

🩶Billionaire Dom

🩶Celebrity FMC

🩶She has a stalker

🩶Blush-inducing steam

🩶Standalone with interlinking characters from a wider series

RELEASE ME

RIAN:

What's worse than falling for my best friend's sister?

Falling for his wife...

One deep, stolen conversation at their engagement party, and my heart was ripped from my chest.

Years of craving. Aching. Burning.

I've lost myself in hundreds of women trying to forget her, but every time I close my eyes, it's her face that haunts my darkest fantasies.

Now she's in my club every weekend, her husband's latest betrayal written all over her face.

Watching my best friend destroy the only woman I've ever loved is a special kind of torture.

I'm running out of reasons to keep my distance...

But taking what I want could start a war—and fighting an enemy is one thing, but betraying my best friend is another...

REBEKKA:

I married the devil's prodigy to save my family's business—but my husband's true talents lie in sabotaging everything he touches—including me.

When he flaunts his latest conquest through his best friend's club, it's the final straw.

I'm done playing the perfect corporate wife.

Done playing by the rules.

Done fighting the heat in Rian Beckett's eyes each time they devour me.

My body aches for his touch, and there's only so much pain I can take.

It was supposed to be a fling.

But somehow, Rian became my everything.

Which is terrifying because no matter what I do, or where I go... my husband will never release me...

💜Best friend's wife

💜Forbidden romance

💜Billionaire playboy

💜Reverse age gap

💜Pining

💜Forced proximity

💜Who did this to you?

💜Touch her and d*e vibes

💜Blush-inducing steam

Learn more here.... **RELEASE ME**

LA Gallagher also writes super hot steamy romance under Lyndsey Gallagher... be sure to check out:

Falling For The Rockstar At Christmas

THE COLDEST HOLIDAY OF THE YEAR IS ABOUT TO GET BLISTERINGLY HOT...

SASHA

Ten years ago, I inherited our family castle and sole care of my youngest sister. More Cinderella, than Sleeping Beauty, at the mere age of twenty-eight I have a teenager to raise and a hotel to run. If the hotel is to survive past Christmas, I need a lottery win, a miracle, or Prince Charming himself to sweep in with a humongous... wad of cash.

When my super successful middle sister announces she's coming home for the holiday season, I'm determined to put my problems aside and make this the most fabulous Christmas ever. Especially as it might just be the last one in our family home.

I didn't factor in the return of my first love, Ryan Cooper. Back then he was the boy next door. Now, he's a world famous singer/song writer. We were supposed to go the States together. He left without me. Now he's back. Rumour is he has writers block. Apparently this is a last-ditch attempt to find inspiration before his record label pulls the plug permanently.

And guess where he wants to stay? You have it in one- the most inspiring castle hotel in Dublin's fair city.

Every woman in the city wants to pull this Hollywood Christmas cracker. Except me. I'm going to avoid him at all costs.

Easier said than done when he's parading around under my roof, with enough heat exuding from his molten eyes to melt every square inch of snow from the peaks of the Dublin mountains...

Falling For The Rock Star At Christmas is an OPEN DOOR steamy, love conquers all, stand alone romance, with no cliff hanger- and a guaranteed happy ever after.

Get FALLING FOR THE ROCKSTAR AT CHRISTMAS here...

Falling For My Forbidden Fling

WHAT GOES ON TOUR STAYS ON TOUR, RIGHT?

CHLOE

Even the name **Jayden Cooper** sends a hot flush of irritation through my veins. His rockstar brother might be about to marry my darling sister, but that does **NOT** make us family.

Thankfully, there's a continent separating me from his ridiculously attractive but super-smug face. And his arrogant tongue.

I'm rapidly carving my name in the glittering world of celebrity event management... and what better event to manage than the final farewell tour of my sister's fiancé, Ryan Cooper.

It's the biggest gig of my career.

Eight cities.

Eight concerts.

Eight opportunities to propel my business to a global level.

I couldn't turn it down if I wanted to.

The catch?

It involves working with closely with Ryan's agent– his brother, Jayden-Super-Smug-Cooper.

Going on tour with Jayden is almost as inconvenient as the hate-fuelled lust that steals the air straight from my lungs every time he's near.

Someone somewhere is testing me, but I've survived worse. And I'll survive him.

As long as I don't melt under the intensity of his smug but admittedly smouldering stare ...or fall foul of the talents of the aforementioned arrogant tongue...

Especially when technically...like it or not, we're about to be related.

JAYDEN

I've been through hell to get to where I am today.

I'm *the* best agent in Hollywood's cut-throat industry because I clawed and dragged myself there inch by excruciating inch.

Which is why I refuse to be bossed around by a pushy, Prada-wearing princess when it comes to organising my Rockstar brother's farewell tour. I've got bigger fish to fry, starting with upholding a promise I made a lifetime ago...

But Chloe is about to find out the hard way, what goes on tour stays on tour.

Get FALLING FOR MY FORBIDDEN FLING here...

Falling For My Bodyguard

I'M TRYING TO PROTECT HER. SHE'S TRYING TO KILL ME- ONE INDECENT LITTLE BLACK DRESS AT A TIME.

VICTORIA

As a student doctor, I deal with bullet wounds on a regular basis, but one teeny nightclub shooting is all it takes for my sister and her rock star husband to send me a new bodyguard/ babysitter.

The last person I expect to turn up is Archie "can't-bear-to-look-you-in-the-eye" Mason.

Now we're roommates until graduation. I can't turn around without tripping over him. If only I could trip underneath him. Because he is every bit as alluring as he was five years ago. And equally as unavailable.

But when my night terrors result in us sharing the same bed, our situation sparks a brand new danger.

One that could hurt both of us irreparably...

ARCHIE

I've been *obsessed* with Victoria Sexton for years.

If my boss and friend, Ryan Cooper, had any idea how bad I have it for his wife's little sister, he'd sack me on the spot.

Living with her is testing every inch of willpower I possess.

How can I watch her back when I can't stop imagining her on it?

Falling For My Bodyguard

DATING IN THE DEEP END

Savannah:

When He-Who-Has-Never-Been-Named knocked me up and ceremoniously knocked me down with the revelation, "I'm actually married," I fled back to Dublin. There, I dusted off my big girl (maternity) pants and launched my blog, chronicling my life as "Single Sav."

Fast forward six years, and I've built a lucrative empire on that premise, which is precisely why I haven't so much as looked at the opposite sex for over half a decade.

Well, apart from slyly perving on my twin daughters' swimming coach, Ronan Rivers, a former Olympic gold medalist.

The man is ridiculously easy on the eyes. He's also a complete manwh*re who lives to torment me with his filthy mouth and decadent innuendos.

When Coral Chic, Ireland's hottest new swimwear brand, offers me a million euros to represent their new swimwear range, it's impossible to turn down. Becoming the face and body of that campaign has the potential to take my Single Sav brand global.

But there's one tiny problem... I can't swim and the photo shoots are in the sea.

When Ronan offers to give me a crash course in the deep end, the only thing I'm drowning in is his mesmerising baby blues.

I've built my entire brand on being single.

The one man who can save me is also the same man who can sink me...

Ronan:

I've been obsessed with Savannah Kingsley since she crashed into my Aston Martin two years ago, but Single Sav is the one woman I can never have.

Which is precisely why I spend Saturday mornings tormenting her with my tongue, and Saturday nights wishing I could tease her with it, instead of embarking on yet another meaningless, lackluster liaison.

When fate forces us together in the form of one-to-one swimming lessons, her skimpy yellow bikini betrays the extent of her body's baser needs and no amount of water can dampen the sizzling attraction between us.

But while she's floundering in the shallows, I'm already in deep.

Can I turn the tide and persuade her to shed her single status?

Click here for Dating In The Deep End

Dating In The Deep End: A hot, single parent romcom! (Dating In Dublin)

DATING THE DELINQUENT

Being with a bad boy never felt so good...

Ashley:

I've always played by the book. As the principal of a prestigious all-girls Catholic school, my life is as orderly as the plaid on my students' skirts. My future was perfectly planned—until a humiliating public proposal ended my decade-long relationship.

It turns out, playing it safe was the riskiest move of all...

Now it's time to let loose.

Which is precisely why I've decided to swap my notions of a ring for an orgasm-fueled fling...

Enter Damien, my younger, intoxicatingly handsome new mechanic. With his rough, oil-covered hands and dirty mouth, he's the perfect distraction—to the point he's ALL I can think about.

Our nights together are explosive, but the days we spend together are what could truly burn my future to the ground.

Because it turns out, Damien is even badder than I could have ever imagined...and it's not just my heart that's on the line—it's my entire world.

It's time to choose between my good girl reputation and the bad boy who's hijacked my heart...

Damien:

Falling for a saint was never in the cards for this sinner...

Life's taught me that sometimes you have to take the fall to protect what's important. I paid a price in the shadows for reasons only I know. Now, I keep to myself, avoiding complications—until Ashley walks into my garage with an overheating motor and an urgent pressure issue—in her panties...

She's everything I'm not—polished, composed, and completely out of my league. But her eyes tell me she's looking for an escape, and I'm reckless enough to offer her one.

But with each day that passes, the weight of my past grows heavier, threatening to pull us both under.

She thinks I'm just a bad boy, but if she knew the truth, it could unravel everything.

Now, I'm faced with the hardest choice: keep hiding the darkness within or let it come to light, risking the only connection that feels real...

My Book

Dating The Delinquent: A hot reverse-age-gap, opposites-attract romance. (Dating In Dublin)

DATING FOR DECEMBER

Ava:

My perpetually single status hardly serves as a shining advertisement for HeartSync, the dating agency I own. Nor is it likely to convince my incredibly successful movie star brother, Nate, to invest in my business. Which is precisely why I agree to fake-date Cillian "can't-crack-a-smile" Callaghan for the month of December.

Sure, his role as a stoically single father and a notoriously grumpy divorce lawyer is far from ideal, but his silver eyes, sculptured shoulders and sharp tongue tick all the right boxes.

Even boxes that are supposed to remain, ahem, unticked...

One mistletoe kiss sparks a lust that could melt Lapland, and frosty fake dates blaze into something feverishly real...

Cillian:

I'm the country's most successful divorce lawyer. It doesn't take a genius to figure out why I don't date. Add in the fact that I'm a full-time single dad, even if I had the inclination, I don't have the time. But when my cheating ex blows back into town, the only way I can convince her it's over for good is by fake-dating someone else...

Enter Ava Jackson, with her infectious laugh, long legs, and luscious lips.

Throughout December, her witty one-liners and effortless bond with my daughter thaw my every defence.

She's everything I never knew I needed.

I'm an expert at breakups... but perhaps this Christmas, it's time to master a love that lasts...

Click here for Dating For December

ACKNOWLEDGMENTS

I hope you enjoyed Sean & Layla's story. Thank you so much for reading Reveal Me. Without you, dear readers, I wouldn't be able to dream up walking red flags and call it work! I'm beyond grateful to all of you that read my words.

I need to say a massive thank you to Margaret Amatt, Lona McCombie, Jennifer Brooks Brown, Heather Hunt, Tammy Beck, and my entire Facebook reader group, **Lyndsey's Book Lushes**. I appreciate your friendship and support. I love our daily check-ins, the inappropriate memes, and just hanging out with you all.

If you'd like to hang out with us too, we'd love to have you. https://www.facebook.com/groups/530398645913222

Last but not least, thank you to my AMAZING husband who wipes my tears, brings me endless amounts of caffeine and wine, supports my dreams, and helps with my research! 😅

If you enjoyed Reveal Me, please consider leaving review on Amazon, Goodreads & Book Bub.

ABOUT THE AUTHOR

L A Gallagher writes swoon-worth contemporary romance featuring billionaire bad-boys, blush-inducing steam, and copious amounts of glamour. She lives in the west of Ireland with her own book boyfriend (that accent–swoon!), two crazy kids, and an even crazier fur baby.

Come hang out at her Facebook reader group Lyndsey's Book Lushes to find out more! https://www.facebook.com/groups/530398645913222

Or check out her equally spicy Lyndsey Gallagher books here...
   https://www.amazon.com/Kindle-Store-Lyndsey-Gallagher/s?rh=n%3A133140011%2Cp_27%3ALyndsey+Gallagher

Printed in Dunstable, United Kingdom